ANGEL'S DEVOTION

A PARANORMAL ANGEL ROMANCE

ELEMENTAL ANGELS

AIMEE ROBINSON

AMR PUBLISHING LLC

To Kerrigan Byrne, and all the dark heroes we can't help but love

ELEMENTAL ANGELS

Angel's Target

Angel's Duty

Angel's Devotion

Angel's Light

CHAPTER 1

Steel had seen something he shouldn't have, and that was a grand fucking problem.

The vehicles he was following had led him to the very neighborhood he didn't want to be in. More specifically, the very neighborhood he didn't want *them* to be in. The polite suburban clusters of cookie-cutter bi-levels sat unassumingly in their neat little rows of manicured lawns. The last thing the Rockwellian inhabitants needed were the four dually pickup trucks growling down the asphalt at eleven thirty at night.

A brisk breeze swept under Steel's wings, and he angled higher with the small current. What the hell were they doing here? The skin under his collar pinched, and that familiar prickle of unease skittered along his spine. His elemental energy homed in on whatever cases of metal were in the beds of those trucks, and they sure as shit weren't garden-variety steel bars and galvanized flat sheets most DIYers loaded up with. No, this metal was something different, something . . . off.

Steel's looming shadow canvassed the caravan as he soared directly above them. The pickups had turned off the main thoroughfare and rolled farther into the sprawling development. His stomach sank. The Glen Ridge section of Aurora was a recently built complex of single-family homes and townhouses. The big draw of the darling little community? Easy access to one of northern New Hampshire's busiest suburban-commuter-required interstates. That meant eight lanes of wide open spaces and high speeds that would make Steel's job a heck of a lot harder once those vehicles reached it.

He cursed and banked right. In the dim glow of the street-lights, his celestial senses scanned the flashes of bold dark letters etched in white across the pickups' front driver and passenger doors. When Steel had positioned himself at an angle close enough to read the words, his heartbeat quickened. *Torrey Mountain Resort.*

That name—holy hell, what he wouldn't give to never see that name again. But even with those letters blazing right in front of him, it was a simple thing to call bullshit. He tamped down a growl and deftly reached for his daggers. The worn hilts of his weapons sitting comfortably in his palms did little to improve his mood. The obnoxious vehicles had all the trim-mings of an official operations fleet for the nearby tourist center, except no group of legitimate mountain maintenance employees would be caravanning away from a demon nest in the middle of the night—and sure as hell not *here.*

Steel gritted his teeth and, not liking the scene around him, tucked his wings more tightly against the biting wind. The damn weather was intensifying. He briefly entertained the idea of transforming into his metallic skin to protect himself from the forecasted storm, but he decided against it. He'd be far too visible, even at night. His steel wings would have to be barrier enough, despite the possibility of detection, even with his evasive flying. Between the moonglow and all those ridiculously close streetlights dotting every spare patch of road, he couldn't risk the reflection, no matter how chilly his balls got.

Familiar names flashed across street signs, and his sweaty

palms pumped around his daggers' hilts. Fucking hell, he didn't want these trucks here. It was too close, far too close, but he couldn't risk calling the other sentinels to aid him either. That specific resort name on the trucks, this neighborhood.

Steel slammed his eyes shut, jerked his head, and willed the tightness in his chest to ease, willed the memories back, but that hot breath of remorse and guilt still licked at his insides. It always did, and it always would. No, his brothers could not come here.

The pickup trucks' red brake lights flared brightly below, then eased into muted crimson when the caravan paused, then rolled through a stop sign. Steel hesitated but quickly corrected his position, dropping lower. As the last truck pulled through the traffic stop, the corner streetlight illuminated the truck's cabin long enough for the passenger's face to flash in the side rearview mirror. Instead of mortal flesh, swirls of teal and gold patterns splayed out over near-translucent skin. The tattoos snaked over the man's bald scalp like creeping ivy. His unnaturally golden eyes remained trained on the road.

Charmers. *Demons.*

All thoughts of the other angels left him. Steel's wings snapped back, muscles tense, and he dove from the sky. He slashed his blade into the truck's back tire with lethal precision before backflapping to avoid the bracing pop and screeching of torn rubber. The truck braked frantically, its rear fishtailing. Its front tires careened up onto the curb and squealed to a stop. Steel reared back in the sky and swapped his daggers for throwing blades. Power roiled deep in his gut. His muscles trembled and shivered with the first kiss of it licking up his skin and over his flesh. It was always like this when he unleashed his angel fire. The blue flames were a searing caress of eager menace. His arms and thighs strengthened, engorging on the only remaining celestial energy he could call forth.

His head whipped toward the other vehicles. A soft curse left him. Instead of stopping to fight him like Steel hoped, the charmers in the three pickups sped faster down the boulevard. Another few hundred feet and they'd reach the exit ramp to the interstate.

"Fuck."

Before he could decide whether to head after them, the front doors of the damaged pickup swung open. The air sizzled with wicked energy. Steel cursed again, banked quickly to the right, and crossed his arms in front of his head. Bright hissing magic erupted against his forearms, clashing with his angel fire. He grunted as he was pushed back mid-air.

"Stupid move, angel."

The driver, whose stocky build and gangly beard fit right in with any other nightclub bouncer, stood at the rear of the battered truck. The demon from the passenger seat slowly joined him. With a shimmer of green light, the driver's mortal appearance faded to reveal the same pale flesh and inky tattoos as his partner.

Steel's eyes darted from the threat in front of him to the potentially greater threat that was speeding away. He gritted his teeth and clenched his weapons tighter. The odds were not in his favor, and the charmers in front of him damn well knew it.

"Ticktock, Cupid. I've got all night, and I'm always ready to throw down with you," the driver needled.

They were too exposed. Any minute, siren wails would permeate the sleepy neighborhood and the dim glow of bedroom lamps would flicker on through gauzy curtains. Worry sat like a leaden weight in his gut, anchoring him to the spot.

The house was too fucking close to where they were.

"Let's take this somewhere else," Steel barked.

"Uh-uh. You blew out my truck. You claimed this spot. Now, let's at least make this interesting." The charmer flashed a vicious sneer and launched his magic.

A moment before the blast hit, Steel ducked a shoulder and

heaved his blade. A sickening thump rent the night air as the metal pierced through the charmer's skull. Shock painted the impaled demon's face. His partner fell back and growled, but he didn't dare touch the knife. Blue flames spidered out from the blade, searing and swallowing every inch of the charmer's translucent flesh. The body jerked once, twice, then dropped to the ground with a thud.

Steel shifted toward the other charmer, his second blade gripped and ready to fly, but halted. The demon, whose body was lankier than the other but still hummed with magic no less deadly, scrambled to his feet and began swirling his arms, casting his magic into a funnel cloud. Steel launched himself higher into the air and drew his Spartan sword. The wide flat of the blade, along with the curved edge and narrow tip, would stab as well as deflect. With a roar, he drew his wings back and held the sword high, but nearby voices had him jerking back.

A block away, half a dozen teenagers were climbing over backyard fences and hopping through hedgerows. A larger boy fell over the lip of a shadowbox fence and grunted when he hit the grass. Based on the not-so-silent shushes and muffled giggles, the kids were doing their pathetically teenage best to sneak back home after curfew without getting noticed.

Fat fucking chance.

The charmer leered at the kids, then grinned, and Steel's heart clenched.

"Don't!" Steel hollered.

But the demon merely cocked his head to the side in a jerky inhuman motion. Then the charmer whipped his arms out and fired dark magic straight at the teenagers.

"Fuck!" Steel took off. His wings cut through the air at breakneck speed. The meager choices available to him flitted through his mind, but none of them were good. Bracing wind lashed his body, but he pushed himself harder, faster.

The teenagers were about fifty feet away and had grown

quiet. The far-too-young mortals' uncertain eyes darted through the darkness as if trying to place a sound.

Shit. Any nose-to-the-window Peeping Toms who'd heard the commotion couldn't witness this. How would the mortal world explain away a gaggle of teenagers embroiled in a demon attack, especially when massive fireballs were involved? They couldn't. Mortals could not know of their world and for good reason. The demons would have an open season on easy prey. It would be chaos, turmoil, mass fear and panic—and that bastard charmer knew it.

Sick dread lurched in Steel's stomach, but he managed to swallow it down. Resigned determination shot through him.

There's no other way.

Right before Steel flew into the teenagers' lines of sight, he extinguished his fire and angled his wings into the funnel of magic.

The impact jolted him from his trajectory, hurtling him through the night sky. Magic sizzled and bled along his metallic wings, seizing up every tendon and muscle. A roar left him as he spun out wildly.

And then he was falling—no, plummeting. Steel struggled to right himself, but his heavy wings had turned to solid sheets of metallic dead weight, dragging him headfirst toward whatever was below. He tucked his head to his chest and braced himself as best he could. A moment later, sickening cracks and crunches rang out. His head smacked against a hard surface. Pain erupted through his body, and all thought left him.

CHAPTER 2

"I can't believe you're wasting the remaining dregs of your Friday night on the phone with me when you've got a gorgeous-as-sin man waiting for you in your bed." Bridget Olsen's needling dripped with all the sardonic mirth a younger sister instinctively reserved for an older brother. As expected, the groan that rumbled through the phone was one of the most satisfying sounds in her life. It was on par with baby coos and puppy dream murmurs and something she always aspired to coax out of her brother. Apart from reading and graphic design, teasing him was among her favorite pastimes. She simply loved the way her big, tough police sergeant of a sibling would get all hot and bothered.

Freaking delicious.

Bridget shut off the lights in her kitchen and smiled at what Ryan must have looked like on the other end—ears red at the tips and that subtle blue vein over his stern brow bulging out just a tad more than usual. But c'mon, like the thing wasn't used to its permanent state of tension at this point?

"You know, that's not as big of a threat as you think it is.

Michael made *buldak* tonight. There's a reason the Koreans call it fire chicken, so please, you're welcome to him anytime."

"No thanks! You chose what you chose."

"I didn't choose the chicken," he remarked pointedly.

"And you know I wasn't talking about the food." Bridget bent down, scooped up Elliot, and headed for her bedroom. The orange tabby cat gave his usual soft yelp of feigned protest before snuggling into the crook of her arm.

"You turning in?" Ryan asked.

"Soon, yeah. Just want to get some reading done first."

"That's good. That's, uh, yeah . . . That's good."

Bridget paused and let Elliot squirm out of her hold to jump on the bed. "Why are you stuttering?"

Ryan scoffed. "I'm not stuttering."

"Fine, hedging . . . like you're about to beat around the bush or something. It's very un-police-sergeant-y of you."

"That's a whole lot of landscaping terminology you're throwing my way. And I'm a sergeant, not a detective. The actual words I use are far less important than how I use them."

"Okay, I can't with this. Hang on." Bridget plopped down on the bed, pulled her phone away from her ear, and enabled the video call. A moment later, her brother's infamous scowl filled her screen. On any other person, it would be intimidating, but with her, it was just annoying. "There, now you can properly see my eye roll. Pause for effect." She did her best *Mean Girl* impersonation, throwing in a hint of Cher's as-if attitude from *Clueless*, and leveled her eyes on her brother's baby blues. "There, better?"

"Brat."

"Spare me. Now, let's talk like adults—specifically, adults who excel at communication with other adults." She slapped her chest. "Hit me, I can take it."

Ryan's wide shoulders lowered with a great sigh, and Bridget's smirk sank. *Oh boy. This wasn't going to be good.*

"Did you see the mail I took in for you today?" Ryan asked.

Bridget tensed. *And here we go again.* "Yeah, I saw it."

He brought his large arm up and scratched behind his neck. It was unnerving to see her older brother so, well, unnerved, but she was hardly in the mood to save him from himself—not if he was seriously thinking about poking the bear . . . again. "Did you get a chance to look through it at all?" Those blue eyes, so like her own, darted off-screen for a second before pegging her once more.

Shit, but she hated this line of questioning. "I thumbed through it, yeah."

"There was a flyer in there from the Chilton Museum of Arts and Digital Mastery."

"Yup." She nodded woodenly.

"They're doing an exhibit on graphic design. That Alfred McDermott guy is giving some opening remarks. I thought it might be a good event for you to go to. It's at ten o'clock tomorrow morning. Mike and I would love to take you, if you—"

"I'm good, thanks."

Ryan winced, glanced off-screen again, and mouthed, "I'm trying," before turning back to her. Pain and trepidation outlined his sharp features, and Bridget blanched. God, when he looked at her like that, she wanted nothing more than to crawl under her covers and never come out. For the past four years, it had always been like this between them. He'd encourage her to get out and join the supposedly wonderful land of the living again. She'd shrug it off and insist she was fine where she was— because she was. His whole body would sag with defeat, and he'd drop it. She'd be racked with guilt and give him an inch, usually in the form of inviting him and Michael over for dinner, until some deeply rooted big-brother guilt would flare up and Ryan would try all over again.

Round and round they'd go. It was a tiring dance, but one

she knew well. Familiar steps were safe steps, after all, but just because she was a pro at their little sparring match didn't mean she had to be cruel about always being the victor. Those victories were important because she had to win every time, while Ryan only had to win once. Her track record was a point of pride and more than a little bit of necessity. But still, Ryan loved her, and he was trying.

Fine.

"I know who Alfred McDermott is. Everyone in graphic design knows who he is. He's the CEO of LightSpark Animation, and from what my coworkers tell me who have worked for him in the past, he makes the word 'tyrant' seem benign. The man loves to throw his dick around, along with his money, and expects nothing short of blood, sweat, and tears from anyone under him. But"—oh, she hated to admit it but couldn't help herself—"the man's brilliant. The teams he's developed, I mean —he's assembled some of the best designers and animators in the business. His studio is swallowing up talent and putting out work my studio could never hope to compete with."

Nor would she ever want to, which was something she'd tried and failed many a time to convince her beloved brother of. Perhaps it was Ryan's line of work, where flamboyant displays of abundant male power were commonplace. But where others like her brother saw McDermott's sort of male high-handedness as a sign of strength, the idea of working in that environment made Bridget's blood curdle. The atmosphere men like Alfred McDermott fostered was sickening and soul-crushing. Deadly.

Bridget snapped herself back to the conversation. "Besides, Pixel Dream is great for me."

"Pixel Dream is safe."

"And what's wrong with that? They allow me to be a fully remote employee, the work is manageable, and the salary is perfectly adequate for what I need." Her chin lifted higher.

"Sure, if by *manageable,* you mean boring as fuck, and by

perfectly adequate, you mean just enough to keep the lights on and keep your reading habit well-fed."

Bridget glared. "Not all of us feed off cutthroat ambition. Can I not just be content to live as is?"

"Not when you don't leave the damn house!"

Silence settled over them. There, he'd said it. Ryan cringed, despite being the one to land the blow, and dragged a hand over his ragged face. Even though it was his attack, the blame pressed down heavily on her shoulders. Remorse and guilt twisted in her chest while Ryan's hurried words fell from him.

"Look, I'm sorry. I just—"

The phone jostled, and Michael's handsome smiling face filled the screen, though the corners of his eyes dipped downward in muted resignation. "Hey, Bridgerton." It was his most often used pet name for her—an ode to her beloved romance novels. It stung that he'd use it on her right now. She didn't need to be coddled or cajoled.

"Hi."

"The exhibit tomorrow is showcasing a section on industry trends. It's all sponsored, of course, but we thought you'd like to see it. They're going to feature artists who will talk about merging 2D illustrations and 3D graphics. Haven't you been talking about that?"

She lifted a shoulder but couldn't bring herself to speak in long sentences just yet. The truth was that she *had* been talking about it, incessantly, and damn Michael for tugging on that particular heartstring. When she first saw graphic artists blend the two elements, it had been fascinating. The process appeared seamless and would go a long way toward grabbing viewer attention, especially in the commercials she worked on—a highly coveted skill given consumers' short attention spans. But because she was the sole remote-only employee at her studio, her opportunities to discuss it with her colleagues were slim. And unfortunately, due to her minuscule social circle, that only left her brother and Michael to listen to her animation ramblings.

The sad truth of the matter was that she *did* want to go, so badly her fingers nearly shook with anticipation. And it wasn't as if she *never* left the house. Bridget was perfectly at ease at Ryan and Michael's place, as well as at the Taekwondo studio Michael owned—provided it was off hours. But the museum would be different. The crowds of people, the *types* of people, all stepping on one another for the chance to kiss McDermott's ass and kowtow to his cruel brilliance, regardless of what he'd expect from his colleagues to bring that brilliance to life . . .

"There's plenty online to learn about it. I saw some continuing ed courses floating around. I'll just sign up for those."

Ryan joined Michael in the video. They were a unified front of sad disappointment. God, she wanted to throw up.

"Look, I'll think about it, okay?"

Ryan nodded. "No pressure. We love you, Bridge."

"Ditto," replied Michael.

"Love you, too."

Bridget couldn't end the call fast enough. She clunked the phone down on her nightstand and grabbed her book, fully intent on escaping through the fantastic lives of totally made-up people. It was all the interaction she could handle without crumbling into a shaking mess on the floor. If she never had to withstand the oppressive pity on her loved ones' faces, it would be too soon.

She shook her hands out and rolled her shoulders back, then slowly stretched her head from side to side, relishing the tight pull in her neck muscles. It was a sort of cooldown procedure after these types of phone calls. Bridget snorted. Who else needed to work so hard to right themselves after melting down over an invitation to an exhibit she actually *wanted* to go to?

No one. No, hers was a particular kind of defect, but it kept her safe and content. Wasn't that enough?

She had just arranged the bed pillows to her liking when Elliot leaped off the bed and landed on the windowsill. His tail flicked up and down in insistent thuds. Blown feline eyes darted through the sky.

"Oh God, what now?" She threw her covers back.

The crash shook the house before her feet even touched the floor.

CHAPTER 3

Bridget careened down the stairs, following the blaze of orange fur. At the bottom, Elliot whipped around the corner toward the kitchen. Her heart hammered out a tortured rhythm. While her sock feet did their best to steady her on the hardwood floor, instinct had her scanning the streetside windows first. A tree must have fallen, most likely Mrs. Willis's old decrepit sugar maple, which neighbors had been after her for months to have taken down. But even as Bridget peered out her living room's large picture window, there was nothing. No giant leafy disturbance blocking the boulevard or even a crumpled car frame lodged against a utility pole.

No, her sleepy street was as sleepy as ever. Sure, a lamplight here and there flickered on, and Bridget could just make out the subtle swishes of curtains being pulled to the side before falling back into place, but otherwise, a whole lot of middle-of-the-night normal stared back at her.

"What the hell *was* that?" Perhaps something had misfired with her old oil heat furnace? Lord knew it wouldn't be the first time. Her poor beast of a heating system was about as ancient as her Irish grandmother's grudges.

Bridget turned the corner and hurried toward the basement door. She halted, however, at the insistent swishing of Elliot's tail over her kitchen's linoleum floor. The small cat stood before her back door, his graceful body arced and threatening, his fur high in warning. Fear tightened in Bridget's chest once again, but logic and stubbornness wrestled it back down. She was in her home, dammit.

I am safe here.

Ducking below her kitchen windows, she inched toward her knife block and pulled out her chef's knife. Meanwhile, Elliot's low growl resonated through the thin faux tiles. "Yes, buddy, I know. I'm coming. You just keep doing what you're doing," she whispered.

Her legs quivered with the strain of her uneven weight as she half squatted, half crawled over to the back door. Sweat slickened the knife's handle against her palm. For Christ's sake, what the hell was she doing? An action hero she was not, nor was she even one of those quick-thinking heroines in her romantic suspense novels. She stalled and made to pivot back toward the stairs where she could freak out quietly behind a locked door, when Elliot's low snarl ticked up an octave.

Shit.

Abandoning her plan, Bridget inched her other hand up alongside the edge of the wall near the doorframe and flicked the outside light on.

"Ouch!" Bridget cried out when Elliot frantically turned, embedding his claws' sharp hooks into the tops of her feet before bolting toward the living room. "Some guardian you are," she muttered, but when she'd shaken her feet out and looked out through the back door at her deck, she understood the cat's reaction.

Sprawled out among her beloved overly stuffed outdoor furniture and lying facedown on the deck's planks was a man. Long limbs splayed every which way and tangled between the legs of her patio furniture like a mass of weeds punching through rock. The bulk of his torso was wedged beneath the table while his head, twisted at what must have been a painful angle, was caged between two chair legs. The man hadn't just fallen onto her deck but had somehow managed to enmesh himself into her furniture as if he'd had a running start and been shoved bodily into everything.

Curiosity, not fear, urged Bridget forward until her nose was practically pressed up against the glass. Even though the man was lying facedown, motionless, that wasn't what unnerved her the most. At first, she thought what she saw was a trick of the light. Her deck's lighting fixture wasn't one of those fancy floodlights with motion detection, much to her brother's chagrin. Nope, hers was a simple outdoor wall sconce with a sixty-watt bulb that she only turned on when she needed to take out the garbage. So, of course, the dim lighting must have been the reason for the strange shadowed outline rimming the reflective metal that jutted off the man's back in long, wide panels. She squinted, allowing the cool glass against her forehead to do what it could to ground her, then sucked in a sharp breath.

Those wide inexplicable metal panels were neither flat nor angular. Instead, the edges arced up and outward with a curved flair, culminating in delicate and clearly defined tips. Wing tips. Beneath the dim light of her woefully inadequate sconce, flat feathers of gleaming platinum shingled along the great sloping lengths. Despite their metal appearance, the wings didn't behave like her brain told her they ought to—and wasn't that just the most delusional thing? Instead of hard metal planks scratching her deck and crushing the poor man, the wings lay still and draping, almost wrapping around him like a weighty blanket.

Bridget's mind whirled. *Maybe he's a cosplayer?*

And then the man's smoothly capped shoulder slowly lifted. Even in the paltry light, the hem of his T-shirt sleeve was visible as it clung against a taut bicep curved from strain. There was no outright bodily damage that she could discern, but there were definitely other bodily things she couldn't help but appreciate. The clean-cut lines of him, even mostly hidden by those costumed wings, swept down his agile form like smooth facets of a finely carved gemstone. Everything about him was honed. Battle-ready, absurd as it sounded. It wasn't a common look among the men Bridget knew. Even her brother, who was fit as a horse, would never be able to manage the subtle strength this man possessed. Perhaps he was one of those CrossFitters who also favored endurance running. Odd, but not impossible.

A prickle of curiosity fluttered through her. Then came the tidal wave of common freaking sense. She should be running. She should be sprinting upstairs for her phone to get her brother over here or, at the very least, call the police. Bridget, however, did none of those things. Instead, her fingers drifted idly toward the door handle.

The instant she gripped the cold enameled metal, the man's body sagged and stilled again.

"Shit." The whispered word was more of a desperate plea than an outright exclamation. He needed help, but no way could she allow visitors here. She didn't *do* visitors, especially not strange men. No, never men.

She dropped her chin and stared at her toes, wincing at the new snagged holes courtesy of one frightened tabby cat. *What to do? What to do?* A shuddering breath buffeted through her. If she called her brother or the police, there would be far more than one stranger in her house. Not only would people be invading her home and property, but patrol cars would line the street, along with an ambulance. Flashing lights and blaring sirens would shine a glaring spotlight on her, and her neighbors would do far more than peek curiously through a window. Oh no, they'd come out on their front lawns to pry, as if their home-owners' association fees entitled them to privacy invasion.

With a single call for help, Bridget would bring the entire town to her doorstep.

A sharp crack rent the night air. She jerked her head up in time to see a bolt of lightning cleave the sky. "Dammit, the storm."

She'd forgotten about the weather, primarily because she'd planned to be in bed well before it started. *Crap crap crap.* Bridget braced herself for the second thunderclap and glanced at the fallen man.

The sheets of feathered metal, which had lovingly draped over their wearer a moment ago, now shimmered with an iridescent sheen. The starkly angled curves faded until the metal wings were but ripples of translucence—here one instance and gone the next. Bridget could see clear through to the man's broad back and trim waist. Did the wings somehow *absorb* back into his body?

"Holy shit! Okay, that's not a costume." Another bolt of lightning flared, this one illuminating the swarms of storm clouds fast approaching Bridget's house. She peered behind her at the stairwell.

Phone or home. Phone or home.

"Phone. Definitely phone. Ryan can keep the emergency personnel here to a minimum."

She took one uneasy step away from the door and made to turn toward the stairs when a wailing moan drifted through the glass. The sky had opened up, pelting her deck and the man's back with fat angry raindrops. Thunder boomed again. The trees around her property groaned and swayed their protest against the wind. Lightning cracked, and a memory flashed, one of another night just as stormy. *A swerving rural road, crunching metal, blood rushing to her head, unknown hands pulling her out . . .*

She swallowed down the threatening lump. Her misted eyelids shuttered with the barest of tremors. No, she wouldn't think about it. While she willed the visions back to the depths of her memory, one piece, however, still lingered.

She had been rescued, and right now, despite her fears, this man needed rescuing as well.

"God, I can't believe I'm about to do this."

Bridget scrambled toward the coat closet, threw on her raincoat, boots, and gloves, and ran toward the back door. Biting wind licked at her skin, and rain beat down on her face beneath a hood that struggled to stay up.

"Sir! Can you hear me? Are you okay?" His left foot twitched, though whether autonomic or in response to her, she couldn't tell. Then he dragged his right arm lower, as if attempting to get his strength under him to rise. Still, he didn't respond. His face, wedged between two chair legs, was turned away from her, so she couldn't see whether he was trying to speak.

Or trying to breathe.

Bridget carefully pushed the table forward and yanked away every chair surrounding him until she'd untangled his sprawled, soaking body from the deck adornments. She was just about to lay her gloved hand on his back when she paused. A long brown leather scabbard, strapped to his frame by crisscrossing bands that snaked around his front, sat snuggly along his spine. At the top of it, kissing the base of the man's neck, was a plain bronze grip. A sword. But like everything else with this man, something told her that too was different. The way it settled smoothly against his muscled frame, almost as if it was an extension of his body, hinted at the weight of it. No, it wasn't a costume or play sword, nor was the wearer unused to the feel of it on him.

It fit him like a second spine.

Do I really want to help a man who can hack me to pieces Gladiator-style?

Before she could think better of her situation, the man groaned and moved beneath her. A mess of soaked blond hair plastered over the man's brow and eyes at harsh angles. Water fell off his long aquiline nose in steady drips. His teeth were clamped shut, and it pulled his fine features into sharp slants.

"Sir?" Bridget tried again, louder this time. His eyes flew open, and blue irises the color of a frosted glacier snapped to hers. Never in her life had she seen such a chilling vibrant blue, and that was saying something given all the color palettes in her animation software. Those blue eyes widened a moment, then darted around the rest of her deck.

"Get inside," he rasped.

"You first. C'mon. Storm's getting worse." Bridget extended her hand toward his shoulder, but he wrenched away from her.

"Don't be foolish. Inside *now!*" The man managed to pull his knees under him, but even that small maneuver had him panting as though he'd just run a 5K. His arms trembled supporting his body weight alone.

"I'm trying to help you here," she snapped. "I have no idea why you're on my property, but I'd rather you not die underneath my patio furniture."

The man slammed his eyes shut and shook his head. Rain sheeted off his hair and pattered against the backs of his palms. "You don't know what you're doing. You need to be inside."

"I'll tell you what. I'll go inside if you come with me. Deal? Because if I'm being honest, you don't look so hot, and I don't necessarily want to be out in this storm any longer than you think I do. So, let's find a way to help each other, shall we?"

The man muttered a string of curses, but they were too low for Bridget to make out. She *did*, however, make out the *stubborn woman* loud and clear.

"Fine," he groused.

"Great. Here, lean on me." Bridget wedged her arm beneath his shoulder. Together, they rose. She nearly buckled under the weight of him. Even slouched and off-balance, the man was still a good head taller than her.

"Fucking hell," he gritted. His stride was slow and clearly

painful, and Bridget got the distinct impression this man was unused to this sort of vulnerability.

Buddy, I can relate.

His uneven gait forced more of his weight onto her, and she grunted against her body's protests. Her back screamed under the load, but she still dragged him as best she could.

"If you drop me, I won't blame you for it. I know I'm heavy. You shouldn't be doing this."

"One more step over the door sill. C'mon . . ." After the obligatory *one, two, three,* the two of them roared a combined grunt and spilled onto the kitchen floor in a sagging heap. Bridget clamored up and quickly sealed out the storm.

"Basement," the man barked out through open lips that were nearly kissing—perhaps borderline eating—the linoleum.

"I don't have a basement. Let's sit at the dining room table. Or perhaps the couch, which would definitely be more comfortable, but it's more of a shlep—"

"Yes, you have a basement, and you'll take me there. Now. I need to be underground."

She scoffed and crossed her arms. "You're hardly in a position to be giving orders." She pointed her chin at him to emphasize his dilapidated state on her kitchen floor. "And need I remind you that I didn't have to rescue your ass at all? I could have left you out there, you know."

"No," he breathed out quickly, "you couldn't have. Oh, you most definitely *should* have, but you're not that smart, apparently."

"Hey, asshole, I just saved you from that storm out there! So, *you* should be the one following *my* instructions."

"I'd be more than happy to take . . . orders . . . once I'm . . . underground. Now, the basement . . . *please.*"

Oooh, he's dredging up his manners now. Must really be desperate.

"I already told you, I don't have a basement—"

"There." The man gestured toward the door opposite her coat closet. Her basement door.

What the hell? She took a step back until her kitchen counter blocked her retreat.

"Look, I won't harm you. Never. But I need to get underground, and—" Another pained wince flitted over his features. "I know you saw me." He lifted his head, and again, those icy-blue eyes pinned her with an uneasy awareness.

"You had wings," she stammered. "And then you didn't."

He held her gaze for a heartbeat, then dropped his chin slightly. That single nod of affirmation scraped icy shards of fear down her spine. She stayed frozen against the kitchen counter.

The man puffed out a resigned sigh. "I'll answer all your questions, but I need your help. Get me underground and once I'm healed"—his eyes flicked away from her, then reluctant bitterness filled his face—"you can have at me."

"I should call the police."

"Yes, you should." No defiance, no judgment.

Who the hell is this guy?

Bridget stood there for a time. God, what the hell was she doing? Was she seriously considering this? But as she stared down at the injured man and the sopping puddle beneath him seeping into the faux grout lines of her otherwise normal kitchen floor, her long-dormant sense of curiosity, which had been bottled up and denied for so long, screamed for attention.

Pity and concern punched through her gut. The man was all weak limbs and had as much energy as a new mother following thirty-six hours of grueling labor. Her brother's voice, and one of his favorite oft-used expressions, flitted through her mind. *A good fart would knock him sideways.*

Vulgar, yes, but she could hardly deny its accuracy at the moment. No, this man wasn't a threat to her, at least not like this.

"Fine. Basement it is. But unless you plan on me barrel-rolling you down a flight of stairs, we're going to have to master the slow descent method."

The man dropped his head onto the meager cushions of his shaky forearms. "Thank you."

"Don't thank me yet. I still haven't ruled out violence." Bridget squatted down next to him, and together, they began the agonizing trek down the basement.

It wasn't until they were nearly at the bottom that she wondered how he knew, with such certainty, her house even had a basement.

CHAPTER 4

The climb down to Bridget's basement was only fourteen steps, yet every time Steel descended the next riser, he would have bet his favorite leather jacket the damn staircase grew longer. It was a literal stairway to hell, made all the more aggravating by the sprightly woman supporting him. She had all the determination of a secondborn child eager to please but also sported a hefty dose of self-satisfying manipulation common among thirdborn children.

Any way he sliced it, he was fucked.

His tender back muscles bunched and quivered beneath her light hold. He gritted back the pain and had no choice but to lean on her otherwise. The only slight blessing in all of this was his dark, soaked clothes. Any bleeding on his back wouldn't look as bad when he'd finally peel off his shirt. Perhaps he'd convince her to let him tend to the wounds himself and prevent her from seeing that bloody show altogether.

His feet found the level concrete floor with a thud, and his back teeth met.

"Here, over to the couch." Bridget grunted again and angled him toward the right.

"No, the floor is fine."

"If you wanted to pass out on a cold, hard surface, I could have just left you on my deck."

"I told you to. You didn't listen."

"Because you're delusional and I didn't want half the neighborhood thinking I was as well. Couch. Now."

Another insistent yank forced his shoulder to change direction. His sad body got in line and followed the leader. There was a brief whoosh of air, and then his face settled onto soft, worn microfiber. Every one of his limbs fell lax, effectively giving up the ghost. Before he could resettle himself, quick footsteps shuffled back up the stairs. A moment later, they returned. He managed to loll his head to the side long enough to see Bridget standing in the corner of the basement gripping a simple pull chain. A tall floor lamp next to her flared to life, but its glow was soft and weathered. It wasn't at all like the garish insistence of LEDs that needed to make their presence known, but the muted sepia notes of a bygone sixty-watt bulb relegated to occasional dark corner illumination. A shadowed movement flashed beneath the lamp's glow. Grunting, he angled his head. Bridget was waving something at him.

"You try anything funny and I'll have the police here in under two minutes."

Steel groaned and tried to lie on his side. He managed the feat with all the grace of a hippopotamus on Ambien. Holy shit, was he feeling every single one of his immortal years. "Didn't you already mention something about not wanting half the neighborhood to know you're delusional?"

"I never said I'd call 911, smart-ass." She planted her fists on her hips, and for the first time since their encounter, Steel was finally able to get a good look at her.

Inky-black strands hung in damp sheets around her face and curved under a pert yet slightly round chin Steel suspected had just as much practice in defiance as its owner's acerbic tongue.

Her face's delicate oval frame was the perfect canvas for her subtle cheekbones and expressive features, which glowed with a misted sheen from the rain as she stood under the lamp's light.

It was a stark contrast to his wet dog look.

Her neat nose and sleekly curved brows punctuated an effortless femininity, but it was her eyes that truly captivated him. Pools of muted blue, so unlike the edgy harshness of his own, anchored her quiet beauty. Even her irises commanded a level of reservedness, as well as proffering a battle cry to those foolish enough to challenge her: *never apologize, never explain.*

A pang shot through him, and he settled his head farther into the pillow. "Don't hold out for my sake. Please, enlighten me."

She huffed and held the blocky object higher. Her phone. "My brother is a police sergeant."

"Ah."

A heavy weight landed in his gut, and a familiar sick, sour feeling coated his insides. She'd chosen to bring a stranger into her home, rather than allow a large presence of people near her, even if those people were called to keep her safe.

Nothing's changed, then.

Her microshort list of emergency go-tos still consisted of her brother and not a whole lot else, apparently. And if her brother was unavailable or gone? Who would she call for help? Would she even bring herself to risk it?

"Yes, *ah.* So, don't even think about—"

"What's your name?" Steel's words cut through his morose analysis of his savior's circumstances. Of course, he already knew that information, but he needed her to get it out in the open so he didn't have to worry about slipping up and revealing more than he should—again. He couldn't bring himself to regret the basement maneuver, however. His drained ass had to get down here, and desperate times were desperate for a reason.

She bristled, clearly not used to being interrupted. "Bridget."

He nodded as best he could. "My name is Steel."

"Steel? What are you, in some motorcycle club or something? Like some MC brotherhood?"

He chuckled and then winced. Curse her cheekiness. "If by *brotherhood* you mean *have brothers,* then yes. No motorcycle club as far as I know, but one of my brothers does own a Ducati. And Steel is what I go by. You can think of it as a nickname if you'd like."

"Why the basement? And how the hell did you know I even had one?"

Lumbering breaths replaced his previously steady ones. "All the single-family homes in this development have basements," he lied smoothly.

She glared at him. "How would you know?"

"Because I came to an open house here when these units were first built. I remembered the layout of the bi-level and figured yours was the same." He stilled under her assessing stare.

"You were considering buying a house here?" She arched a single delicate brow.

"Yes." *No.*

"So, you live around here, then?"

"No." *Yes.*

Haunting moans battered the house's lowest-bid aluminum siding. Upstairs, javelins of pelting rain hammered the windows, deck, and roof. His back muscles tensed alongside the sheets of water pummeling the house. Battered and tender skin tightened more harshly with each show of the storm's strength, reminding Steel of a far more pressing matter. Already, his celestial energy was searching, scanning for the nearest source of the undiluted metals and minerals he'd need to replenish his angel fire. When he hurled himself in front of that charmer's magic, the hit had been on par with kissing a fire hose whose valve was cranked all the way open. Brutal pressure had battered his body and tossed him through the air like a clay target, but thank the mages it was only that—a pressure-packed punch intended for mortal teenagers. If the hit had been laced with magic specially crafted for him or any of his brothers, however, he'd have a much bigger problem on his hands. If he'd even still have hands at all.

More scuffing echoed through the basement, followed by the *squish-clop, squish-clop* of rainboots. Bridget squatted next to the couch and revealed a small pile of neatly folded clothes. Shit, he hadn't even noticed she'd brought them down with her. The woman could have grabbed a kitchen knife to go along for the ride while she was upstairs, and he would have been too out of it to notice until the thing was already four inches into his gut.

Good thing she didn't give off stab-happy vibes.

Those dangerous steel-blue eyes settled on him again. "These are my brother's clothes. He's a bit stockier than you are, and not as tall, but it's the best I can do." She held the clothes out to him. A peace offering of sorts, or more like an exchange: dry clothes for explanations.

Steel accepted them and, finally, after exhibiting far less dignity than he'd have preferred, got his butt upright on the couch.

"Thanks." His response was short and given to her back as she retreated up the stairs.

"I'll give you privacy . . . and five minutes," she threw down to him over her shoulder. "After that, I'll decide whether and who I'll be calling."

"I can heal fast. I just need rest," he replied thickly.

She stopped at the top of the stairs and turned to him. "Needing rest is a no-brainer, but I'll be the judge of the healing. You're obviously breathing if you're able to talk, and I don't see fluids leaking out of you, but if you need anything beyond basic Girl Scout first aid . . ." She worried her bottom lip, and the corner of her jaw ticked ever so slightly, as if the ramifications of that idea didn't sit well with her. "Just change if you need to. I'll be back."

The door clicked behind her. Finally alone, Steel dropped to the floor, with only the weak light of the lamp to illuminate the massive clusterfuck he'd found himself in.

IN THE SECONDS it took Bridget to pull her head through her sweatshirt's collar, the time on her phone kicked over to twelve fifteen in the morning. She grabbed the phone, pulled up her contacts—which consisted of her brother, Michael, and her boss—and hovered her thumb above Ryan's name. It would be one second, one simple second for the call to connect, then another ring while she waited for him to pick up. Perhaps two if he was already in bed with Michael. In his world, he was used to middle-of-the-night calls. Never from his sister, though. All she had to do was slam her thumb over her brother's face and his lazy smirk and he'd be rolling up her driveway in the time it'd take her to triple-check Elliot was still hiding under the couch.

She didn't, though. No, instead she threw her phone into the center pocket of her hoodie, gripped the thing like doing so would magically blitz her back in time forty-five minutes, and marched her butt back to her waiting patient.

Patient. Ha! If her dilapidated childhood Barbies and string of numerous deceased house plants were anything to go by, she had zero business playing the part of doting caregiver. The only reason she even had Elliot was because her brother insisted she needed some sort of daily exposure to another carbon creature, if only for his peace of mind. And because she loved her brother —and the automatic cat feeder and water dispenser he'd set up —she'd obliged.

But a blond stranger in her house, especially a stranger so large he nearly crested the top of her basement doorway despite his hunched state, who did his best to still support as much of his substantial weight as possible as she helped him hobble down the stairs? This wasn't just uncharted territory. It was a complete fantasy! And then there were the wings . . .

Despite the phone in her hand, her fingers itched to grab her stylus pen and tablet. Even amid all the nastiness Mother Nature was throwing their way, the deluge and wind hadn't obscured the sight of those wings. Long, clean lines had arced up and out of Steel's muscled back like mystical sheets of carved ice. Platinum-tipped arches peaked with glinting points before sloping back down in a brush of shingled silver.

Even as her sock-clad feet scampered down the stairs, her mind whirled at a matched pace. Freaking wings! Unbelievable. Already her thoughts were a blaze of color samples and contoured highlighting. Which colors would she pick if she were to draw them? Which darker tones would she shade into the silver to enrich their depths? And the size of them! They had nearly been as long as her deck was wide, and she couldn't help but wonder at the mechanics of them, or how they faded into glittering nothingness as soon as she'd gotten a good glimpse of them. Were they like turtles, shrinking into their shells at the first sight of movement?

Her quick feet cleared the bottom basement step. "OK, let's get a damage report here—"

The couch was empty, save for the pile of dry clothes she'd left.

"Hello?"

Nothing, and she was sure she'd have heard him if he had gone back up to the main floor. But c'mon, the man could hardly stand upright, and she had been a hairbreadth away from rolling him down the stairs for all the good his legs were doing, regardless of how powerful they looked.

Bridget took a left and walked over to the side of her basement that wrapped around toward the back of the stairs, where her washer and dryer hung out. Had he somehow summoned enough strength to throw his wet clothes over there? But when she was again met with a whole lot of dark and quiet, her skin prickled.

"Hello? Steel?"

Turning to her right, she padded toward the only other vacant area of the basement—the small alcove that housed her water heater, boiler, circuit breaker, and the tangle of pipes responsible for easy living. The sole lamp was far from this corner, but there was enough light to make out the long tan bare legs stretched out before her.

"Shit!"

Steel lay sprawled on his stomach on top of the cold concrete floor and wore absolutely nothing save his black boxer briefs. Rumpled clothes—his own, not the ones she'd left him— sat in a soggy pile by his feet.

Bridget did her best to scramble toward where his head was, but he had somehow managed to squeeze the top half of himself nearest to the pipes jutting from the wall. What the hell? She reached for his shoulders, intending to yank his upper body away from the wall lest he wake up and bash his beautiful blond head against the iron pipes, but something about his arm placement had her halting.

Unlike when she had found him wedged underneath her patio furniture, his position was different. Yes, he was still on his belly, but his arms were straight out in front of him, as if reaching for something. She followed the long lines of him and tried not to dwell on how the shadows dipped and curled over the taut bands of muscle, how his body rippled with honed strength even in the darkness. When her gaze reached his hands, surprisingly, they were frozen in a vice grip around the solid iron pipe of her main water service line. Oddly enough, the image made her smile and called to mind lazy summer afternoons when she and her brother would hold the garden hose to their mouths and drink greedily before returning to endless sprinkler play.

"Steel?" She leaned closer to his ear and said his name more softly. And even though the cut lines of his arm muscles were visible, they didn't seem unnaturally tense despite his death grip on the pipe. No, there was almost a casual ease to them, as if the pipe were a pillow and its contact made for deeper sleep and sweeter dreams.

Bridget ducked her head farther to inspect her curious patient. Beneath the short fall of haphazard blond waves, a calm serenity softened his features. His eyes were closed, and light lashes—long for a man and more beautiful because of it—kissed the tips of his angled cheeks. Those full lips still held the slight tension she remembered when he was awake, but his lower lip boasted a subtle softness, even as it sagged slightly, allowing his mouth to fall open with each breath.

Breathing. He was definitely breathing, and not the short, raspy breaths of someone with fever or hypothermia, but the long languid inhales of someone knee-deep in some quality REM sleep.

A soft chuckle escaped her. "I'd rather cuddle with Elliot than an iron pipe, but I'm hardly one to judge. Exhaustion does funny things to people."

Content that her patient wasn't going to die on her, she braced her hands on her thighs and stood up. The dim lamplight's muted glow lay differently on him than it had from her vantage point on the floor. From up above, Bridget had a glorious bird's-eye view of a whole lot of mostly naked male. Even as she shifted toward the staircase, she couldn't tear her gaze away from all that was laid out before her.

Good Lord, his body was amazing. A golden Adonis bathed in shadowy perfection. Each dark curve of the light's absence painted his broad back in sweeping strokes of brutally carved beauty. Commanding power trailed lower, almost sizzling beneath his solid form. Her eyes danced over the dip of his lower back before the curvature rose again, brushing the muscled arc of his backside. For the second time in fifteen minutes, she longed for her stylus pen, ached to record the beauty of this stranger before the sun rose and whatever bizarre dream she was living was shunted to the recesses of her mind.

But to draw it, capture it, even allow herself one moment to imagine what it would feel like to . . .

Bridget slammed her eyes shut and exhaled. "Stop. Just stop."

Oh, but who was she kidding? Even her internal reprimand lacked any sort of true bite.

A sharp snort broke through her paltry battle of wills. She opened her eyes and took in the behemoth once more. Wide shoulders rose and fell in a steady, even rhythm. As he inhaled again, a soft snore rumbled through him.

She smiled. Definitely no fever or imminent death. No, she had nothing more to worry about from him tonight and could finally turn her attention to tending to her own exhaustion.

"Sleep well," she whispered.

Tomorrow, she would call her brother. Yes, tomorrow.

CHAPTER 5

Steel had woken up in a lot of bizarre places during his eternally long life, and he was well past the point where surprises were . . . well, surprising. The bracing cold surface against his cheek and chest seemed vaguely familiar, as did the circular iron pipe still kissing his palms. What wasn't familiar, however, was the soft cocoon of the cotton-polyester blend his toasty back half found itself nestled under.

Groaning, he unclamped his stiff fingers from the pipe and stood. A cloud of burgundy blanket tumbled from around his shoulders and pooled in a fluffy pile at his feet. Odd. He didn't remember any blankets down here. No, aside from the pile of dry clothes Bridget left him, there hadn't been any other creature comforts of that nature. Perhaps it had been folded and sitting on the back of the couch? As soon as the thought came online, however, he dismissed it. Why have a blanket folded and at the ready, on a couch no one used, in a basement that was as uninviting and utilitarian as they come? Unless . . .

Bridget had brought it to him while he slept.

Bridget.

The night came back to him, along with his rush of poor

34

choices and bad penchant for oversharing. Crap, how much had he told her? His mind ran through everything, from his encounter with the charmers to landing on Bridget's deck to her asking about his wings.

"Shit."

Like a bad penny, his desperate words from the night before floated back to him.

I'll answer all your questions. Get me underground, and once I'm healed, you can have at me.

Steel bent down and picked at his sodden clothes, but he let them plop right back onto the concrete. Never one to look a gift horse in the mouth, he threw on the clothes that were left for him. Whoever they'd belonged to—her brother, Bridget had said—was indeed stockier but not so far off that he couldn't make the digs work. A few rolls of the waistband had the sweatpants settled where they needed to be, even if he was flashing more ankle than he'd prefer. The long-sleeve T-shirt was a tad baggy but manageable. He spotted the dryer in the corner of the basement and threw his clothes into the drum, set the dial to timed dry, and punched the start button.

By the time he'd walked into the kitchen, the smell of medium roast did an excellent job of setting his priorities to rights. It wasn't French press, but it also wasn't gas station insta-drip. Again, another win.

He took a step forward, but a blur of orange and white shot across his feet. "What the—"

"Oh, that's Elliot. Hey, you're up. That's a good sign. You survived. Ta-da!"

Across from the breakfast bar, Bridget was stirring something at the stove while sipping from a steaming mug. She quickly set the cup down and scrambled to pick up the cat.

"He's very friendly, I think." Her reassurance was questionable.

"You think?"

"Well, he doesn't get a lot of visitors." Her short nails tended to a spot behind the cat's left ear, and that feline closed his eyes and sank into what looked to Steel like the ear scratch of a lifetime.

"May I?" He gestured toward the chair at the counter. Bridget nodded, then brought Elliot to the floor. The groan of Steel's chair legs against the linoleum may as well have been an air siren. He caught Bridget's gaze, then the expectant lift of her chin.

Aaand just like that, his grace period had run out. *Time to talk, buddy.*

"So, I guess we should start with—"

"Before we start, I need to know where—"

They both stilled, but Steel casually gestured for her to continue.

"I just mean, I hope you, um, slept okay, and if you're up for it, I'd like to ask you some questions. Oh! And breakfast. There's breakfast, too." She whirled around to the stove and scooped out some steel-cut oatmeal into a bowl. "There's already maple syrup and cinnamon in here, but I have dried cranberries and sunflower seeds that I also like to add. Sometimes walnuts. Oh, did you want walnuts? Wait, you don't have a nut allergy, do you? That would suck, as I'm pretty sure my cabinet doors are held together with peanut butter, I eat so much of it. There's coffee, too." She dropped the wooden serving spoon into the bowl, heedless of the scant half-serving she'd portioned out, before flitting to a nearby cabinet. "Yup, walnuts," she said with a proud nod of her chin, as if she'd just claimed some small victory for accomplishing a hostess duty she was worried she'd fail at. Walnuts in hand, she walked back over to the bowl and finished scooping out the oatmeal.

Steel held his tongue, and dropped his hands beneath the counter, where she couldn't see the shameful rage curling his fingers into angry fists.

Four years of this.

The coffee's sweetly bitter aroma turned sour in his nose, twisting his gut into tight coils of wretched guilt and foul memories.

". . . the half-and-half is already out, next to the coffee pot. Oh, do you drink dairy? Some people don't, I know, but it's what I prefer. Although, I think I have some of that shelf-stable almond milk my brother likes. Let me check." She placed a bowl of steaming oatmeal, bejeweled with glistening dried cranberries and dotted with smooth ovals of sunflower seeds, in front of him. Craggy walnuts bobbed in neat defiance of the viscosity they now found themselves in. The little beige earthen islands amid a sea of sweetness had no choice but to accept their fate. He could relate. With a dip of his spoon, Steel sent them under.

"I need to know where you put my things."

Bridget walked back to the counter, a carton of in-no-way-is-that-real-milk in her hand. "Your clothes?"

"Try again." He shook his head and took a bite. *Mm-hmm.* Never in a million years would he have tried dried cranberries in the oatmeal . . . and the sunflower seeds? He licked his spoon clean and shoveled in another bite.

"Oh, the, um . . ."

"My weapons and phone. I kind of need those."

"Yeah, well . . . I kind of *don't* need you to need those right now. I'd prefer we talk first."

Steel settled the spoon in his bowl, then took a sip of coffee—with real dairy—and eyed her speculatively. Even though her lower half was largely hidden by the breakfast bar, he wouldn't have been surprised to see a pair of giant brass balls hanging out loud and proud, especially knowing what the woman had endured. Hell, even some of his brothers would have gone prickly and offensive had they been in her situation. It wasn't every day you found yourself harboring a fallen angel with more edged weapons strapped to his body than could be found in the Smithsonian's sword and scabbard exhibit.

In the light of the new morning, Steel couldn't help but study her further. So different up close. Her straight raven hair had been neatly smoothed so it curved softly around her cheeks. A smattering of freckles dusted the bridge of her nose, and the contrast struck him. In all the time he watched over her from afar, he'd never gotten close enough to notice them. So unusual for someone with her dark hair.

Just like her willingness to see an armed stranger fed when she had every reason in the world to shut him out worse than all the others. And the first thing he threw her way was not a word of gratitude but a bark of inquiry over what she did with his weapons?

By the mages, he was an ass.

He set the spoon down. "Thank you. I am truly humbled and beyond grateful for the aid you showed me last night and this morning. Please forgive my rudeness."

Those searching blue eyes assessed him a moment longer. Then she nodded. "Forgiven."

"And you have not called your brother yet."

"No, I haven't. But I will," she rushed out. "I will if I need to. He always checks in while he's at work anyway, so . . ."

"And he's a police sergeant."

"Yeah." No threat, just a statement. Then she turned to finish fixing her own bowl of oatmeal. "Your stuff is in the closet across from the basement door. I didn't want Elliot running into any of it." Read: she didn't want her cat slicing off his tongue or fur when curiosity would inevitably have him rubbing and licking all over Steel's very real and very sharp blades.

"Again, thank you."

She shrugged, then lifted her coffee to her lips. The heavy silence between them settled thickly over every surface of the kitchen until the elephant in the room could no longer be avoided.

He took one last bracing sip of medium roast. "What do you remember?"

"What do *I* remember? I should be asking you that question."

"Humor me."

"Well, I was in bed reading. Elliot heard a loud bang and bolted. I went after him, and then I found you face-planted on my deck. As soon as you were semi-conscious, you kept yelling at me to get inside. I gather you remember most of what happened after that." Curious eyes bore into his. "How did you wind up in my backyard anyway? What happened to you?"

Mages give me strength. And more caffeine.

Steel rose from his seat and walked over to the coffee pot. Flecks of cinnamon lightly dusted the carafe's handle. He followed the simple trail of spice along the gray and white swirling marble until he took in the sienna-brown smudge on Bridget's fingertips. The corner of his lip lifted. "You don't go light on the cinnamon, do you?"

"What? Oh, no, I guess I don't." She quickly wiped her hand on her jeans, effectively painting her pants in the honeyed brown spice.

He busied himself with fixing his coffee and doing his best to bite back the moan at her further coating herself in his favorite flavor. "Tell me, have you noticed any strange vehicles driving through the development, especially late at night?"

"What sorts of vehicles?"

"Operations vehicles—pickup trucks, vans, anything that might hold cargo."

Bridget pursed her lip in concentration. "Like from the resort?"

Steel dropped the spoon he was using to stir his coffee. "Torrey Mountain Resort, yeah. Official vehicles from there."

"Sure, I see them from time to time." Her eyes shifted in

eager avoidance.

"How often?" His voice turned icy.

"I don't know. Once or twice a week, maybe. There's always a bunch of them. I don't pay much attention, honestly."

"Last night, a caravan of those vehicles came through the development. I was following them."

"Okay . . ."

"They were not official resort vehicles."

"Then what were they?"

"That's what I was investigating when I got . . . injured."

"How did you get injured and wind up in my backyard? That's the answer we're both dancing around, isn't it? You don't think I should know the answer because you've inadvertently creamed your cup of coffee twice already. I'm pretty sure it's undrinkable now, unless you like chugging coffee-flavored half-and-half."

He peered down at all that unintended cafe au lait in his mug, then shifted against the counter and ran a hand through his hair. How could he tell her? Where did one start? But the fact remained that the charmers had been so close to her. So *close*. Had they known one of the very souls the demons had been searching for resided in the same development they'd been traipsing through night after night? One of the very souls he and the other sentinel angels had sworn to protect?

"Look, there are things you're going to hear from me that might sound . . . different."

"Different how?"

"Different as in skewing toward the unbelievable."

Spit it out. Spit the fucking words out. You don't have the time to be pussyfooting around the truth.

"Like . . . your wings?"

He looked up at her. A half-smile lifted her lips, and her eyes were alight with a sparkling curiosity. Not fear or trepidation, but genuine interest, as if wings sprouting from a man's back were a common occurrence and she was eager to compare colors and wingspans.

Ridiculous. Foolish. Who was this woman? She should be running from him, and yet . . .

He slowly nodded, and to his immense astonishment, that half-smile of hers grew to match the brightness in her eyes.

"Tell me, Bridget. What creatures do you know that have wings?" Crap, his heart threatened to punch through his chest. He was really doing this, leading her down a road she could never turn back from. He should stop, grab his shit, and leave right the hell now, but those haunting misted eyes pinned him where he stood, as if knowing, accusing, blaming.

She narrowed her brows. "Well, birds, bats, that sort of thing. If we go back further, you've got those flying dinosaurs."

He was doing this. He *had* to do this.

"What other sorts of creatures have wings?" He gave her a look of what he hoped was encouragement.

She shook her head. "Um, I don't know. Harpies, griffins, winged horses like Pegasus."

"Keep going. What else?"

Her lower lip fluttered. "I . . ."

"Think." It was a flat-out command. If she could connect the dots on her own . . . "What creature with a human appearance would have wings?"

She sucked in a breath, and he detected the moment she'd latched onto what he needed her to imagine. To *believe*. Her eyes darted around all that open-concept living space as if expecting the very thing no doubt painting the front of that imaginative brain of hers to jump from around a corner.

It's already here, Bridget.

"No human . . ." The words trembled, but even as she shook her head with uncertainty, the one phrase he all but demanded to hear tumbled from her shaking lips. "Angel."

Bingo.

CHAPTER 6

ngel.

The word fell from Bridget's mouth before she could take it back, before she'd had an opportunity to explain how the notion was just a byproduct of her quirky sense of humor. She was a graphic designer who moonlighted with delusions of being an animator one day, so yeah, she had a thing for mythical creatures and fantasy entertainment. The operative words there being *mythical* and *fantasy.* Angels were about as real as pixies or bridge trolls or rock star goblin kings.

She tittered out a laugh, but when those glacial blue eyes remained focused on her, when he didn't return or even acknowledge her forced attempt at levity, her tight smile fell.

The silence stretched on again. God, she hated the silence, hated it even more so because the man in front of her had an equal opportunity to bust right through the thick stuff, and yet he wasn't. Why the hell wasn't he talking?

"Please say something," she pleaded.

Thick blond brows slanted, and the corners of his eyes fell slightly. "You guessed correctly."

"I didn't guess anything! You asked what winged creatures I knew of, and I answered."

"You saw me," he said pointedly.

"There was a freaking storm outside. It was nighttime. My outdoor lights are crap." Even as she said the words, some secret part of her didn't believe them, knew they were only frantic offerings from the little princess in her mind trying to protect her.

"You still saw me."

"I couldn't miss a body sprawled out on my back deck!" The oatmeal had turned leaden in her stomach. She couldn't be considering this, couldn't *actually* be considering what the man before her was hedging her toward.

And yet you *brought up the wings.*

"What do you remember?"

"You asked me that already, and I told you." God, she sounded petulant, like a straight-A, front-of-the-class third grader in the principal's office stomping her foot in denial when accused of cheating.

"What do you remember? *Really* remember?"

Her mouth had gone dry. The lingering coffee's essence had turned rancid on her tongue. She shook her head frantically and braced a hand on the refrigerator.

No. No. No. He couldn't be serious, could he?

But those icy eyes of his dipped slightly, as if she wasn't the only one warring with an impossible truth. His fists bunched at his sides. "Why haven't you called your brother yet?"

Words froze in her throat. Why hadn't she? She sure as hell had a good enough reason to do so. The closet of knives and swords—*real* knives and swords—should have topped the list, but her phone still sat nestled in the back pocket of her jeans.

"May I help?" he asked softly.

"Help?"

He nodded. "I have a suspicion why you haven't called your brother yet or any other authorities."

"Oh?"

His chest deflated with a sigh, and he leveled sad eyes on her once more. "Because it's one thing for you to acknowledge the inexplicable to yourself, but it's another thing entirely to speak it out loud, especially to others who may want to interfere if what you tell them seems a little . . . far-fetched."

The impact of his words slammed into Bridget with a bludgeoning force. Even if she were to acknowledge the wings—those truly fascinating and powerful wings—how would that come across? Would her brother, or anyone else, believe her when she wasn't entirely certain she believed herself, even if a growing part of her wanted to . . . was even exhilarated by the prospect of giving in to the belief?

The refrigerator's compressor kicked on, and the gentle hum of its vibration tickled her palm and fingertips. It reminded her of another humming vibration that stuck in her mind from years before—a low sputtering growl of a dying vehicle's engine. The cold asphalt under her backside and feet was a sporadic memory that loved to make itself known. Another time where her fate had been shrouded in something inexplicable, where concerned and doubting faces were the only receptions she'd received, despite her yells, her screams.

"I'm not crazy," she rushed out.

"No, you're not." Then he smiled encouragingly. "Between you and me, you're the sanest one in this room."

"What game are you playing at?"

"No game, I swear. Just trying to help the cause."

"What cause?"

He stuffed his hands into his pockets, a submissive casual gesture. "Trust."

"You want me to trust you?" She scoffed.

"I want you to trust yourself, trust what you saw."

"What I saw—"

"Was real."

Bridget shook her head. "No."

But then he shrugged a shoulder and relaxed farther against the counter. "You tell me. And whatever you decide, whatever you say, I'll believe you, because it'll be the truth."

"You're crazy." She threw the barb at him, the very one that had been flung at her countless times over the years, but he just leaned there with an air of easy encouragement.

"What do you remember?"

Without a viable escape route, her addled fury relented to the man's troubling line of questioning. *What do I remember?*

Bridget squeezed her eyes together tightly, as if doing so would block out the cold pressure in her chest and leave room for the burgeoning kernel of hope and wonder that had nestled inside her when she'd first beheld him.

What do I remember?

"Everything," she breathed out, her eyes still closed, but her heart a bit lighter. "I remember everything. I remember the inexplicable . . . power, I guess . . . thrumming off you when I found you on my deck. I remember my confusion and fear, worry at your unconscious state, but trepidation—"

"What else?"

"I remember you weren't moving at first, but there was no blood, no cuts or slashes or anything. And then your body shifted slightly . . ."

"What else?" His prodding grew more insistent.

"I remember . . ."

"Say it, Bridget. What do you remember?"

Her eyes were pinched closed so tightly, but already her chest was lighter, her breaths more even and deeper. She couldn't stop, *wouldn't* stop, regardless of the consequences.

"Wings. I remember long sheets of platinum wings jutting from your back." Her eyes flew open. "They were large and looked heavy, not weighed down like something sodden with water, but draped and still, like a layer of protection. Like those old Scottish plaids from Highlander tales, where the weave was so tight and fine, it would keep out the most brutal of winter's ice and wind. There were feathers too but not those gossamer tissue-like feathers on Valentine's Day cupids and Christmas tree toppers. No, these looked strong and were shingled in row after row of what seemed like an impenetrable yet fluid metal. Funny thing, I actually had a thought that it was an improvement on the original design, you know? That perhaps angels *should* have indestructible wings instead of flimsy feathers."

Bridget's cheeks ached at the crests. To her shock, she had been smiling—no, not smiling but beaming. Then her face fell but only slightly. "They were gone before I knew it, though, just disintegrated into a translucent swirl around you. There were no markings on your back to indicate they'd been there, no tears through your shirt, no remnants of feathers or metal or anything. It was as if I truly *had* imagined it all, and then you woke up."

Shame at her confession heated her cheeks, and she braced for the inevitable chastisement of her impossible imagination, of more of her brother's words on how she'd been holed up in the house for too long and desperately needed time in the real world.

The response she received, however, nearly knocked her to the floor.

"Thank you."

"What? What do you mean?"

"For your trust."

"I haven't given you any. I just told you what you were hounding me to share."

"Oh, you have, and I'd like to return the favor."

Bridget shook her head in disbelief. "You're crazy."

Steel pushed away from the lip of the kitchen counter and

walked into the living room. "You said that already, and yet you still haven't called your brother."

Before she could reach for her back pocket, Steel was already standing in the room across from her. His powerful body glinted in the new sun's rays, dappling the tan skin of his neck and profile.

And then he released them—two massive glinting sheets of silver wings.

TRUST WAS A FUNNY THING. When given freely, it could be a gift, a gesture of appreciation, or it could serve as many other happy tidings full of agreeable sentiments. Pennies on the dollar, really. However, when trust was given under skepticism, when it was offered up under scrutiny and had a mighty big job to do to turn things around, well, King Midas wasn't rich enough to pay that price.

So, there Steel stood, his angelic wings fanned out and, along with a hell of a lot more of him, offered up as his own show of trust. He flexed them wide, straining his shoulders and tensing his muscles, which had come a long way in a few hours below ground. The rich iron in the water service line had been more than sufficient to feed his metal and recharge his power's essence. But still, even fully healed and with his power restored for the time being, he worried how he'd fare under the continual wide slash of Bridget's gaze currently battering him.

That was something he was powerless against.

"Holy shit. Holy shit! It's real. They're real, I mean. No, *you're* real. But what are you, exactly?"

He grinned a fool's grin at her babbling and the little crinkle that furrowed its way onto the center of her brows. He couldn't help it. "You had the right of it before."

"No, because before, I said 'angel' and—"

"And as *I* said, you are correct."

She froze, still standing sentinel by the refrigerator door. "You're an angel."

"Yes."

"A real one."

"Yes."

"With wings."

"That usually is part of the package, yes."

That thick silence filled the room again, and he relaxed his wings behind him. He couldn't go on like this, couldn't have her spinning her wheels and questioning her sanity. Not again, not because of him.

He walked toward her, and to his great relief, she didn't run. She simply stood there with a mix of wariness and wonder sketched across her face.

"May we sit? I would very much like to explain myself, and I'm willing to venture a guess you'd like that, too."

"They're real, the wings. And you're an angel, standing in my house."

"If you prefer, I'll retract my wings. Then you can finish your breakfast"—he gestured toward her now-cold bowl of oatmeal—"and we can talk. Just talk. Nothing more."

"Don't," she cut in. "Please."

His stomach sank at her refusal, but he simply nodded.

"No, I mean, you don't have to retract your wings. They're stunning, and I can't stop looking at them. But not in a creepy way, I promise. I just . . . Wow, that's real metal, isn't it? Platinum?"

The starch left his shoulders, and that great leaden weight in his gut lifted slightly. "Steel, actually."

Her eyes widened. "Your wings? The same as your name?"

"Yes, they're one and the same." He walked toward her and offered to take the bowl from her hands. When she let him, he swept his arm out toward the couch in the living room. It was such a simple thing, eating together, talking, seeing her settled on the sofa so he could rewarm her breakfast and bring it to her. Purely domestic acts of a whole lot of nothing special. But as he stole glances from the kitchen to trace the delicate curves of her brows, her nose, her lips, a great loss punched through him. Aside from her brother, there had been no one else to offer her such simple affections.

Steel made quick work of his kitchen duties, then joined a still-stunned Bridget in the living room. He was mindful to take the loveseat, leaving the couch for her alone. He eased onto the cushion and couldn't help but smile as he tracked her watching him. Those dusty blue eyes immediately arced up and over his shoulder, never leaving the crest of his wings, even as he adjusted himself so his wings would rest over the back of the loveseat.

He sighed. "I wish this was easier."

"I'm not sure I do, to be honest. I still can't believe it." Bridget kept looking at him in that wondrous way. It was the shining look of dreamers and visionaries, of those who were in awe of long-kept fantasies come to life. For a moment, he wondered whether shopping-mall Santas received the same gleeful adoration from little ones who—hand to God, as the mortals would say—really believed a lumpy man in a rented velour suit would answer their every toy-related wish.

Though the sentiment humbled him, it was little more than another shovel of shit piled high on his black conscience. He forced a smile and did his best to shirk the thought, though tension still pinched the corners of his mouth.

"It's true. I am an angel. My brothers and I are sentinels who have long ago fallen from the Empyrean—what you might think of as heaven's highest realm."

"Fallen? You're a fallen angel?"

He nodded, and he didn't miss the trickle of unease that tightened her features.

"Why did you fall? How?" Such a tiny voice now, and he silently cursed the reason for it. Steel was well aware of mortal tales regarding fallen angels and how they painted celestial beings in condemnation for choices usually doused with a heavy helping of sin or insubordination. Ridiculous.

"To preserve heaven and the Empyrean, to keep it safe, we had to enact the Sealing. It was a final act of defense that sealed the gates, but it could only be accomplished from beyond its walls. My brothers and I took up the power and succeeded. In doing so, however, the resulting force expelled us from the realm. We landed here quite some time ago."

Bridget leaned so far forward on the edge of her seat, Steel worried she'd wind up on the floor in another moment. "What were you defending against, exactly?"

He took a deep breath. "Charmers. What mortals think of as demons. They're residents of the dark realm who had made a run on heaven and tried to snuff out its eternal light and the light of all the souls who dwell there." He gritted his teeth. "They view the Empyrean and all sources of light, whether celestial or solar, as threats to their existence because they cannot abide it. Darkness is their sanctuary. Light of any sort kills them, including the light of mortal souls, which all humans carry. They want it all gone and for darkness to reign."

Her lips parted, and she stared vacantly into her cold coffee.

Just rip the bandage off.

"Those operations vehicles I told you I was investigating? The ones from the resort?"

She nodded woodenly.

"Well, they were being driven by charmers."

Her head whipped up at that. "What? The ones that drove through my development last night?"

"Yes. I was fighting them when they made a cheap shot at some teenagers a block away. I intercepted the hit, but it blasted me out of the sky. You found me where I had landed."

"I don't . . . I don't . . ."

"I don't know why they're driving through your neighborhood, but we've got a bigger problem." His words were icy rage.

"What problem?"

"They know I'm tracking them, know that I went down somewhere in this vicinity."

"Okay . . ."

"Charmers can't be exposed to light of any kind. That includes daylight. So right now, with the sun out, they're no threat, but as soon as night falls, they'll be back here."

"Back here, as in my development."

"Yes, but more likely, they'll try to track where I landed."

"Wait!" She shot to her feet. "Are those things going to come to my backyard to try and find you? You need to leave. You need to leave right the hell now." Bridget whirled and began shuffling still-full dishes to the sink, no doubt giving herself something to do in an otherwise helpless situation.

He *should* leave, grab his gear and hightail it out of there so fast his ass groove on the loveseat cushion wouldn't have time to inflate before he was airborne, but shit . . .

"Do you have someplace to go?"

She turned, heedless of the water she left running in the sink. "Why do I need someplace to go? You're the one they're tracking, right?"

"Call your brother. Now. Stay with him if you need to."

"I don't need to go anywhere. I'm perfectly fine where I am."

Steel glanced around the contemporary single-family home, with its overstuffed furniture, neutral-colored walls, and sweet mass-market signs erected over entryways—signs like "Friends Are Like Fine Wine, They Get Better With Age" and "Cook for People What You Love and Everything Else Will Be Fine."

He was almost certain that if he walked into the bathroom, he'd find another sign above the crapper asking "Everything Come Out Fine?"

Bridget leaned on that four-letter F-word like a damn crutch, as if outsiders looking in would see *fine* plastered everywhere and think, *Yup, yes you sure are. So sorry to have intruded. Please, as you were.*

Fuck, she was so much worse off than he'd realized. What did he expect to happen by his big reveal? That he'd flash her some wing, tell her to keep an even lower profile, and pretend he hadn't just made her paranoia ten times worse?

He sighed and pressed his eyes with his thumb and forefinger. "You're not fine. You're anything but fine," he said with his head dipped low.

She killed the water and flung a dish towel over her shoulder. "How the hell would you know a damn thing about me?"

Because your fine little hell is my fault. Because every day for four years, I've watched you through that picture window.

"You know what I am, and I can't hide that anymore. Willing your ignorance back won't change reality, and it won't change what has to happen now." Oh, she was not going to like this, but in the immortal words of his brother Chrome, too bad, so sad.

"Nothing has to happen." That stubborn chin lifted his way, but he didn't miss the slight tremble to her bottom lip.

So much strength buried under all that fine-fine-fine.

Steel stalked toward her but halted when he reached the opposite side of the breakfast bar. "You've been exposed because of me. So, until I can figure out what the hell those demons are doing in your development, I'm not going anywhere."

He only wished she didn't hate him for it.

CHAPTER 7

There was only so much troubling news one could handle before nine in the morning and certainly before a second cup of coffee, and yet here Bridget was, waist-deep in a whole lot of outside-her-comfort-zone. The behemoth blond angel she was locked in a staring contest with certainly wasn't helping matters.

"For your information, this isn't the Hilton. I don't give out guest passes and complementary mints on pillows."

"So, does that mean I have to pay for the mints instead?"

"What? Ugh!" Bridget threw the towel at him. To her exceeding annoyance, the jerk caught it with one hand—his left hand. Of course, given the theme of the past nine hours, it was probably his nondominant hand to boot. At her feet, Elliot was meowing up a storm. She glared down at him. "You better not be playing favorites." Thankfully, the cat had the good sense to flick his tail and meander back over to the automatic feeder.

Mm-hmm. That's right.

"What I'm saying is, you can't stay here."

"I won't stay here—"

"Good—"

"During the day. Just at night."

"Excuse me?" Oh, she was fuming now. "Look, I don't care if you have wings, fangs, or a forked tongue. I am not inviting you to stay here. I don't know you, I don't care to know you, and as far as I'm concerned, you could be making up all that stuff about the charmers and resort vehicles."

He shot her a look as if to say, *Really? Do you regularly find unconscious angels ass-up, wings-out in your backyard?*

She rolled her eyes. "Fine."

As soon as she said the word, his shoulder tensed, and his lips thinned. The reaction caught her off guard and bothered her for some reason. "Is there—"

Her phone trilled from her back pocket, and she eyed the microwave clock above the stove. Eight forty-five on the dot. She accepted the call and mouthed, "My brother," before putting the phone to her ear. Steel simply nodded, but his body was still stiff. And why did she give him a heads-up at all about who she was talking to? He wasn't anything to her, and she'd already told him her brother would be checking in on her soon.

"Hey," she said, rummaging through the high cabinet to get more ground coffee.

"Hey yourself. Your neighborhood fare okay in that storm last night?" The crackle and commotion in the background told her Ryan was walking through the main open area of the station on the way to his office, most likely with his phone tucked against his shoulder and fisting two cups of black coffee—one to drink immediately and one to rewarm and gulp down approximately ten minutes after he finished the first one.

"Uh, yeah. We didn't lose power or anything. Though it looks like there were some large tree branches that fell in the street." Bridget busied herself digging out the coffee scooper inside the bag while her eyes tracked Steel, who was headed toward the hallway closet across from the basement.

"Whole town's a fucking mess. The southside of Aurora

went dark around two thirty last night—or this morning, I guess, hell. Electric crews are still on scene. I've got a scheduling nightmare clogging up my morning. I had to pull a quarter of the officers from the northside and assign them to traffic duty in the south because of all of the damn road closures."

"Yikes." Bridget did her filter-and-scoop routine and snapped the coffee machine lid closed. Behind her, subtle sounds of creaking leather and gentle clanging tickled her awareness.

"I don't need this shit," her brother groaned.

"At least all the town schools are on spring break. That's good, right? Not as many people on the roads?"

"Normally, sure, but since a good chunk of our officers are parents of those very kids, we're short-staffed. I did my best to accommodate everyone's time-off requests and even had to say no to some, but it still bit me in the ass. Fucking April storms." Papers rustled through the phone, along with the telltale chime of a computer waking up.

"But I still love you?" Bridget smiled and gripped the carafe before bringing it over to the sink to fill it up.

A familiar grunt rumbled through the phone, then a longer-than-normal pause. "Say, uh, have you given any more thought to that exhibit?"

Crap. She did *not* want to have this conversation now, again, here, ever—and definitely not with a fallen angel within earshot.

"Um ..."

She rested her hand on the tap, just about to fill the carafe with water, but stilled when the hallway quieted as well. Bridget turned and nearly dropped her phone. At the far end of the breakfast bar, which wasn't very far, Steel stood hunched over a small pad of pastel sticky notes. His large hand practically swallowed up her favorite kelly-green gel pen as he scribbled furiously across the paper's surface. Every weapon in that closet was now strapped and fastened to his body, making him look even harder and more formidable than she thought possible. True, she'd seen him armed before, but he had been nearly unconscious, drenched from head to toe, and had all the coordination of a newborn giraffe. Now, however, he was a sight.

His surfer blond hair was the only thing casual about him. Everything else was pure, sharp savagery. Powerful shoulders, tightly muscled arms, strong torso, everything honed to withstand the weight and balance of all those blades strapped to his body—blades that she knew the exact weight of because, while he was sleeping, she'd nearly crumpled to the floor after dragging the damn heavy things up the stairs and into the closet. Here he was, however, wearing the things without a thought, like she would wear earrings or a necklace.

"Earth to Bridget. You there?"

"Yeah, I'm here. Sorry, Elliot was scratching the carpet again."

Steel's lips quirked at the very obvious lie she told, then he finished off his note with a flourish. He didn't even make eye contact with her as he threw the pen down and slid the note across the counter. Before she could even read the thing, he walked toward the back door—to the place where it all began—and left. She whipped a curtain aside to try and track him, but there was absolutely nothing to track, nothing to see, not even a shadow on the ground to watch fade away.

"Ryan, I gotta go. I, uh, yeah, I don't think I'm up for the exhibit. Thanks anyway, though."

He sighed. "Okay, fine."

Remorse twisted her gut. "But I love you." She threw out her tried-and-true expression again, because God, she *did* love him, but what if, one day very soon, love might not be enough anymore? "Do you want to swing by for lunch?"

"Nah, can't. With the way today's shaping up, it'll probably be my ass in a patrol car managing traffic duty around that time."

"But you'll make such a cute traffic cop."

"Can it. I'll text you later."

"Love you," she said.

"Love you, too."

Call ended, Bridget scrambled for the note.

Back at 6 p.m. I'm cooking. Enjoy the coffee.

"Huh?"

Then Bridget glanced down at the coffee carafe still in her hand, the one she had meant to refill with water at the sink a moment ago. That was when she finally registered the weight of the thing, and the slight heat seeping into the handle against her palm.

Freshly brewed coffee sloshed at the bottom of the pot, just enough to fill her favorite twenty-ouncer, which had been set out beside the coffee maker, along with the half-and-half and a clean spoon.

———

THE SUN'S buttery rays baked the backs of Steel's wings. Below him, blue spruce trees blanketed the little valley at the foot of the White Mountains. Normally, when he made his descent into the tiny thicket of trees that housed the entrance to his and his brothers' den, it was with confidence and an overwhelming sense of calm. He imagined it was a bit like the feeling mortals got after gorging themselves on a heavy meal at home, where they relished the absolute freedom to unbuckle their belts in front of their loved ones and relax, unapologetically sated, in their chairs.

Instead of Steel relishing such great ease and comfort, however, his shoulders and limbs may as well have been carved from the very mountain he lived beneath. So much tension coiled in his frame, he wouldn't have been surprised if the lightest of taps sent him shattering.

I'm not going anywhere.

He hadn't intended to threaten Bridget, especially not after seeing the larger scope of just how bad things had gotten for her these past several years, but the truth of her circumstances—of *their* circumstances—couldn't be overlooked. He'd sooner slice his gut open with his favorite Lakonian short sword than see her further embroiled in anything having to do with those demons.

A granite slab nestled against the sloping side of a small mound. The scrap of earth was no larger than one a bear might use for its den. Crouching in front of it, he placed his palms against the stone's smooth surface and let his power free. All along the rim of the stone, a solid gleaming seam of metal began to sweat, then soften, until finally, the seal liquified enough to free the slab from its rigid confines. A twist and push later and Steel dropped into the opening of a long dark tunnel. After flying back up to replace the stone seal, he snapped his fingers. Blue flames of his angel fire flared brightly before him, dancing and licking along the entire span of his hand.

At the end of the long, dank tunnel, its granite walls alive beneath the soft glow, Steel halted in front of yet another slab, though this one spanned from floor to ceiling and was made entirely of iron. He extinguished his fire and placed his palms upon the cool metal. His power's connection to the steel embedded within the handleless door made quick work of gaining entrance, and he slid inside.

"Well, look who the cat dragged in. Another few minutes or so and we would have had to send a search party out for you." Chrome's gruff greeting contained more antagonism than actual worry.

Steel groaned. "We don't have a cat." He turned to the large angel behind him and took in his brother's steaming mug of coffee. "Really? A search party? And was that going to be before or after you poured yourself a fresh cup?"

The angel—who was all motormouth and muscles with a military-style fade—threw a hand up in mock offense. "This is only cup number two, man. I'm virtually useless before that, and you know it."

"Right."

Steel lumbered through the den's great room. He and his brothers had carved out the cavernous space eons ago when they first fell to the mortal realm. With its curving granite walls and smooth support columns, the underground sanctuary was as large as Chrome's coffee cup was bottomless. Normally, after a night like he had, the connection to his home and the metals and minerals found within the base of the great mountains were soothing and restorative. The elements called to his celestial makeup, as they did for all his brothers, recharging and bolstering his metallic energy and fire. Even now, his metal hummed and sang below his skin, like a jubilant puppy excited to be let out of its cage and frolic in its own territory. It was a far cry from cuddling up to a mortal-made iron pipe all night, but iron was iron. As his metal was an alloy primarily made up of carbon and iron, it did the job.

He had slept in far worse conditions.

Now, however, instead of squaring off with his brothers and explaining more than he cared to, all he wanted was to fly right back to Bridget, fall onto her cream-colored sectional, and see how she fared. Did she tell her brother about him? Were there other signs of charmers on her property? Would she even allow him back?

He scoffed, remembering the Trojan Horse that had come barreling through her neighborhood. Oh, he'd be back in that house come sundown. No approval required.

Steel stalked toward the double-door refrigerator and yanked the thing open. Bright garish light accosted his vision and was an optical eyesore against all the muted warm lighting of the den's electric lamps. "Who the hell put my tomatoes in the fridge?"

Chrome clanked his coffee cup down on the counter and eyed the red globes in question. "Who the hell worries about cold vegetables at nine thirty in the morning?"

"Tomatoes are fruits," Steel huffed out, rescuing the produce from their frigid prison, along with some basil, parmesan cheese, and holy hell, was that *garlic* next to the cream cheese? But when his brother didn't take the bait to flex his stubborn (though incorrect) knowledge on the tomato is a fruit/vegetable debate, Steel glanced around the fridge door. Chrome stood there, those thick eyebrows settled low over a broad brow and his brawny frame nearly filling out the width of the kitchen's entryway.

"Going somewhere?" Chrome asked.

"Just taking stock of what we have to eat around here."

"You're really going to throw that bullshit at me? Like I can't sense when I'm being played?"

If you only knew.

Even as the thought struck him, his gut wrenched. Over the past several years, deception had become second nature, even when there had been no need for it. Why lie about this, after all? What purpose did it serve? By the mages, he was a sentinel angel of the celestial realm, and here he was, embroiled in a web of secrets he had no hope of extricating himself from. The ruse had been erected for far too long, however, its grimy stones nearly as solid a foundation as his own truths. Whatever those were.

Then calm blue eyes flared brightly in his mind . . . eyes that flashed with panicked worry when he'd informed Bridget of the demons caravanning through her development as casually as an ice cream truck in peak summer.

Determination straightened Steel's spine. He couldn't lie anymore, but dammit, he couldn't reveal the whole truth. He settled on something in the middle. "What do you know about the Torrey Mountain Resort?"

"That it's a tourist resort used more so by local companies who think team-building exercises and an open bar will make employees overlook the fact that their pay is shit and their hours are shittier. Why?"

"I saw a caravan of trucks from there driving through the Glen Ridge housing development."

"Okay . . ."

"At eleven thirty at night, being driven by charmers."

Chrome's eyes, rimmed with lethal menace, flashed a blinding silver. His hulking form rippled with the surge of his angel fire dancing just below his skin's surface.

"There were four vehicles. I took out the last one, but not before the other three made it to the exit ramp for the highway. There were kids. Teenagers. The demons used them as bait, and I willingly took it. The kids are fine, but the hit made for a rough night. I had to hang low."

Chrome nodded curtly, then waved his hand in an understanding dismissal.

"Those trucks had cases in the back," Steel added.

"Cases of what?"

"Metal. But it was different, not pure elemental or alloy. I don't know."

Chrome paced in front of the counter. "If they've commandeered official operations vehicles, they've got a base there." He shook his head. "Something's brewing."

Steel nodded. "I'm going to be patrolling the development for a few days. Damage control, in case those teenagers piece together what they saw and any other residents start chattering. I mean, everyone and their mother has those fucking wireless security camera systems they all run from their phones. I've got to make sure no one picked up anything more nocuous than a raccoon rummaging through the garbage or a neighbor swiping packages. Plus, that property is huge. If the charmers are using it as a trade route, there's bound to be more activity that needs to be hidden from the mortals."

"Fucking hell." Chrome dragged his meaty hand over his still-not-caffeinated-enough face. "All right, I'll get everyone on board."

"There's a vacant unit in the development. One of the townhouses that hasn't sold yet because there was a flood in the basement from the previous owners. I'm going to hole up there for a few days, keep an eye on things, and see what I can learn."

"Sure, okay. I'll talk to the others about the resort." Chrome stalked away, his coffee forgotten, but before he made it to the hallway that led to the living quarters, he turned back to Steel. "You come up with anything on this Bridget woman yet?"

Steel froze. His back was a solid shield of ice against the fiery words that hit it. "No," he replied.

"Damn." Chrome gently punched the side of the doorframe. "I was hoping we'd get further along in finding her before our resources got diverted, but I guess that wasn't in the cards."

A cold calm blanketed Steel's features. "I guess not."

Only when the footfalls of Chrome's heavy boots turned to little more than whispers on stone did Steel resume his grocery hoarding. Agitated, he whipped out two large totes and began cramming everything he'd need for the night and then some. He had a dinner to prepare for and a neighborhood to patrol.

As he whipped out the freezer packs after deciding to swap out one of the totes for a cooler, he pulled taut yet another silken thread in his vile web of lies.

CHAPTER 8

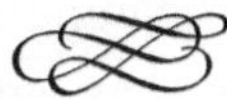

Bridget's eyes glazed over the paragraph in front of her. It wasn't the heroine's fault Bridget couldn't stay glued to the woman's inner monologue, even after rereading the damn thing for the eighth—or was it ninth?—time. She was sure the prose was lovely and vital on some nose-in-the-air literary level, but every time the heroine would wax on about the color of the hero's eyes, Bridget's mind would wander to the crystal-blue eyes of another man, or the silver slope of his armored wings.

She sighed and glanced at the time on her phone. It was nearing four thirty in the afternoon, and there had been no sign of angel boy.

Who are you kidding? There's nothing boyish about him.

She groaned and shifted her thighs slightly, trying to will some blood to return to them after she'd been plastered on the couch all afternoon facing the picture window. Elliot, who sat curled up on her lap, stood following the slight hint of his sleeping spot's disturbance, spun so his butt was facing her, and plopped it back down. Bridget didn't miss the tail twitch.

"You can move, you know, if my fidgeting's too much for you."

Another *thwack* of his tail.

"Ugh, fine. That's fair, I suppose. Why should I be the only one on edge?" When she didn't get a response—because, hello, cat—she closed her book and brushed her fingertips along the fanned edges of the pages. The mindless activity gave her all the space she needed to go completely out of her mind.

Angels were real and so were demons. Humans had souls—well, that one she could believe—but they were somehow illuminated, and a race of evil existed that very much did *not* cohabitate with any sort of light, heavenly or otherwise.

Bridget thought back to the moment she saw Steel lying on her back deck. There had been no blood or physical gore, thank goodness, but she couldn't ignore the pain and debilitating weakness that had left a man of Steel's formidable size and strength unconscious.

And the things capable of doing that to him were *here*, in her neighborhood?

Her mind spun around her situation more fitfully, keeping time with the frantic fluttering of the pages beneath her fingers, when a soft rap on her back door had Elliot leaping from her lap.

The jolting shudder skittered through Bridget's heart. She held her breath and closed her eyes. *One . . . two . . . three . . .* Once the tense storm within her chest had calmed slightly, just enough for her to lay her book on the coffee table without her hands shaking, she turned toward the noise.

As usual, her meager little outside light was doing its I-think-I-can best at illuminating the presence at her back door, even though sunset was a good two hours away and the light's efforts were wasted. Just tick another mark in Bridget's *winning as a homeowner* column for turning on her outside lights in pure freaking daylight. Woo-hoo.

Despite her lighting cockup, the form that took up the whole of her rear doorway couldn't be mistaken. Her roof's overhang cast enough shadows to accent the pale yellow glow shining down on tousled blond hair. One side of Steel's profile was visible. The lit corner of his mouth lifted softly, an illusion of innocence, especially considering his slight casual wave mixed with the knowing glint of amusement he offered her through the glass. The other half of him, however, was more obscured by the broken plays of light and meager shadows, but one thing she could make out with complete clarity: there were no wings in sight.

"I guess we're really doing this," she whispered to herself. She discreetly wiped her sweaty palms down the front of her jeans before she rose and walked toward the back door. When she got there, the familiar, if out of place, brown leather scabbard was still draped across Steel's wide chest, but at his feet sat a standard grocery store tote bag, along with a cooler one might take to a cookout. Bridget's brow furrowed in confusion. Through the glass, two long fingers were held out in front of her. Their classic V shape told a universal truth.

I come in peace.

Bridget bit back a smile, which surprised even her. Surely, she could do this. It was one meal with someone who wasn't her brother or his boyfriend. And for some reason, even though Steel was very much a stranger, the idea of a single sit-down dinner with him didn't panic her like it would with others. Oh, her storm of anxiety still brewed beneath the surface, but her curiosity about this man stirred deeper eddies.

In the end, her spirit of inquiry won out, and Bridget slowly pulled the sliding door open. As soon as that barrier was gone, Steel dropped his peace-signing hand and tucked it into his back pocket. He never made a move to come inside.

"Hi," she said.

His grin widened. "Hi."

She winced internally. *Brilliant conversation starter, Bridget. Care to move on to two-syllable words next?* Hell, she was terrible at this. "Um, do you want to come in?"

He merely stared at her for a moment, then ducked his head slightly. "Thank you."

Steel moved through her kitchen with all the confidence of a leopard prowling across sturdy-limbed tree branches. He had only been in her home once, yet this kitchen didn't appear foreign to him. On the contrary, he moved with lithe grace through her cupboards and refrigerator and showed no surprise when he quickly found whatever he was looking for. He had mentioned checking out a unit in the development once before, which was how he'd known her house had a basement and where the entrance was. Perhaps he recalled a similar kitchen layout as well?

"You seem awfully comfortable in the kitchen," she remarked.

He shrugged a casual shoulder. "It's a fairly common setup, and you have things stocked in a sensible order."

She crossed her arms and sat on a stool at the breakfast bar. "Well, I'm glad my kitchen design suits your standards."

"Not my standards, but yours. They simply make sense, is all."

"Oh, well, good to know." His back was to her, and even though his wings weren't out, she had to look away or she'd never stop gawking, never stop wondering what his wings looked like without his shirt to conceal his muscled form. A sudden heat rose in her face, warming her cheeks. She quickly looked down and dipped her chin lower into her sweatshirt, silently cursing her inexperience with the situation. With so many things. It was just a back, for crying out loud! Though, admittedly, a finely sculpted one. Her damned traitorous eyes risked another glance at the angel moving so smoothly throughout her private space as if it was his own. And for a brief moment, she entertained the idea of that very thing, of his strong hands growing familiar in and around her home. *Around her.*

More foolish fantasies.

Quick as a blink, the thought left her, and she returned her attention to Steel.

"So, you said there are demons in Glen Ridge." She paused and then shook her head. "Wow, did that sound as ridiculous to you as it did to me?"

Steel tied an apron around his low hips and flashed that sly grin again. "You're asking the wrong angel."

"Ah, yes, right. You're a fallen angel."

"Just an angel."

"Oh, of course. Forgive me," she said with a mock affront.

"Nothing to forgive." Steel slipped a flat, square stone onto the bottom rack of her oven and set it to preheat at a temperature so high she didn't even know her oven could reach. In front of him, on her counter, were two balls of dough.

"Bread?" Bridget asked.

"Pizza dough," he clarified.

"Ah." Inwardly, she groaned. No way could she do this. No freaking way could she chatter on idly and maintain back-and-forth banter. Any conversational skills she'd known at one point had flown out the proverbial window, along with every other bit of normal functioning prowess when it came to human interaction. God, why was he here? Why her? She shot a look over to Elliot, who lay curled up in his cat bed in the living room. Golden eyes surveyed his home's intruder, but the cat merely resumed his look of superior boredom and laid his head back onto his front paws.

Enter Elliot: The Unhelp.

Steel's casual words broke the silence. "Tell me what you know about the Torrey Mountain Resort."

Her head whipped around to him. "What? Why do you think I would know anything about it?"

Flour dusted the countertop and liberally speckled the front of Steel's black apron. He plopped a dough ball down, and her heart volleyed into her throat at the impact. "I don't, but you seemed to have a reaction when I first mentioned the place."

"I didn't have a reaction."

"There was a look."

"No, there wasn't. I don't give *looks*. My God."

"Fine, no looks."

"Thank you."

"But you were less shocked when I told you actual demons exist and, oh hey, they were the ones driving through your neighborhood last night." He raised his floured hand and pointed to the space between his eyebrows. "You didn't get that little V thing there."

Her jaw fell open. "A V thing . . ."

"It's a tell. We all have 'em. Why do you think those world-class poker players wear such big sunglasses *inside*?"

"You know what? Sure, I'll bite. Yes, I know about the resort. Everyone in the area does. It's a major recreational spot that brings in a good chunk of local tourism dollars. It's got ski slopes, though at half the cost of what you'd pay for any of the other more prominent slopes on the White Mountains, as well as ballrooms for formal events and even conference rooms for corporate stuff."

"That's quite the brochure."

"Well, you asked, right?"

"No, I asked what *you* know about the resort. What you've told me isn't anything I couldn't look up online."

She sighed. "What's the difference? I mean, what's this all about?"

The conversation was going around in circles, only whipping her emotions into an even more frantic frenzy, yet before her, Steel stood as stoic and immovable as the mountains around them. Then her eyes drifted toward the only things that *were* moving: his arms.

The sleeves of his navy-blue shirt had been rolled up to his elbows, creating a perfectly smooth canvas for his taut veins and sinewy forearms. The heel of his palm pushed against the pillow of dough, kneading it with a tender, yet firm maneuver. When his hand finished its insistent press, strong cradling fingers wrapped around the dough and pulled it gently back into his orbit. Another rub, pat, press, then the smooth circular spin of his hands around the soft globe, slowly but firm, until he released his charge from the cage of his fingers. The dough all but sprang from his grasp in a cushioned eruption before his masterful hands called it back home once more.

Bridget couldn't tear her gaze away, couldn't even remember what they were talking about. His hands, with those long skillful fingers, held her entire focus. His maneuvers were effortless, yet practiced, and some unexplored part of her even thought them a bit wicked. For a short moment, she wondered what those hands would feel like on her. A strange shuttering thrill rang through her as she imagined those gifted fingers moving just as masterfully against her skin, curving down the valley between her breasts.

Unbidden, heat soared in her cheeks, yet she couldn't look away, couldn't focus on anything other than those strong hands as they urged the supple dough back and forth, back and forth. Another curious thought occurred to her as she envisioned those same hands warming her skin. Would his nails scrape gently across her peaked nipple as he trailed them over her, or would he curl them under, cushioning the sensation instead of heightening it? Would his palms tease and knead her flesh with such purpose, rolling and cupping each mound until they yielded to his hands in the precise way he wanted? Her heartbeat thundered in her ears while her mind unraveled the thread of her blossoming fantasy.

No, she couldn't be thinking about this—about him. Of all the times her mind picked to wander and explore, this was *not* the time. Enjoying her one-handed reads in the privacy of her bedroom was one thing, but eliciting those thoughts in front of another, in front of a freaking *angel* . . . No, not with him, not ever. She had no interest in powerful men and certainly no use for them. And Steel was certainly powerful, she had no doubt of that.

She swallowed against the dryness in her throat. God, what was she doing? And who the hell becomes utterly undone by a dough ball, of all things?

Frustrated in more ways than one, Bridget crossed her legs and clenched her thighs against a flare of heat. *Down, girl.*

A charming, teasing glint in Steel's eyes sparkled at her, and she prayed a black hole would open up and swallow her and her shameful thoughts right the hell up. *He knows.*

She glared at him. "Are you sure *you're* not a demon?"

His smile tightened with secret amusement as he patted the accursed dough out into a far less enticing and far more familiar pizza crust shape. "Not in the literal sense, but I suppose everyone has a darkness inside them. Isn't that what mortals believe?"

Bridget grunted, but he simply continued.

"Besides, I don't believe for a second you actually think that. You don't give off that sort of vibe."

"And what sort of vibe do I give off, exactly?"

Whatever playful joy filled his expression left as quickly as it had arrived. "The lonely kind."

Flour danced in the air between them, almost providing a blanket of mist to hide in, as if this man somehow knew he'd hit a nerve but would give her a veil of privacy to shield herself behind if she needed to. The oven beeped, and just like that, before Bridget could contemplate his words further, the spell was broken. Steel resumed his pizza ministrations and left her to her thoughts, her secrets.

Just like the secrets he'd shared with her—him being an angel, the soul-sucking charmers. Secrets, she was certain, he would have preferred to keep as such. Admittedly, he'd had little choice in the matter once she found him unconscious on her deck, but that wasn't entirely true. There were always choices. He could have harmed her, threatened her to keep quiet before running off, or worse. He could have left her to the mercies of whatever those demons were up to, but instead, he'd trusted her enough to share his knowledge of the charmers' whereabouts and their proximity to her home.

He could have stayed away, and yet here he was, cooking her dinner and offering her conversation, as strange as it might be. He had no way of knowing it was her first dinner guest outside of Ryan and Michael in four years. This chatter between them, however stilted and awkward it was, had been the first real, substantial conversation she'd managed to carry on that didn't involve family or colleagues.

And it felt *good.* No, not just good but safe. *He* felt safe. It was a feeling that had been in dangerously short supply over the past several years, despite her brother's best efforts, and one she hadn't realized she'd missed so vitally.

Bridget exhaled a trembling breath, and before she could worry over the reasons for doing so, she let the words fly.

"I've been at the resort before, four years ago. That was the first and only time I'd been there, though . . . and I haven't really gone out into the world since."

CHAPTER 9

The clang of the oven door closing was a death knell. Its swift shutter was the only sound in the small kitchen following Bridget's casual allusion to her agoraphobia, as if her words hadn't just ripped open a chasm into Steel's painful past.

Breathing slowly, he willed his tense frame into a semblance of calm, tossed a kitchen towel over his shoulder, and faced the small woman in front of him. Her eyes were downcast, and her lips, normally tinged with a delicate rosy hue, had blanched slightly. A tenuous worry tightened her usually soft features.

"You don't leave the house at all?" Steel asked, though he sure as shit didn't need to.

"No, I don't. I mean, that's not entirely true. I'll check the mail, and I spend time in my backyard when the weather's cooperating. My brother's boyfriend, Michael, owns and operates a Taekwondo studio downtown, and I'll visit there on occasion with my brother, though not during peak hours. I mean, it's not as if I'm a complete social pariah. I spend time at their house, too. Sometimes." That last word was barely a whisper, one Bridget clearly hadn't intended Steel to hear, but darkness wasn't so far off yet, and its steady approach strengthened his angelic senses. There wasn't a sound in this whole house he couldn't capture, including the fervent beating of his strained heart. And hers.

"Do you work at all?"

She straightened her back and glared at him, a bit of fire returning to her wan complexion. For a moment, he debated whether to needle her some more, if only so the glowing flush in her cheeks would keep her solemnity at bay. "Of course I work. I'm a graphic designer for a firm that largely specializes in television commercials, online ad spots, stuff like that. They have remote work accommodations." She shrugged.

The heat in her response, the way her spine stiffened at his knowingly callous retort, would have thrilled him if it also didn't shatter something inside him. All that fire and vitality had no business being locked in a cage. Not for the first time, Steel wondered just how long a passion like that could survive confinement before being snuffed out.

Summoning a calm strength, he chose his words carefully. "I don't think I need to tell you this—"

"Then that's usually a good indicator you can stop right there."

"But that's no way to live."

Bridget rolled her eyes. "You sound like my brother."

"From the way you talk about him, that doesn't sound like such a bad thing."

"I'm happy, okay? It works. I've . . . I've found a way to make it work."

Steel planted his elbows on the kitchen counter and leaned in closer to her than he had any right to be. Her fingers worried and fiddled with her nails, and he couldn't resist the smile that pulled at the corner of his mouth when her nervous eyes darted everywhere except at him. He was crowding her, but a bit of discomfort, even in her own element, could be just enough to rock a boat that had been docked for far too long.

"Tell me what happened, or only some of it, if you prefer. It won't change the fact that I'll still be here all night. And I brought dessert."

A short laugh escaped her. For a moment, her blue eyes turned pleading, almost misty, as if the words were there but she needed some help springing them to the surface. Then it hit him. Some part of her *wanted* to share, but her stiff body and even stiffer mind struggled with its release. The woman before him had been completely frozen in every way for so long, and yet she still looked at him with those lost, searching eyes. By the mages, he'd sooner let his fire run cold than ever be the victim of such a helpless longing look from her ever again. In all the years he'd watched her from afar, he'd never been able to ascertain anything beyond her surface-level discomfort and obvious social fear, but seeing her hidden worries etched along the smooth curves of her face? It was an entirely different form of brutal torture, one he had not anticipated and wasn't certain he could combat. Frustrated, he glanced down at the counter, spying the neat bundles of silverware he'd assembled. He paused, then smiled when a thought occurred to him.

Steel lifted a fork-and-knife duo and held them in his palm. Bridget's expression went from pained to curious as she tracked his movements. With the ease of breathing, he gripped the stainless steel utensils together in his fist and let a pulse of his power free. The metal sang in his hand, responding to his gentle coercion. Steel softened and fused the utensils, then rounded and smoothed out the collected mass before stretching and shaping it into his desired form.

A soft gasp had him glancing up to where Bridget had dropped her worried hands and instead gawked at the malleable bit of silver moving beneath his fingers. Fear and whatever other painful emotion that had clogged her senses had fizzled away, leaving only bright, shining wonder sparkling through her smile. Yes, he had actually gotten her to smile. Something within his chest pinched, then fluttered. He cleared his throat quickly and averted his gaze back down to his hand.

After another quick final tweak, Steel revealed a small silver dragon, complete with a wicked curving tail, slitted eyes, and vicious teeth.

"Oh my gosh!" Bridget hunched over in her seat and, in her excitement, threw her hands out to grab the thing as if it were a precious baby bird, but at the last second, she left her fingers to hover over the tiny trinket.

Steel chuckled. "Go ahead, you can touch it. It might be a tad warm, but it won't burn you."

"You made this? But the metal was, wait . . . This is . . . Oh my gosh . . ." A few more words stumbled out of her with broken haste, but this time, they didn't stop her from snatching up the silver dragon and cradling it to her heart like a child with a kitten. "I haven't seen this since . . ." A dewy mist clouded over Bridget's flushed features. "How did you know? How did you even *do* this?"

Steel merely flicked a gaze to the ornamental dragon painting she had hanging above the couch. Then, in answer to her second question, he added, "I can command steel or any metal with traces of its alloy. And you seem to have a thing for dragons."

"I had one exactly like this—*exactly* like this." Then her head whipped up to face him, and Steel braced himself for an accusation or knowledge he couldn't share. The gut punch came as swiftly as he expected, but the actual manner of delivery was a stunning blow. Instead of scorned blue eyes full of shameful doubt and mistrust pinning him to the floor, those same eyes, now lined with hopeful fondness, kissed a joyous trail along his skin until he could feel it in the base of his spine and, yeah, other base places as well. Gratitude, misfortune, longing, remorse, guilt, joy, they all slammed into him in a barrage of emotions. Then her voice, tiny yet firm, broke through the torrent.

"I had a small dragon like this once. I always kept it dangling from the rearview mirror in my car. Ryan hated it, always said it was illegal because it obstructed my vision, though he never forced me to take it down. I just figured it was another one of those things where, when he didn't like something, he'd just say it was illegal, as if he had a monopoly on legal knowledge that implied Michael and I had no need to go looking things up for ourselves. Spoiler alert, we always did. Regarding the dragon, though, Ryan was right. I shouldn't have had it hanging like that. I wonder if he sometimes blames himself for not forcing me to take it down when he warned me about it originally."

"Why would he blame himself?"

Bridget took a deep steadying breath. "Because four years ago, I was in a car accident after leaving a work event my company was throwing at the Torrey Mountain Resort. It was dark and late, and I was the designated driver." Her fingers played in the tiny grooves along the dragon's barbed back. "Shit, I don't know if I can dredge all this up again."

Steel nodded, then went to work pulling the finished pizza from the oven before sliding the next one in. "Just say what comes to mind, and if you can't, we'll stop."

We'll stop, as in he would stop poking and prodding at her festering wound while she went back to slapping on useless bandages. It was another lie. Now that he'd seen her, really *seen* her, and how she lived as a result of that night, there was no going back. He was well past sticking his finger in the dike, and he'd make damn sure she was as well.

"The work event was a cocktail reception turned dinner dance, some major fundraiser thrown by the board of directors. All employees were expected to attend, as our major clients would be there, as well as prospective clients and other industry professionals. Back then, I was practically buzzing with ambition. I was twenty-four and had just gotten my master's degree in media design the year prior. I had been at my firm for about six months, but I was on a design team with three other designers. To put it bluntly, we were frickin' amazing. A real dream team, despite how young we were. We just wanted it all, and quite honestly, together, we had the talent to go after anything."

"I bet you did." After a few more minutes, Steel removed the second pizza from the oven and began plating up dinner. A solemn silence took over the small kitchen. Bridget's glazed eyes were staring a hole into the counter.

"Yeah, we did," she said softly, a clear victim of her memory. "Brett, Rishik, Lucas, and I were your quintessential big fish in a small pond, or so we thought." She cast him a knowing glance that spoke of all the misguided certainty common among youths. "We were making waves at our tiny firm, as I said, but we wanted more. Our projects had become boilerplate and rudimentary and just altogether stale, you know? And when you're young and dumb, the last thing you want is to feel like your work, your life, is stale.

"One of the big announcements that was being made at that gala dinner was the creation of a new department, with the *very generous* help of our wonderful investors and new clients. It was a test to see whether our small commercial studio could branch out into larger high-production animation, and they'd need animators—not simple graphic designers, but full-fledged entertainment animators—to make it happen. The guys and I were salivating at the opportunity to be considered for the promotion."

"I take it those two specialties are different."

"For us, yeah. Animators primarily produce content for entertainment purposes, while the graphic design we were doing was more marketing based. Ads and commercials and stuff."

"Ah."

"We wanted it so badly—the promotion, a chance to be part of the new department, and most importantly, we wanted to stay a team. It was our best chance to advance."

Steel pushed a simple salad and a slice of pizza in front of her. She accepted it with a polite smile but merely pushed the lettuce around with her fork.

"As you can expect, we had been drinking. I mean, it was an open bar. We were barely out of grad school and still solidly lived by the 'if it's free, it's for me' mantra. We were desperate to make a good impression but realized too late into the evening that we were too drunk to drive home, and racking up a steep expense report of hotel rooms and ride shares on the night we had just fawned over the new department heads wasn't going to endear us to anyone, you know? It also wasn't a good look that we had let ourselves get so carried away at a work event. One of us needed to drive us all home, and because I was the least inebriated of the lot, they nominated me as the driver. I tried to argue the point, but Brett and the others said it would cost too much for a car or ride share down the mountain. Torrey's not exactly around the corner, after all."

Steel nodded but kept his counsel otherwise.

"I was originally just going to call my brother and have him come pick me up, as I usually do in those circumstances. I offered the same to the guys, but they said no, that it would give the wrong impression, that our bosses would see us all being shuttled into a tight car and it would call to mind images of immature college kids. Brett especially . . ." Bridget bit her bottom lip and shook her head. "He was so damn proud, and he could be so convincing when he wanted to be. Something about his old prep school charm, I don't know, but it worked. He was *very* persuasive, and Rishik and Lucas backed him wholeheartedly, even to the point where, when I questioned going along with them, they accused me of wanting to break up the band, of holding them back from the promotional opportunity we were all such a good fit for together. So, in the end, after checking with the resort a *third* time to make sure there weren't any available rooms so we could maybe stay the night and split the expense, I caved."

She lifted anguished, haunted eyes to him. "I didn't want it to be my fault. I didn't want . . . If we didn't get the promotion because I was too scared . . ." Her voice cracked, and she shook her head as if fighting against the memory. "I refused to be the reason they missed out on what they'd wanted for so long. After that, we said our goodbyes, and we all shuffled into my car.

"It was almost midnight, and I kept the windows down even though it was late autumn. I really needed that fresh air to wake me up, as if deep breathing would somehow fix my poor decisions. I don't know. God, what a freaking fool . . ." Her breath caught. She quickly dropped the fork and the dragon and pressed the heels of her palms into her eyes.

Steel's fingers itched to grab those trembling hands, drag them away from her pale cheeks, and replace them with his own, catching every single tear and all the ones to come. The thought surprised him, but he didn't look away.

"I made it to the base of the mountain when something flew in front of me and crashed into the road. I couldn't turn in time, and we hit the thing head-on. My car flipped instantly, sending us skidding out of control and landing up against the side of a rocky outcropping." Bridget swallowed and stared back down at the dragon sitting next to her plate. "They all died, except me. When I was finally able to open my eyes, I was on the ground with my brother hunched over me screaming my name. They said I must have been thrown from the vehicle, while the others were trapped inside."

Then a sardonic smile bracketed her trembling lips. It was a hateful look that should never be worn on a delicate face such as hers. Steel's upper lip rose in a slight snarl. "The official on-paper report says a boulder fell from one of the smaller mountains I was driving past and landed on the road. That's what I drove into. The accident was classified as a motor vehicle collision, with no mention of blood alcohol level tests thanks to my brother's influence and the fact that he got on scene before any other emergency services could refute his claims." A pained gasp choked her, but she threw her shoulders back and lifted her chin high like an ice queen on her throne.

"Ryan latched onto that dragon and how it was always in front of my face while I drove. He believed it obscured my vision to the point where it prevented me from swerving out of the way of the boulder. That stupid toy turned into a lifeline for him, a crazy obsession, because he knew I had been drinking, but he couldn't risk confirming things without possible manslaughter charges being flown my way, and he would never forgive himself if that happened when he could have prevented it. Over the years, it had just become easier for him to blame himself, blame that accident on a stupid lump of hanging silver that he had told me so many times to take down.

"So, no, I don't need to leave the house. I don't need to risk another accident on the road or endure another high-handed attempt by some man's blind ambitions to force me into a decision I don't want to make. I've got plenty of heartache and guilt to keep me company just fine." Then those cold eyes found his once more. "Now it's your turn. Why are you really here?"

CHAPTER 10

"Eat." The one-word command came out of Steel's mouth before he had the good sense to temper it with any sort of softness.

"Talk, and I'll eat."

He untied his apron and threw it down on the counter. "Fine."

Fuck, he really hated that word.

"Why are you so angry?"

"Because this"—he threw his arms wide—"is no way to live."

A simmering boldness lit her eyes, and Steel's muscles flexed, responding in kind, recognizing the raised hackles of a long-trapped animal. As soon as the brilliance in her gaze heightened, it tempered back down just as quickly, as if her very soul was accustomed to cowering and couldn't bring itself to ascend to anything more. Fury tightened Steel's already taut frame, so much so that he had to conceal his hands beneath the counter lest his glowing palms torch every flammable thing within spitting distance. She caught his movements, though, and, like a damn dog with a bone, would not allow him to belabor his point. Instead, her face lit up with a curious wonder.

"What's that?" Bridget jutted her chin toward his fists, still hidden beneath the counter. "Do you have a flashlight or something? What's that blue light?"

"It's nothing."

"It looks like something."

"It's not."

"Then let me see it."

"Just eat, will you?"

"I've never seen a bright-blue nothing before. How do I know it's safe to eat in front of it?"

By the mages, did she always want to play these games? His fingers were a hairbreadth away from punching through the marble counter, but as soon as his frustration started to mount, he recalled how there were so few people in her life *to* play games with. He held his eyes closed for a moment. Once he was sure he could summon words without his literal heat responding in threatening kind, he met her gaze. "For a woman who's holed herself up in a palace of protection, you're going to let a little light spook you? After how you found me?"

"*Especially* after how I found you, yes. You're in *my* palace of protection, as you call it, so show me what you're hiding."

Steel flicked his chin toward her pizza. "Eat."

She lifted a slim eyebrow in response. "Talk."

He groaned and hissed a breath through clenched teeth. "Do you promise to eat if I show you?"

In the span of two thoughts, Bridget had gone from a brooding ghost to a sassy queen of back talk. Calmly, she lifted the slice of pizza to her mouth. White teeth sank into the melted cheese before full lips covered the bite. A quick pull had her tearing through the crust and drawing back until all that was left was a glossy sheen coating her lips. Steel's gaze remained glued to those pertinent lips, even as her small pink tongue darted out and licked away the remnants, leaving a trail of another gloss in its wake. Every swipe, press, and moan of Bridget's mouth rico-cheted through his body, until his cock nearly throbbed in time with each work of her jaw, each swallow of her delicate throat.

Steel stifled a groan and, with little other recourse to avoid his obvious appreciation for her appetite, he turned his back toward her and leaned into the counter next to the stove under the guise of tidying up. By whatever luck the mages saw fit to still bestow upon him, he prayed Bridget didn't notice the firm press of his hips against the marble counter, or how he gritted back a frustrated wince when the pressure of the feeble stone against his swollen cock was a paltry excuse for what he needed. After a moment, once he was satisfied he wasn't at risk of rupturing the fly of his jeans or snapping her counter in two, he allowed himself to face her.

"Eat your salad, then I'll tell you about my angel fire."

Salad. Yes, salad was safe. Crunchy lettuce and crisp peppers would go a long way toward cooling this apparent frenzy he'd somehow worked himself into. But then the damn woman had the gall to pluck up a single cherry tomato, one glistening and gleaming with a sheer vinaigrette, and pop it into her mouth like a grape offered by Bacchus himself. One quick snap between her teeth and Steel nearly came undone at the burst of sweet spring flavor he imagined coating her tongue and slowly sliding down the back of her throat.

Blue fire erupted from his forearms. Bridget sprang back from her stool, nearly toppling the thing. Elliot, to his credit, got good and gone real quick, fleeing into a bedroom down the hall. Meanwhile, great greedy breaths sawed in and out of Steel until his chest swelled and every muscle in his body tensed with enough force to hold back a tsunami. Or ten.

Fucking hell, what was he doing? Did he really just lose himself so completely over a goddamn *tomato*? Would it always be like this every time he offered to feed the woman? It was just food, for fuck's sake. And why, *why* did he respond so fiercely to her of all women?

"That's, um, quite the light show."

Quiet, slightly quivering words cut through his feral haze until those arresting blue eyes—soft and querying this time—danced over the electric blue flames that engulfed his arms. Blessed calm once again stole over him as he leaned into his core power like a weary soul sinking into a favorite time-worn chair.

"This is the only remnant of my celestial power, my angel fire." Wonder so bright and curious had filled Bridget's expression that he couldn't resist smiling back at her, and, yes, even showing off a little, twirling his fingers wide to create blazing blue shapes that writhed in playful swirls around his forearms. "When we fell from the Empyrean, we were cut off from all our power, except this. Our abilities to transform and merge with metal only materialized once we fell and landed here. A final gift of sorts that the mages were able to bestow before the gates were sealed and we were lost to them. Our fire, however, is not everlasting. In truth, it's a scrap of what I once used to wield, but it has served me well regardless."

Bridget puffed out quick breaths, and Steel marked the astonished—and remarkably relaxed—look on her face. "You're not scared?" he asked.

"No," she breathed out in exasperation. "I mean, it's not something you see every day, but it's, well, amazing."

Steel had to chuckle at that. "I suppose I shouldn't be surprised, seeing as how you have a thing for dragons and such."

"Yeah, true. All mythical creatures, actually. I was a big gamer as a kid. I know, hardly a shock there."

Steel couldn't help but enjoy the slight tinge of pink that crept up her cheeks. Bridget Olsen, the timid princess who had locked herself away in her own tower and was content to downplay her talents, was actually blushing.

"Your fire, though, it kind of reminds me of dragons, sure, but more so chimeras or maybe even a phoenix."

"I have to admit, I didn't see this panning out this way." *I didn't see anything about you panning out this way.*

"Yeah, well, that makes two of us." Bridget turned her head away for a moment, but her eyes never left his fire, as if she were afraid to blink for fear of it extinguishing. "Does it hurt?"

"No. It's as much a part of me as any limb. Think of it as . . ." He searched for the words. "It's like how your eyelids blink to protect your eyes from foreign bodies or how your skin sweats to keep cool. My fire is a power I can call into action to defend myself but also defend what I deem as mine, what my soul identifies as needing protection."

"And what does that short list of worthy beings look like?"

"When we dwelled in the Empyrean, my angel fire would be called into service to protect the realm, the souls within, the mages, and any other celestial beings. Here, however, among the mortal lands, it flares only to serve me, my brothers, and any souls preyed upon by the charmers. You," he added slowly, "are also among those souls now."

Bridget's eyes shot to his. If his declaration disturbed her, she didn't let it show and resumed her study of his fire display. "You said there are more of you."

"Yes. I have six brothers, all of whom served with me as sentinels and protectors of the Empyrean, and all of whom, like me, have been cast out, hunting charmers as we find them. They also command metal like I do, as I've mentioned, though different ones."

"Are there other angels aside from yourselves?"

"There were, yes, but none in the mortal realm. In the Empyrean, however, there were many other celestial beings." When her brows deepened in confusion, he added, "There were other angels, but none that were sentinels like us. The others served the mages in different capacities."

"You keep saying that. Mages."

"The celestial mages are our spiritual advisors. They govern the Empyrean."

She nodded simply, as if all of this was no more complicated than the words used to assemble the Sunday crossword, which, for Steel, who was *not* a words person, was very complicated.

He extinguished his flame. Bridget flinched, and then the wonder in her features dimmed slightly, though no hint of relief took its place. Steel lifted a brow. "You're taking this very well for a mortal. Like, eerily so. Did my fire really not frighten you?"

Or is she so tame because she's seen power from the other realms before? Had the charmers already found her? The horrid thought gripped him, and he moved with a panther's grace around the breakfast bar closer to her side.

"I'm a big fantasy nerd, huge gamer growing up, as I said." A soft wistfulness stole over her, and she collapsed onto her couch with an easy levity, her dinner clearly forgotten. Steel joined her on the adjacent loveseat, admiring the ease of maneuvering in her home, feeding her, talking to her. Simple pleasures for those with simple lives, and the mages knew his life was anything but simple.

"There's no real pain in fantasy worlds. It's all glorious fiction, sweeping adventure, epic romance, and the coolest pets one can dream up. Not that I don't love Elliot," she quickly added, "but he's excessively moody on a good day, and I mean, c'mon, he doesn't exactly exude warm and fuzzies."

"In my world, there is very much real pain. My fire, and that of my brothers, is our only means of destroying the charmers, and it is finite." What was it about this woman that had him spilling long-guarded secrets—secrets he and his brothers had barricaded from mortals for eons—like they were no more significant than the code on a bicycle lock?

"How so?"

"When we fell, we lost access to the Empyrean, which is the source of all light and life in the realms, including our fire. Here, our celestial power is limited and held in reserve each day. What is available to us is all we have to use until we can recharge our power among the minerals and metals of the earth each night. It's dangerous but necessary." He threw her a lopsided smile. "Trust me, I am not normally in the habit of snuggling up to iron pipes. We usually sleep underground to aid in the exposure."

She chuckled. "Ah, hence why you were so insistent about finding my basement. Well, that's good to know. But why is it dangerous? What happens if you don't recharge your fire?"

"Our angel fire is the only thing that can truly destroy a charmer. Not injure, not maim, but wipe out of existence. It's the only thing that stands in the way of those demons capturing mortal souls and extinguishing them permanently."

Bridget considered this for a moment. "You said you saw them here, driving through my development."

"Yes."

"And those things can hurt humans? Mortals, I mean?"

Steel sighed. "Yes, gravely. The charmers are searching for something, a special light inside certain souls. These lights have been spawned from the Eternal Flame in the Empyrean, from which all light in the realms was first created. There are remnants, sparks, of that flame here, residing in a select few mortals. My brothers and I are tasked with finding these souls and protecting them at all costs so we might one day use their combined light to reopen the gates and return home. The charmers, however, hope to extinguish them. To do so, they suck the soul out of the mortal using magic, snap the soul free from the body, and disintegrate it until it's as if that being never existed. Once all the sparks are gone, the Eternal Flame will die out, and the Empyrean will fall for eternity."

Silence fell through the room, and Steel was grateful for it.

Just reliving the severity of his brothers' circumstances was enough to freeze his blood. They had been fighting for so long, so *damn* long. Each inch closer felt like an insurmountable stormy sea he'd somehow slogged through with dying arms and wooden legs, and yet that sea had brought him here, to this doorstep, to this living room, to *her*.

His skin thrummed with a need to take to the skies, to scour the streets and build a wall of fire around anything Bridget had ever touched, walked past, or even looked at. Idleness did not become him, and it certainly wouldn't do Bridget any good with a threat looming.

Though, even if you did ensure her safety, what would she do with it? Live out her remaining days trapped within these walls?

Steel shot to his feet.

"Where are you going?"

He stalked toward the same closet where his weapons had been stowed the night before, where the bulkier ones were stored now. "Dessert's in the fridge. Cheesecake. Strawberry sauce is in the container next to it."

Bridget got up as well. "Again, not what I asked."

Steel was already strapping on his remaining weapons, tugging at straps and checking harnesses. "Out. I'll be back at midnight."

"You can't just dine and dash like that!"

A creeping thought hummed through him, tickling the nerves along his spine. "Why? Was there more you wanted to do tonight?"

She gasped, and the flush that followed crept so high it kissed the tips of her ears. Just the visual display of her heated skin spurred him on, his lower abdominals clenching tighter. "What? No! I just thought—"

"Don't do that."

"What?"

"Think."

"Excuse me? Why the hell not?"

Steel stalked past the kitchen, snagged the spare key dangling from the hook beside the refrigerator, and headed for the back door. "Because," he called over his shoulder, "that's the same foolish nonsense you used to convince yourself that living in a prison of your own making was better than living at all. I refuse to risk my life just so you can squander yours, and tomorrow, I'm going to prove it to you."

"And what the hell's that supposed to mean?"

"It means that as soon as the sun rises tomorrow morning, we're going out."

CHAPTER 11

The sky outside Bridget's window had the absolute nerve—*the nerve!*—to lighten from satin-kissed inky black to a dark lavender. Soon, the lavender would brighten even further, until purples faded to pinks, which then would fade to soft oranges before a full-blown sunrise was creeping over her little valley.

That sunrise could stay good and hidden for all she cared. Leave it to the other side of the world or hell, literally anywhere else on earth where people actually looked forward to a new day, because at six thirty in the morning, Bridget sure as shit didn't need to get out of bed. And for what? Just so some arrogant angel in her basement could prove a point about a woman he'd known less than forty-eight hours? Even if she *had* spent all night wide awake and ready to shake, turning over every wondrous, fantastical, and terrifying thing she'd learned about a world she thought she knew, it wouldn't change her.

Bridget flopped over onto her stomach and smothered her face in the overstuffed pillow. In the new darkness she'd plunged herself into, every word Steel had spoken crept back to her on catlike feet, but with *very* sharp claws.

I refuse to risk my life just so you can squander yours.

This is no way to live.

His high-handedness was even present in the demanding way he urged her to eat, as if she was an animal unable to recognize her own hunger signals.

Eat. Don't do that. Stop thinking.

Just who the hell did he think he was? No one, absolutely *no one*, ordered her around. Not her brother, not Michael, and sure as hell not some metal-headed stranger. She didn't care how abundant his shoulders were, or how the cheesecake he made was so smooth and rich against her tongue, she was grateful for the alone time she had with the fork.

Regardless of his divine baking skills, they didn't negate that every word out of his mouth dripped with more of that male superiority and insistent will. Bridget had experienced firsthand just how dangerous that way of thinking could be and how the behavior could squash reason and logic through sheer intimidation.

She could still recall Brett's voice in her head those four years ago, urging her to sober up and drive them home. His will, heightened by desperation and inebriation, had tuned out her objections or cries for reason. All for a shot at a stupid promotion. Even now, her stomach clenched and her face grew hot whenever she thought of that night, or how since then men like Alfred McDermott and his firm had all but ensured that the corporate culture at the big animation studios stayed the same —powerful, intimidating, greedy.

A sharp knock jolted her from her morose thoughts. Her heart kicked up into her throat. She tried to inhale and breathe in deep cool air, but she came away with a whole lot of hot and thin morning breath. Cringing, she rolled over and, remembering her houseguest, promptly chucked the pillow at the door.

The damn thing didn't even have the good graces to at least pretend to give an intimidating thunk against the wood.

"Go away!"

An infuriating chuckle tittered through the door. "Please tell me that wasn't a pillow."

Bridget glanced around for something else to throw, something with more *oomph*. She eyed Elliot briefly, weighing the recent hairball she'd stepped on barefoot with the fact that cats did always land on their feet, but she decided against the use of a feline projectile. That sort of cruelty was a hard line, even if said animal had no trouble crossing the cruelty line himself. No, she wouldn't be a thrower of cats.

Her gaze shifted to her nightstand, and she smiled. While cats were out of the question, she could be a thrower of hairbrushes.

Bridget gripped her plastic paddle brush and heaved the thing. She braced for the satisfying thunk but instead got an earful of near-silent creaking and . . . Was that laughter?

She sat up straighter in her bed and squinted toward the door, which now hung open into her room. Behind it, the hall light's abrasive mustard glow made an angry appearance, throwing its lazy beams across the floor of her bedroom. Elliot voiced his displeasure but never bothered to open his eyes. Loafing ingrate.

Bridget's eyes, however, were very much open. She scurried back higher against her headboard and sucked in a breath. Before her, nestled against the paltry glow of her hallway, stood a dimly illuminated figure of hulking proportions. She knew who it was, so there was no fear, per se, but more so stunned fascination. Her drapes were shut tightly, so little light touched Steel's features, which only added to the captivating menace filling out her doorframe, for that was exactly what he was. A shadowed menace. He wasn't just dappled in darkness. Instead, he owned the shadows, as if his presence and power weren't merely crowding out the light but absorbing it entirely.

Dark amusement lit with a predatory challenge.

With that absence of proper illumination, Bridget's bleary early morning eyes could discern two things.

One: what she had thought of as Steel's casual strength was anything but casual. Clad in muted shadows, his arms, shoulders, and even the cut lines of his torso gave both everything and nothing away about his true power.

And two: said power was being used to toy with her hairbrush, which Steel twirled lazily through his long fingers.

That dimly shadowed frame prowled into the room and hit the light switch.

"Hey!" Bridget threw the comforter over her head, plunging her into a meager darkness, but it did little to drown out the deep timbre of his annoyingly amused voice.

"While I appreciate the leveled-up projectile of a hairbrush, it doesn't make for the best weapon. The back of it is plastic, not even metal."

"If it's metal you're after, go back to the kitchen. Tons of stainless steel to gawk at in there."

"Oh, I'm well aware, but I'd rather gawk at you."

Bridget flung the comforter off her head, then shoved some bits of wild hair out of her eyes. The smug angel had parked it on the corner of her bed, hands in his lap, and was peering over at her like he was simply waiting for a train to come in. His face, however, was a solemn mask of something she couldn't quite read. There were soft features, to be sure, but those crystal-blue eyes, even in the dingy light of her bedroom, flicked with something different. Regret? Guilt? Longing? Whatever it was, she couldn't look away, not when he stared at her as if he had some great confession locked up behind those hard lips.

She had never wanted to know another's secrets so badly. *Easy, girl.*

A gentle smile curved the edges of his tightened mouth. To her horror, she hadn't taken her eyes from them yet. He must have noticed her attention as well because he quickly cleared his throat and bent to give Elliot a scratch behind his ear.

"To be clear," he said gently, "despite what it may have looked like, I never had any intention of barging into your room unannounced."

"I figured."

"I merely wanted to see you."

Those icy eyes—blue in color, not coldness—settled over her, and she had the strange sensation that he was memorizing her. Or perhaps with the starry glaze that arrested his vision every now and again, he was remembering something? Which was impossible, right? That nagging painful curiosity in her chest flared up again, desperately demanding that she learn the source of all those haunted expressions he tried to hide.

But she had no right, even if she did invite him into her home. She, of all people, knew the value of keeping secrets.

"I'd like to take you somewhere," he said.

And just like a frightened groundhog who'd seen its shadow, her heart sank back into the protective pit it had scurried out from. With a sigh, she threw her shoulders back and prepared her usual spiel. "No, that's all right. And please know that I appreciate your concern, but I'm going to tell you the same thing I've told my brother and my coworkers countless times: just because I don't live like you, doesn't mean my lifestyle is something that needs to be fixed. It doesn't mean I'm not happy with how I live my life or that I need to change it to fit the patterns of a majority-rules society."

"Humans, I have learned, are very social creatures. Though there are exceptions, by and large, I can't recall a single society I've witnessed over the years that didn't have some form of connective interaction as part of its core. Even the most remote tribes still had a community."

"You know, I forget how old you are. You don't look a day over thirty-three."

"I drink a lot of water," he said with a wink, and dammit all if one of those golden waves didn't choose that exact moment to swoop down over his brow, painting his features with an eternal easygoing charm. "Helps the complexion."

Bridget threw him a droll look. "And what's your secret for your hair? You telling me angels have effortlessly lush locks, or did you just invent conditioner and are living lavishly off the patent royalties?"

He kicked his head back and barked out a stunning, bright laugh, the first she'd heard from him. Her heart fluttered at the sight and sound, and some foreign part of her thrummed at the prospect of finding a way to elicit that sound again. "Oh, man, you have no idea how much Bronze would appreciate that one."

"Bronze?"

"One of my brothers, who happens to be a tad vain when it comes to his appearance. Go figure. And it was precious metals, not conditioner."

"Huh?"

"While we certainly didn't invent gold and silver and the like, we *have* become experts when it comes to mining and trading the stuff. Makes for a very handy and lucrative form of income and, as you've alluded to, a very lavish lifestyle over the years, especially when you've been alive as long as we have." Then he pursed his lips and assessed her. "I'll tell you what . . . you let me take you out for one cup of coffee in town, and I'll answer any question you'd like. We'll even take your car and can enjoy our drinks from the comfort of the parking lot once we've gotten them. And if it's too much at any time, you just say the word and I'll drive you right back. Even if it's only five minutes out of the house, I'll be happy."

Bridget eyed him. His gaze and offer were both genuine, and she detected no ulterior motives or gotcha moments hanging in the air between them.

"But," he added, leaning so close that she could smell the

crisp night air on his skin, "I'll warn you now, I do have one goal you should be aware of."

Ah, here it is. "And what's that?"

"To make you smile and see what your freckles look like in the morning sun."

CHAPTER 12

For the third time in as many minutes, Bridget retied her shoelaces, even going so far as to double knot the bunny ears that, yes, she still made even as a grown-ass adult. The sneakers were her fourth pair of shoes after rejecting the ballet flats, open-back mules, between-season boots, and finally landing on her tried-and-true athletic shoes. The other shoes had been too easy to slip on and too casual, making for a wardrobe that was flung together, leaving her with nothing to do but focus on how her trembling steps would carry her downstairs to the front door.

But with the laces? Well, the laces took time, especially to get them tight enough. Her first try was too tight, and the tops of her feet protested the confinement. A second time had been looser but uneven between her two shoes, with the right one slightly tighter than the left. The difference would drive her crazy while walking, so she undid the laces and tried again.

The third time was the most successful of the three, but her fingers didn't quite want to be finished fiddling, so she busied them with double knotting.

But now, there was nothing left to double knot. No, she was thoroughly dressed, shoed, and handbagged. There was truly nothing else to stop or hide the slight tremors she'd kept at bay while playing with her laces.

"Oh, for fuck's sake, just walk." Bridget whipped her hands sharply at her sides and marched her way downstairs with the false confidence of a general on the losing end of a battle. It wasn't like she hadn't been outside in four years or hadn't left the house at all. She'd been to Ryan and Michael's house plenty of times, often for dinner at least once a month, and Michael's Taekwondo studio as well.

But she hadn't been in her vehicle. Ryan always drove them in his SUV. The car that sat in her garage was brand new, as far as the odometer was concerned, even though it had been parked there unused for the past four years. Ryan would take it out for a spin once a month for a grocery run and keep on top of the oil, fluids, and battery, but otherwise, the thing was a two-ton paperweight.

The car had been a gift from Ryan after the accident, but she'd never driven it, never even been in it. In five minutes, that would all change because of the whim of a stupid, pushy, charming, not-hard-to-look-at angel.

She could do this. Some small fighting part of her thrummed within her chest, shouting from the depths of her protective cage that, yes, she could do this. It was daytime, Steel would be driving, and the coffee shop was ten minutes away. No mountain roads, just smooth pavement and short traffic lights.

Bridget opened the front door and braced herself against the blinding sun. Her eyes slammed closed, but through the backs of her eyelids, a calm darkening settled in front of her.

"I know, it's bright, but I've always found that coffee tastes better when the sun's good and hot."

Bridget peeled her eyes open. Steel stood before her with his large back and blond mop of hair blocking out the chipper sun. Once again, his features were cast in muted shadows. Around him, the rays illuminated his body's finely trimmed outline, edging him in what seemed like a cut-crystal halo. Of course.

Before she could remark on it, he reached behind her to shut the door, then locked it with his spare key. His sleeved arm brushed against her jacket, and a foreign shiver ricocheted through her awareness, tightening everything on her so intensely that she had to grip the railing for support.

Holy hell, her heart was pounding, but she wasn't entirely sure whether it was the angel's proximity, the beating sun, the prospect of what she was about to do, or a mix of all three.

Ryan's taken you out in the morning before, on super sunny days even, so don't think for a second Mr. Golden Sun or the car has anything to do with it.

"Coffee's coffee," she muttered as she slowly dragged her heavy feet down the three steps to her walkway. "It tastes just fine in my house."

"Nah. It's all about the experience. For example, Turkish coffee is traditionally brewed using sand and fire. The coffee is placed in a pan, which is then heated over an open flame. It's genius because the brewer has total control of the process through mediums that, in theory, one should have no control over. But the heated sand does it all. The cups nestled in the sand stay warm and the temperature of the coffee can be adjusted by how deep the vessel holding the coffee is placed within the sand. It's meant to be shared and is a symbol of hospitality and friendship. You can't get that experience from a barista, no offense to them."

Bridget shook her head in bafflement. "It's just coffee."

"No, it's life. It's entertainment and tradition, refinement and joy. It's drinking a communal beverage while the man across from you beams over the birth of his nephew after years of his distraught sister thinking she couldn't have children. Or it's the woman to your right who hands you a bit of Turkish delight with your coffee, while the small child in her lap with cheeks stuffed full of confections nods encouragingly at you to try some. *That's* what coffee is, what it can be. It's a heck of a lot more than bitter beans and hot water."

Hard metal pressed against the tops of Bridget's thighs, and she halted. Peering down, she was shocked to see that her feet had already carried her to the car's passenger door. When the hell had that happened? She backed away a step and readied herself for the crippling anxiety that always came when she would enter a vehicle, but warm, soothing heat at her back arrested her steps, trapping her.

Steel's tingling breath fanned along the nape of her neck as he just stood there, ushering but not caging her into the car. In the next stolen breath, however, reality and fantasy slammed into her with a roaring familiar blow.

"I can't do this. No, I'm not ready for this." She spun and looked up into his serene face, a foil to her frazzled nerves.

His angular, strong features shone down on her but didn't contain a hint of sadness or even the resigned frustration that often painted her brother's anguished expressions. Steel's beautiful arctic eyes simply danced over her face with all the care of a faithful guardian, yet spiced with something heated and forbidden below the surface. There was no censure, no disappointment, not even a lick of concern or worry. No, something else entirely lurked behind those eyes.

Confidence. Trust.

"Coffee is an experience. *We* are about to share this experience. But any experience with me comes with other expectations as well."

"Oh?" The word was little more than a squeak. She would have been mortified if her brain wasn't still busy processing everything she'd seen written on his face.

"Yes." He moved closer and ducked his lips to her ear. That warmth again filtered through her, melting the thin layer of ice around her nerves that formed whenever she got near a vehicle. But this was different somehow. This was . . . more. She lifted her chin slightly and turned toward his strong jaw, enraptured by his neck bobbing on a thick swallow before he spoke again.

"First off, I want you to know that you control everything. If I drive too fast, tell me. I don't give a shit if I have people honking at my ass for going ten miles per hour in a twenty-five. They can fucking wait. If there are too many people, just say the word and we're gone. Anything that's too loud, too small, too foreign, or anything that just feels wrong to you, tug my sleeve and I'll get you out of there."

Steel's arm hovered in front of her abdomen. All it would take was a simple nudge forward, not even a movement of feet, and Bridget would feel that toying hand pressed against her stomach, even through her clothing layers. Christ, why the hell was she thinking about that right now?

"Second, I don't go into any situation unprepared. In this case, I'll be by your side the entire time, even if that means standing still on a sidewalk while you slowly place the next foot in front of the other. I have no hidden agendas here, and I'm in no rush." The sparkling glint of his smile arrested her and froze the very breath in her lungs. "I've got no short supply of patience. Kind of comes with the whole being immortal thing."

She nodded jerkily, though the heat rising in her cheeks caused the skin along her neck to prickle. God, she couldn't stand here another moment, not with him so close and yet not touching her. She lifted her mouth higher, closer to his, which was braced mere centimeters from hers. Bridget couldn't bring herself to raise her gaze to those brilliant eyes, but oh, she had no problem staring at that full mouth, bracketed by faint lines that hinted at frequent laughter.

"All right," she breathed out, daring to inch closer still.

This was torture on so many levels. Pure freaking torture, and strangely, she was totally there for it.

"And third," he whispered. His mouth was a scant breath away from hers, and she was as frozen as an ice carving. Dammit, she had no experience with this, with men, with angels.

"Third . . ." Bridget's eyelids fluttered closed.

The heat vanished, replaced by the cool kiss of an early spring breeze. Huh?

She opened her eyes. Next to her stood Steel, arm and body leaning against the open passenger door. That charming smile lit his face. He looked like one of those car models who walk around shiny waxed vehicles with their hands roaming hard bodies while the audience *oohs* and *aahs* over the coat of paint and the leather interior.

She was right. He did smile often, and damn if it didn't look good on him. Damn if she didn't smile right along with him.

"Third, my drink of choice is a London Fog. It's sooo good. Strongly brewed English breakfast tea with extra-hot steamed milk, infused with lavender and vanilla."

Her eyes narrowed. "Wait . . . what? That's not even coffee! You spent all this time waxing poetic about coffee, and you don't even drink it?"

"Oh, I drink it, and plenty of it, but the London Fog is an experience all its own. I've tried to replicate it, but Jan, the barista in town, has her method locked up tight. I have yet to charm it out of her, though I'm not ready to admit defeat so soon."

Her mind spun out in disbelief, then she blinked away what she was sure was a dazed expression. Was he *toying* with her like she was one of his buddies chumming it up over beer and darts at a bar? Silence spanned between them, and then her roaring laugh burst free. She bent over so abruptly, she nearly knocked her forehead on the doorframe. Her heart clenched tightly, and her sides heaved, but she couldn't stop herself. Another wave of laughter roiled through her, and Steel's soft chuckle joined the chorus.

"I . . . must look . . . ridiculous," she panted, swiping at her eyes in between fits. "Imagine what . . . the neighbors . . . must think, me cackling like this."

"They'll think you're happy. Now, inside, Sunshine." He bobbed his head toward the car. "You're my date for the day, if you'll have me."

Bridget could hardly see through the tears, but they didn't stop her from smiling at him.

Steel paused and squinted at her for a moment, then smiled back. "Interesting."

She cocked her head. "What is?"

"Your freckles."

Her eyebrows shot to her hairline. "Excuse me?"

"I told you I wanted to see what they looked like in the morning sun. And I'm coming away with . . . cinnamon." He nodded with no small amount of certainty.

She laughed lightly and did her best to ignore the creeping blush that heated her cheeks.

"Yes." He stretched the word out like a cat drawing out its time in the sun. "Definitely cinnamon."

"What am I? Some sort of confection?"

A hungry searching gaze darkened Steel's expression. His eyes lingered on her, flitting over every curve and hollow as if he were mapping her and deciding where true north should be. Again, her skin prickled under his bruising awareness. Her breath hitched within her traitorous lungs, and she did her best to collect herself, but before she could fire back at him, the heat in his eyes dissipated. Those cool easy blue eyes met hers. Then he bobbed his head once more toward the car.

"Whenever you're ready."

A shuddering breath rushed out of her. The action wasn't as tense as before, but her heart still fluttered behind her ribs.

You can do this. You can totally do this.

Before she could think better of the situation, she gripped the doorframe and slid into the car.

CHAPTER 13

As far as parking lots went, the one Bridget's little sedan was hunkered down in wasn't bad. It was small and had one of those annoying entrances where, if you weren't looking for it, you'd missed it, but even given its size, the openness to the lot made every breath she struggled to hang on to release just a bit easier.

Steel had chosen a parking spot perpendicular to the entrance and facing away from the bustling street. While the chain-link fence in front of her car was standard-issue for the Aurora business district, what lay beyond was anything but.

The small lake in front of them sat nestled alongside the town's recreation facility. In the distance, a playground stood out among sprawling green athletic fields and winding walking trails. Pods of people were sprinkled throughout. Some walked in pairs. Some corralled dogs that were so darn happy to finally be outside after the hard winter they'd had. And others ran about in teams on the fields chasing one ball or another.

But the lake was different. True, it may have started out as a man-made endeavor, something to lend appeal to the burgeoning community decades back, but the flora and fauna didn't know that. It simply didn't matter to them. The turtles sunning themselves at the lake's edge hardly cared who placed the rocks they lounged on, nor did the lily pads concern themselves with whether the water they sprawled on top of was from rain or some other source. The entire landscape, small as it may be, was simply an open and lively home for the critters and creatures that claimed it. There were no expectations beyond that.

Bridget released another rattling breath, then proceeded to worry her bottom lip accordingly, but she couldn't steal her gaze away from the lake. Around her, the car still idled, even though they were parked. It struck her that Steel had brought her here without expectations. He hadn't even turned the car off yet, but instead, he waited for her to take the lead. One word from her, he'd said, and he'd drive them right back home. The realization unnerved her, but for a reason she'd never before considered.

Was no expectation actually the greatest expectation?

Neither of them spoke. It was as if, by mutual silent agreement, they had let the car's idle sounds and what noises managed to drift through the window from the outside speak for them. And the sounds did on some chilling level. The engine's muffled groan, the tittering trills of the parkgoers' lazy chatter, even the singsong chirp of the pedestrian crossing signal all spoke of a welcoming embrace that Bridget, deep down, desperately wanted to be a part of. Every time she forced her hand to reach for the door handle, however, some tense crippling thing held her back.

Fifteen minutes passed before Bridget, feeling like she owed Steel some sort of explanation, finally said something. "I don't know why it's so hard sometimes," she whispered, drawing little circles on the window glass.

"I could spout some well-meaning motivational quote to make you feel better. Something about 'You can do hard things' or 'Anything that comes easy isn't worth having,' but I think that's all bullshit."

She looked at him in surprise.

"We tell ourselves what we need to in the moment, but those outwardly spoken words are more for other people's benefits than our own."

Bridget didn't say anything and returned her attention to the window.

"If I were to say, 'I'm going to eat a well-balanced meal,' in front of my brothers, I'd be announcing a declaration that comes with the expectation of their assessment. They might see my plate, see how I have a slightly beefier helping of mashed potatoes than chicken, and one would comment that I'm loading up on too many carbs. Meanwhile, another would see that I chose mashed russet potatoes instead of mashed sweet potatoes and declare that russets don't have as much fiber and I should change my choice of starch around."

She gave him a knowing chuckle. "That sounds familiar, especially when my brother starts a new spring fitness routine every year. God, I hate mashed cauliflower." She shuddered, recalling Ryan's attempts to pass the bland vegetable off as anything other than it was.

"Exactly. But if any of them stopped to talk to me, they'd learn that *my* goals regarding what I'm aiming for with a well-balanced meal have absolutely jack squat to do with the types of carbs *they* think I should be throwing in my mouth."

"Oh?"

"Sure. Not that it was any of their business to begin with, but what if my well-balanced plans were more focused on color than substance? What if my goal, from which my declaration stemmed, was all about eating as many different colors of food on my plate as I could? Maybe I wanted to see if I could eat the rainbow."

"Why would that be your goal?"

"Why not? Does it matter to them or anyone else what and how I choose to eat?"

She sat silently as the message he was crafting slowly wiggled its way into her mind, kneading and untangling the cords of tension that had been knotted so tightly since she'd left the house.

"None of it matters, Sunshine. They only threw their fuel onto what they perceived as a fire because I spoke first and opened things up for scrutiny. Spoken expectations are nothing more than strong beliefs that the speaker hopes will come true. And since that sounds a lot like betting on chance and circumstance with the hopes they'd turn into a sure thing, I'd rather not say anything at all and just do what feels right."

His words went against everything Bridget had been told would be effective, against every litany of motivational tools Ryan had amassed for her to stow away into her mental health arsenal. Willpower, repetition, speaking truths into the ether and learning to separate the actual from the perceived—these were what she knew. And they hadn't helped at all.

"What do I do, then? Not say anything?"

His knowing gaze stayed trained on hers. "You come get coffee with me."

"It's just that easy . . ." But that dark, perpetually frightened part of her couldn't stop marveling at the prospect of it, of the freedom that might come with not constantly clarifying or explaining her actions to others. In her mind, that iron-caged door had slowly crept open, now large enough for her worried subconscious to step through if it wanted to.

"The only thing you have to decide is what you want to drink. Though if you're interested, I'm happy to give you some suggestions," he added lightheartedly.

God, everything about Steel was lighthearted. No, that wasn't true. He certainly was intense at times and other times forlorn or a bit difficult to read, but overall, he was *easy*. It was easy to be herself, damaged and deranged as she was, around him. Her initial need to apologize and change whenever she spoke to someone had been dashed away by his mere presence. Yes, he had been vocal about his concerns regarding her desire to stay home, but he had also given her choice and agency where others hadn't.

With something like a click, the cage door in her mind slammed open.

"I'd like to try a London Fog, except without the lavender. Save the flowers for the garden."

Steel gave her a knowing smile, though she could have sworn something like relief and admiration flickered through his features. Then he simply nodded. "I'll ask them to replace it with cinnamon instead."

THE BELL'S delicate jangle above the door announced their entrance into Jan's Java Hut. A ridiculous name, Steel had always thought, but he'd happily come here as often as Bridget would like just to see her stroll over that threshold again and again. Though, true, it didn't need to be here. If she wanted, he would have taken her to a park, a low-traffic grocery store, or even an abandoned office complex if it meant he'd get to see her surrounded by anything other than the cream-colored walls of her house.

The coffee shop wasn't necessarily busy, nor was it empty. The morning rush had come and gone, thankfully, and the regular guard was swapping out from the commuters to the stroller brigade. They had a few more minutes until the pleasant coziness of the cafe was made even cozier by the stay-at-home moms and post-school drop-off crowd. The walls were painted in swaths of lavender, accented with great sweeping strokes of rich mahogany. Plenty of hanging plants spilled over the ornamental shelves, barely grazing the shoulders of a few patrons in some cases. There was no shortage of cheeky, deliciously cringeworthy signage displaying all the coffee banter you'd hope and damn well expect in a mom-and-pop coffee shop. Everything from the hand-painted wooden Perk Up! plaque above the espresso machine to the Give Me Matcha Got sign standing on an easel in front of the tea bar was a challenge to every customer to see how far they'd get into the shop before the owners could convince them to smile and relieve them of their money.

"Steven! Is that you?"

At his side, Bridget tensed. The entire walk from the parking lot, she'd stepped with sure, if a little slow, footing, like a house cat who knew the treats her owner was offering were safe but was always still wary of the reason *why* she was getting treats. Bridget hadn't been skittish, per se, but Steel didn't miss the way her eyes immediately tracked the people in the coffee shop, who left and who stayed, and how close they were to her. But she was here, and it was a better start than he could have hoped for.

"Jan!" Steel threw a charming smile at the middle-aged woman peering out from around the corner of an espresso machine.

"Steven?" Bridget whispered.

"Just go with it," he said out of the side of his mouth. "It's a more common name, and I don't have to explain anything when they holler to tell me my order's ready."

"I guess you've thought of everything."

"I try." He winked. "I'm going to go say hi to Jan, who's the owner, and order our drinks. You're welcome to come with me if you'd like, but you don't have to."

"I know that," she replied, but her fingers were already fiddling with the strap of her handbag.

"Take your time. Whatever you need."

Steel walked toward the counter and smiled widely at the

coffee shop owner. As usual, her curly gray hair was pulled back into a sweepingly long ponytail that barely kissed the small of her back. A forest-green apron was cinched tightly over generous hips, drawing in an abundant waist and highlighting more-than-ample assets up above.

"What'll it be today?" Jan settled a hand on her wide hip and eyed him in challenge, as if she were daring him to even conceive of ordering anything other than what she intended on making him.

Steel leaned closer over the counter and flashed a smile that was all teeth, fully aware of the pleasing effect he had on women. "You know what I want."

"Pretty boy features and striking smiles are not going to get you anywhere close to *that.*"

"Then how close *will* it get me?"

Jan chuckled while she punched an order into the register. "If I had a nickel for all the men over the years who have asked me that question, I could sell the shop tomorrow and retire, start taking those river cruises in Europe John's always salivating over."

"Oh, I don't doubt it."

She smiled at him, but the sly upturn of her lips spoke more of amusement than actual secrets regarding long-lost lovers. "Your usual?"

"Yes, no—" Steel caught himself. "I mean, two London Fogs, but one with cinnamon instead of lavender."

Steel followed Jan's gaze over to where Bridget stood. A knowing light sparked in the coffee matron's gray eyes before she went back to punching in the order. "Brew the tea in the milk."

Steel's eyes widened. "No . . . really?"

She threw him a saucy look. "You questioning me, boy?"

He let out a laugh. *Would she still call me boy if she knew how old I* really *am?* He leaned over to kiss her proffered cheek. "Never. I value my life too much."

"That's what they all say. Order'll be out in a few. Gotta get some things from the back."

"I'll try not to eat all your sample cookies in the meantime," he said, reaching for a madeleine next to the tip jar.

Jan, never missing a beat, merely tossed her hair and threw him a wink over her shoulder. "Again, that's what they all say."

Steel chuckled around his mouthful of cookie, enjoying the rhythmic hisses and grumbles of his favorite coffee spot's machines. By the mages, he wanted to show Bridget this, wanted to introduce her to his favorite haunts, his favorite people. Show her the power of a bright sky and sunny day—or maybe that was merely what he thought was needed to outshine his shadowy guilt of her circumstances. He let the thought settle over him for a moment before his attention drifted to someone else's words. Words that had not come from Bridget or Jan.

"Ho-ly shit. If it isn't Bridget Olsen out among the living." The voice was low but melodic. A woman.

"Hi, Angelina." Bridget's voice, on the other hand, was small and meek, nothing at all like what his brazen brunette could sound like—*had* sounded like when he was alone with her.

He turned to face the group of people who had just walked in. There were four of them, the woman—Angelina—as well as another woman and two men, all of whom were dressed in what could only be described as mother's-basement-turned-corporate-glow-up.

The man next to Angelina was larger than the others and bald by choice if Steel had to guess based on the man's fresh face. He spoke next. "Oh crap, did you drive here, Bridget?"

"No. I mean, someone drove me."

"I'm sure that was such a relief for you. Hey, how's your department going? They still letting you work?" the man asked.

Even from Steel's distance, his heightened celestial senses

narrowed in on Bridget's whitening knuckles as she tightened her grip on her handbag strap. She shot a glance to Steel, then the door behind her, but looked right back at the man who addressed her.

Before she spoke, however, Angelina chimed in again. "Of course they're letting her work. They couldn't let her go after what happened, but it's not like they could have promoted her to our jobs in animation either."

"Here you go, Steve-o!" Jan placed his drinks on the counter, but Steel stood rooted to the floor. They were colleagues then, that group of people who were presently crowding around his ray of sunshine and quickly dimming her spark.

These were the people who, after Bridget's accident, had been promoted to the new animation department she and the rest of her design team had been vying for . . . before her life had been shattered.

CHAPTER 14

Fear did funny things to a person, and not just emotionally. For example, how Bridget's hands could have both sweaty palms *and* frozen fingertips at the same time was truly baffling. It made for a damn challenging time hanging on to her handbag. But c'mon, like she'd brought the thing to be anything more than a massive emotional support fidget toy?

The steadily increasing thrum inside her chest, however, was a familiar sensation, and she couldn't think of anyone she'd rather *not* experience an emotional breakdown around than the four people standing before her.

Angelina, Tom, Kiara, and Manuel hovered in a circle, all wearing the same expectant, yet skittish expressions. She'd seen those looks before, and she fucking hated them. There was sadness and guilt, sure, but just below the surface of those garden-variety emotions lingered more than a lion's share of morbid curiosity. It was the same cringing temperament that drew museum patrons in droves to specialty exhibits just so they could glimpse torture devices from the Middle Ages or learn how the voyagers journeying to the New World for the first time truly lived at sea for ten weeks, vermin and all. It was always like this. Perhaps it was part of the human condition, but there was just something about people who couldn't look away from an explosion, despite their horror and remorse. They needed to know every gory detail, as if their mere existence gave them the right.

"I'm doing fine," Bridget said, wincing at the meekness in her voice. Her shoulders crept higher around her ears—ears that were near to bleeding from the heightened clamors of the coffee shop around her. She needed to get out of there, but how? She couldn't just run, not in front of them.

"Oh, chin up, Bridge," Angelina cooed, then casually pulled her dirty blond hair into a messy bun, which belied the tailored blazer draped over a video game graphic tee. "We know how hard it was for you."

You know nothing, and you never did.

"But I've been meaning to ask you," she added, and a sparkle of something Bridget couldn't easily detect gleamed in the woman's eye. "Did you want to shadow us sometime?"

Surely, she hadn't heard her right. "Shadow? As in watch you animate?"

Angelina casually lifted a shoulder. "Sure. I mean, it's the least we can do. None of us would have gotten into the department without you."

A force slammed against the cold iron bars of Bridget's mental prison, shutting her back in. Following the accident, the deaths of her colleagues, and the miserable miracle that was her survival, there had been catastrophic fallout—for her. For the studio, however, after the messy business of HR's dealings with the families were over, things quickly turned to business as usual, and the four designers in front of her had seized the opportunity Bridget and her team had been planning for. What her colleagues had died for. No, she hadn't just lost her friends, but following a few mandated months of time off, she'd lost her dream as well.

And the four colleagues pressing around her were doing a bang-up job reminding her of that. Now they wanted her to watch as they flaunted it in front of her?

"No thanks," Bridget whispered. Her eyes had dropped to the black-and-white checkered tile at her feet and decided to stay there until her paralyzed legs could move her out of the blast zone.

"You sure? I mean, the production company we're working with is *amazing*. Total creative freedom. Actually, come to think of it—Tom, have any of the designs we've submitted to them *not* passed creative review?"

The bald designer at her side shifted on his feet as if even *he* no longer liked where this conversation was going. "Uh, no."

"See? It's been so insane. I *never* had that type of feedback and encouragement when I was still doing marketing work. Is that still going well for you? I guess as well as it could be, right?"

Out out out. Bridget needed to get out *now!* She turned toward the door and muttered, "Uh-huh," but her legs wouldn't move. Chilling tingles blanketed her thighs and calves, quickly spreading along her abdomen and arms. It was a painful, paralyzing distraction from what she tried to mentally order her insubordinate legs to do.

C'mon, move!

Then Manuel, the tallest of the group and perhaps the most charismatic if his stylish horned-rimmed glasses and casual appearance were anything to go by, leaned closer, and dammit, she couldn't even bring herself to back away.

"I hope it's not too intrusive, but I've always wondered about this. What sort of compensation did the studio give you after the accident? We all know you got more than the standard short-term disability HR offers. I'm just curious about the bargaining aspect because I've got this procedure coming up.

It's an eyelid lift, which is *technically* plastic surgery, but my doctor said I can argue that it's not because it's medically necessary in my case. My eyelids are way too droopy, especially for someone who just turned thirty, and my hindered peripheral vision is starting to impact my pickleball game. But at any rate, I want to see how much I can squeeze out of the company. They gave you off for a few months, but your injuries weren't that bad, right? I mean, all things considered."

Concussion, fractured femur, herniated disc, more stitches than all the balls in a sporting goods store, but sure, they weren't that bad, I guess. Prick.

He threw his hands up and had the nerve to appear sheepish for all of five seconds before he continued. "The animation department's been killing it, and I kind of want to flex my muscles a bit, you know? Test my worth and see if I can milk more out of them like you did."

Dead. Three people were dead, and he wanted to know how she bargained for more time off? How she had somehow *milked* her company into time away from them, from that heinous toxic environment that would lead hardworking people to make foolish decisions?

Her heart pounded in her ears, and the checkered tiles at her feet began to blur into overlapping squares. Nausea rose in her gut. She needed to leave. To go go go before—

"Sunshine."

Bridget's gaze was yanked away toward that deep rumbling voice that was capable of crumbling mountains and shattering icebergs with just the right pitch and tone. Steel's shoulders were thrown back and his legs braced as if preparing to hold up the building should it come crashing down around them— should *he* send it crashing down around them. He wore no weapons, none that she could see, anyway, but the challenge and ferocity simmering in his icy gaze hardly needed any accessories to make their points known.

Gone was her carefree teasing angel. In his place stood an avenging one.

"These guys bothering you?" He tossed his head to her colleagues but never bothered to look at them.

"No, not . . . not really."

"We work together," Angelina said with more cheerfulness than the situation called for. Whatever nerves had been present in the woman's eyes a second earlier had vanished as soon as Steel joined their circle. Angelina sidled closer to him and quickly ushered out of the room any lingering uncertainty she may have had, only to replace it with brazen fire. "I'm Angelina." Her questioning eyes darted between Bridget and Steel. "I don't know how well you two are acquainted, but I'm happy to give formal introductions."

As if it would be impossible for someone like him to ever regard someone like Bridget.

"Don't bother," he sneered. Steel stalked over to Bridget. Tom and Manuel hardly had any time to get out of the way before Steel's shoulders decided for them. Then possessive hands wrapped around Bridget's stiff frame and hauled her to him, shackling her against the wall of his chest. "She's mine."

There was no time for a shout of protest or even surprise before his fiery mouth claimed hers.

IT HAD BEEN a long damn time since Steel had given himself over to his possessive instinct. Oh, it had been straining to burst free, always bubbling just below the surface of the cool, calm demeanor he so effortlessly covered it up with, but millennia-honed stamina and guided precision had done well to keep it at bay.

No more, not with Bridget's mouth finally on his. Fuck, like he was going to let her be treated that way? Made to feel ashamed, guilty, belittled when she had already suffered so much? And after he'd convinced her to leave the house with him, to entrust her care to *him?* The signs had been there before he'd even heard one word from those pissants' mouths. Her pulse beat in time to the pounding blender behind him and was giving the thing a run for its money. In his rage, Steel's heightened senses observed every tremble, every bead of sweat collecting at her hairline that had not yet fallen.

The very fire within him quaked and had his steps quickening toward her. In his frenzied vision, the coffee shop had narrowed until it was just the two of them. He only needed to reach her before she combusted fully, before her feeble mental barriers crumbled so completely, he wasn't sure he'd ever be able to build them back up again.

Words were said, but he hardly tracked them. He had apparently responded in some fashion because a whole lot of surprised faces flashed next to him as he leaned down and clutched Bridget to his chest.

"She's mine."

The raging beast prowling beneath Steel's skin snarled, then bayed when Bridget's mouth found his. Shock froze her lips and limbs and halted her breathing. Then he pressed further, plying and kneading until the soft gates of her mouth eased a touch, then a touch more. Her sharp inhale robbed the breath from his lungs, and he happily relinquished every part of himself to her. Tenuous kisses turned bolder. The curve of her back deepened, and Steel gripped her impossibly tighter. She opened her mouth, parting her lips in time with his own.

Steel pulled back and let out a cry. A ferocious energy eddied in the base of his core, collecting and gathering every powerful piece of him until it raced through all the veins and muscles in his body. Blue electric flames erupted over him, and his back was yanked into a painful arch. Pain, however, quickly turned to power as his full angel fire engulfed his entire frame. His chest heaved against the onslaught but quickly calmed. This was *his* power, *his* weapon, and no one could wield it but him.

But how?

Around them, screams rang out, piercing through the fog of his power-drunk mind. Frightened shopgoers knocked over tables and ran for exits, while some stupidly stood there scrambling for their phones.

Shit, this is bad. One photo . . . all it would take is one photo and there'd be questions.

In the corner, by the front door, hung a red fire extinguisher. He shot his hand out and commanded the steel in the canister forward. The tank *thudded* into his palm. He yanked the pin free in the next breath, and white clouds of chemicals sprayed all around him. He kept releasing the mist, taking no small amount of joy in turning Bridget's colleagues into ghosts, until the canister sputtered on empty. Gags and wheezing coughs took the place of screams. Under the chemical cloud clover, Steel called his fire home and grabbed Bridget, who had fallen on the ground and had her face as far away from the spray as possible. Despite her best efforts, even she wasn't immune to the coughing fits.

Steel hauled her to her feet and hurried them toward the door. "C'mon. We need to get out of here."

"What . . . What the hell? You were on *fire!*"

"Yes, and no. I'll explain more later, but not here. Too many cameras." Too many witnesses.

They dashed across the parking lot and climbed into the car, but it wasn't until Steel had peeled out of there and was a good five minutes away from downtown that he finally started to breathe at regular intervals. Sweat prickled along his spine, and it had absolutely nothing to do with the heat they'd just escaped.

He tensed behind the wheel and flexed his fingers more tightly around the smooth leather. How the hell could this have happened? He turned the events over in his mind on repeat and couldn't come up with any other plausible outcome. In that moment, two very cold truths gripped Steel by the balls.

He had just wielded the full force of his angel fire, a feat he had not been able to do since before he fell to the mortal realm.

And it had been entirely out of his control because Bridget had been the one to pull the fire out of him.

CHAPTER 15

Steel's piss-and-vinegar mood had turned into full-on broody by the time he locked Bridget and him up tight in her garage. He hadn't even managed to turn the car off before she opened her door and scrambled through the entry to the house.

"Shit." He took his time following her, though he wasn't sure whether it was to collect his thoughts or because she probably wanted to be around him about as much as calves just loved that final trek to the slaughterhouse. "Fuck. *Fuck!*"

He didn't lurk or sulk, however much he wanted to, and made damn sure his presence was known as he stepped into the house and headed toward the kitchen. She wasn't there. No surprise.

"Bridget!" he called up the stairs, but no sound greeted him. Through the ceiling and the drywall, groans and creaks sounded. She was in her bedroom or perhaps the room across from it.

Steel's heavy steps dragged him up the stairs. Careful placement of his footing and weight ensured she'd be able to detect him as he rose higher. When he finally reached the top of the stairs, he waited. Tension swirled in his chest at not knowing what he'd find when he reached her. Would she have reverted to the cowering introvert he'd observed from afar the past four years, or would some small glimmer of that amiable fire still linger?

"Bridget," he said more softly. Still nothing. At the end of the hallway, a faint light crept through a partially open door. The light wasn't as strong as the morning sun was outside, so perhaps it was being muted through a film of airy curtains. Across from that room was a shut door, one he had not entered before. Instinct had him moving toward the light, however.

"May I come in?"

More silence greeted him, but he still didn't reveal himself through the half-open door. Fucking hell, he had forced her to do so much today. So foolish, so stupidly foolish.

"Are you going to light the bed on fire?"

He halted, then a sharp chuckle burst out of him. When she didn't say anything further, however, he took her silence as permission to proceed and stepped into the threshold. Bridget sat curled up in the center of her bed, with her back nestled against the pillow-padded headboard and her knees tucked up tightly against her. She looked so small amid the poofy comforter and even poofier ornamental pillows, but he wasn't sure whether it was her stature or fear that made it seem so. Both were unforgivable.

"Not unless you want me to."

"Why on earth would I want that?"

Steel expelled a deep breath. "Because it was you who brought it out of me."

Her back stiffened, and she lifted her chin from her knees. "What?"

"I touched you and—"

"No, you kissed me."

"Yes, and I had to touch you to do that," he said. She glowered at him but didn't respond. "When that happened, my full celestial fire was ripped free from me, though it wasn't by my hand but yours."

That curious fear returned to her wide eyes. "What?"

"May I sit?"

She nodded, and Steel walked over to the edge of the bed closest to the window and settled in front of the hazy sun struggling to break free through the gauzy curtains.

"You're special, Bridget, and not in the way that every mortal can claim to be."

She eyed him incredulously.

"Each mortal's soul holds some light that originated from the Empyrean, but a few contain something more, something far more valuable and precious." Steel lifted his chin to the meager light trying to stream in through the window and wished it was greater, wished it was as powerful as the full strength and glory of his fire, which had since receded to its limited stores within him. Whatever she had brought out before had been soul-crushingly temporary. "We've learned recently that a few sparks of the Empyrean's Eternal Flame reside in select mortals, though these mortals have always been hidden from us, and we have no idea why the sparks have chosen those souls in particular. As long as these sparks live, however, the Empyrean can never fall." He faced her and leveled all the weight of his immortal existence into his gaze. "Your soul must have one of these sparks because when I touched you, it called to my celestial fire. Well, not so much called to it as ripped it out and swung it around by the balls."

She snorted and did her best to school her features again into the harsh mask of hurt and sadness, but she failed miserably when the thin crease of her lips lifted ever so slightly.

The bed dipped beneath him as he turned more of his body toward her. Solemn memories rose unbidden, and that familiar tension in his jaw returned. "My world is hell, Bridget. I'm not going to sugarcoat it."

"No need. I still have the dents in my patio furniture, remember?"

"I'll reimburse you for it."

"How do you know I won't jack up the price, tack on some pain-and-suffering fees?"

"Oh, I expect you to, but don't worry. I assure you I'm good for the money."

The teasing light fell away from her eyes a bit. "And that kiss?" she asked softly. "Was that another form of payment as well?"

"No. I kissed you because you needed to be kissed."

She laughed this time. "Says you and every other male in existence—"

"There are no other males." That fiery possession flared hot in his chest again, and for a moment, he had to glance down at his arms to make sure his fire hadn't been summoned once more. He mentally shook his haze away. Fuck, what was happening to him?

"No, there aren't." An unnatural tremble warbled her voice, and mages damn him for putting that fear in her. Concern lashed through him while Bridget plucked at the fringe of the pillow in her lap. "And there haven't been."

The strange words echoed through the room.

"There haven't been . . . what, exactly? I'm afraid I don't follow."

Bridget cast pleading eyes to Elliot, who sat in the hallway silently lording over the proceedings as a talk show host might before the results of a paternity test were revealed. When she received no help from their feline voyeur, she stared back at Steel with pinched features. "There haven't been any other males . . . men. That kiss in the coffee shop was my very first one."

Mortification ebbed higher within the pit of Bridget's stomach, so high she nearly gripped the featherdown mass of blankets in her lap, threw them over Steel's shocked face, and ran for the door like she would when she and Ryan were teenagers. The first kiss of her life happened twenty minutes ago, and as far as major life experiences went, she couldn't say she'd chosen things to go down quite the way they had.

Nor, however, could her lips forget the smoky honey flavor of his.

"How the hell is that possible?" Steel's voice rose higher, with something akin to anger coloring its timbre. "I refuse to believe that not a single mortal man with eyes in his head and blood in his cock wouldn't have at least kissed you once you reached maturity, let alone manage to stay away at all."

Blood flared hot in her cheeks at the forwardness and absurdity of his words. "It wasn't like it was my choice or that I'd planned it that way!"

"How have you made it to twenty-eight years of age and not have been kissed before?"

"There just wasn't— Hey, how did you know how old I am?"

Steel closed his eyes and jerked his chin to the side, as if biting back words balancing on the tip of his tongue. Then he resettled his attention on her. "I saw your license. Now, explain. Please." Though his last word was courteous by nature, nothing in his tone implied anything remotely civil.

His words were more curious than condemning, however. Bridget briefly wondered when Steel had seen her driver's license, as she couldn't recall ever showing it to him, but she brushed the concern aside when his fingers curled so tightly around the edge of her mattress, she nearly held her breath for fear he'd grow claws and puncture the thing. Did angels even have claws? The angels she'd always imagined certainly didn't turn to metal, so who the hell knew?

"It just never happened." Her decade-long confession was as acrid on her tongue as it had been in her soul. God, this was mortifying. She didn't think it was possible to shrink any farther into the pillows, but when her back had fallen nearly flat against her cushioned palace, she had her answer. For Christ's sake, she never even told her brother this, though she figured he'd suspected after all these years.

She groaned softly and continued. "I was an anime- and manga-loving nerd in high school and then a solid romance and fantasy lover for years after that. Add in the fact that I had an older brother who, though not exactly a star athlete, per se, was athletic enough and very much loved by the popular and glamorous types to be well noticed, and I wasn't even a speck on the radar. Which was honestly fine by me. I was the dorky kid sister who got dragged to his games in a show of solidarity but who happily and quietly got to read on the bleachers or in the corner.

"College was different but . . . not. I kept my head down, focused on my design work, and mainly interacted with people through the video games I played. Any in-person friends I had were all design nerds like me and were definitely *not* ones I could ever see as more than friends. The few guys I had a fondness toward, however, never reciprocated, so I left it alone. I wouldn't beg, but nor would I seek it out. Grad school was more of the same, and that was when I first felt unusual being single and not having progressed intimately. My classmates were coupled up, some were even engaged, and I hadn't been kissed or gone on a real date yet, so I stopped thinking about it and did my best to avoid situations and gatherings where my single status would be noticed and commented on. After I got my degree in design, I started working right away for Pixel Dream. I wasn't there long before . . ." That familiar tightness threatened to clamp down again, but lucky for her, full-fledged embarrassment was stronger. Yay. She sucked in one more bracing breath. "What can I say? Meeting people hasn't exactly been on the top of my to-do list for the last four years."

Steel sat on the edge of her bed, though it might as well have been the precipice of a vast canyon. A skittish yet somehow virile energy rolled off him. If she looked closely enough, she'd have sworn she could almost make out pulsing ripples of the menacing stuff swirling beneath the smooth tan skin of his neck.

"You were hurting back at that coffee shop," he gritted out. He had turned from her during her confession, never taking his eyes off the floor in front of him.

"I was." The small whispered concession was to appease the beast before her, but then she hurried to add, "Though it wasn't because of you."

A single laugh filled with dark mirth was all the response she got. Then he leveled his eyes on her, and she gasped. Irises swirling with white-hot heat gleamed before her. All traces of that stunning glacial blue had vanished, leaving behind a colorless fire that had no equal anywhere. Instinctively, her body understood what she was seeing, what Steel was showing her.

His angel fire.

"I've done many terrible things in my life, Bridget, but I like to think I've done many good things as well. This house, this cage"—he gestured around them—"is not for you, nor are those fucking assholes you work with who build themselves up by tearing others down. I know this because that light inside of you is the purest thing in existence. It's the very thing I fell from the Empyrean for and swore an oath to protect. And for me to have tainted it as I did, to have stolen a kiss from you when you had never given one to another—"

"Hey! You didn't steal anything. Okay, maybe you did, technically, but I don't regret it. Not in the least. The outing was just a lot. Being around *them* was a lot. But not the kiss. No, that was pretty great."

The white flames in Steel's eyes cooled and simmered, until finally, those arctic baby blues shined down on her once more. Heavy breaths filled the air between them, along with magical confusion and heated confessions. What had they both just admitted to? And why could she not keep her eyes from tracing the curve of his lip or wondering what the warmth of his fire would feel like if he were to cup her jaw and capture her mouth once again?

Slowly, emboldened by some foreign brazenness, she kicked out of the blankets and moved closer to him, until the length of only one tufted square of the comforter beneath them separated their legs. Steel's eyes flicked to her mouth and lingered. Holy hell, that gaze—it was only a look, but it somehow raked over every single inch of her, until there wasn't a patch of skin that didn't feel somehow heated by him. She let out a shuddering breath, and that shy feminine part of her delighted at the flare of heat that flashed in the angel's eyes.

She wanted to kiss him. Lord, did she want to kiss him. A rushing chill swept over her, tightening her nipples. Breath and heat thickened the space between them.

"Had I known you existed, I'd have kissed you good and often." Then he dipped his head toward her mouth.

A door downstairs banged open, and her brother's familiar heavy steel-tipped boots stomped a mean streak through her entryway.

"Bridget? What. The. Fuck."

CHAPTER 16

"**S**hit!" Shit shit double shit.

Bridget flung herself away from Steel and scrambled off the bed.

"Ryan's here, which means he can't know *you're* here. Hide!" She waved frantic hands at Steel and shooed him away, but he didn't move. She even went so far as to grab his wrist and yank, but the large man on her bed merely sat there. His face was still and unreadable. "Please, you need to leave. Now!"

There was no way in hell she was about to explain a male's presence in her house to her police sergeant brother. Not that she had to answer to him for anything, but some sisterly part of her wanted any new people in her life to be introduced properly, not under a haze of secrets. She may be twenty-eight, but she respected and loved what little family she had far too much to have them stumble onto something like this. When she eventually presented Steel to her brother, it sure as hell wouldn't be during a gotcha moment in her bedroom. Cringe.

For half a second, Bridget was stunned that some part of her even assumed the angel would meet Ryan at all, but what was more so unnerving was that the thought had been a foregone conclusion. She couldn't think about that now. Unsettled, she tucked that kernel away to analyze later and turned her frustrations back to Steel.

"I'm not leaving," he said, though he finally had the wherewithal to rise from the bed.

"Oh, yes you freaking are."

"Bridget! You upstairs?" Ryan's shouts were no longer echoey as they had been when he'd called up from the front door entryway. He was closer, possibly at the base of the stairs.

"Uh, yeah! Just a minute!" she yelled.

Steel glared at her with stony eyes, completely heedless of the situation's urgency or maybe more aware of it than she'd realized. "Does he always talk to you that way?"

"What? He's my brother. We talk like that all the time." Well, not exactly *all* the time, but Steel didn't need to know that. "Besides, he's a cop. He practically had to take a course in foul language and attitude problems when he went through the police academy." Still not a complete truth, but it sure as heck didn't seem far off.

"He seems upset," Steel countered. Below, the hardwood stairs groaned and creaked in protest as someone much larger and bulkier than Bridget started scaling them.

"Ryan, I'll be down in a sec! I'm in the bathroom."

"I gotta talk to you."

"Not if I'm in the *bathroom*."

"I'll talk through the door. This can't wait."

Steel whirled at the door and gritted out, "What the fuck does he have to say to you that can't wait until you're out of the bathroom?" He made to move toward the door.

Crap! If Steel started walking around, Ryan would hear more than two people upstairs. No no no, this couldn't be happening.

The wood in the hallway creaked louder as Ryan passed that notoriously extra squeaky step, the one she always managed to dodge in the middle of the night when she had to go downstairs because it was the last step that the hallway bathroom's light could still reach when it was on.

Wait . . . the bathroom.

A thought occurred to her. A possible, though embarrassing, way out of this. The bathroom door at the top of the stairs was still closed. It could work. Bridget inhaled a deep breath and cupped her hands around her mouth, preparing to scream loud enough as if the bathroom door separated them.

"I just got my *period*, asshole!"

Every sound in the house went still. Even Elliot, to his credit, stopped licking his hind legs and simply stared at her in a subdued expression of feline shock. Steel's back went ramrod straight, and his head slowly swiveled in her direction. The expression on his face was nothing short of mortification and panicked horror. *Serves you right.* She stomped around him and went to the edge of her bedroom but didn't go out into the hallway.

"If you'd be so kind as to bring me a fresh box of tampons and leave them outside the bathroom door, I *might* be in a better mood when I come out. Or would you rather storm in here and help clean up this mess?"

Not a single male moved, and that was perhaps the only smart decision any of them had made in the past five minutes. Steel finally managed to close his mouth, but he had suddenly taken an acute interest in a bit of nicked wood at the corner of her dresser.

That's right, you better look away. I am sooo not in the mood right now to referee this would-be pissing contest.

From the stairwell, Ryan's words had transformed from fiery to beseechingly clipped. "Where do you keep 'em?"

Bridget smiled in smug satisfaction. "There are extra boxes in the basement, in the storage cabinet across from the washer and dryer."

"And do I— That is—" Ryan cleared his throat. "Do you need a specific kind or something?"

She debated twisting the knife a bit and telling him she was actually out of the kind she liked and that he should run to the store to grab her more. Perhaps send him on a wild goose chase as punishment for not calling ahead and have him ask the drug store clerk where the heated tampons were or where he could find the extended-wear ones that you could go a week without changing. The lies and foolish made-up errands kept flashing through her, and she briefly wondered whether she shouldn't be a little more shocked that this type of revenge suited her so well, but she ultimately resisted. Bridget loved her brute of a brother, so no, she wouldn't do that to him, but she *would* resort to calling his boyfriend if he really didn't stand down. That would fix his ass real well.

"Just grab any blue box you find, so long as it says 'super' on the front somewhere."

"Super?" She hadn't heard that tremulous tension in her brother's voice since that first day after he'd had his ass kicked in the academy. Hearing it again was oddly delicious, if not a wee bit remorseful. It was a *very* wee bit, though.

"Yeah, as in 'super heavy.' Oh God, I'm really making a mess here. Better grab the super plus ones."

"Super . . . plus?"

"No, the ultra! Definitely going to need the ultra ones here. The box with the dark purple stripe on it. And would you hurry up already?"

Ryan's steps hammered out a steady retreat, but it wasn't until the floor under those heavy steps changed from wood to concrete that she finally exhaled the tight breath she'd been holding.

Bridget turned to Elliot, who still lay in the corner of her bedroom. She jerked her head toward the hallway. "Go bother Ryan for treats."

The orange tabby clearly didn't need to be told twice that someone was willing to feed him again only an hour and a half after breakfast. A swish of his thin tail darting into the hallway and down the stairs was all she saw before she turned to face Steel.

Her pale green curtain danced softly against the light breeze trickling in from the open windows. It was the only disturbance in her room and the only clue to the angel's sudden vanishing act.

THE ASPHALT ROOF shingles beneath Steel's ass weren't the only things grating him. Oh, sure, after he got through the dumbfounded shock of Bridget's admittedly brilliant lie, clarity regarding the situation also had the opportunity to snake back into his senses. Because, honestly, what did he plan on doing? Pummeling her brother to a pulp for using language that, if Steel had to guess, came more naturally to her than three-quarters of the pearl-clutching suburbanites on the block? No, it wasn't so much the tone and phrasing that triggered his heightened alert, but *why* her brother was there when he should have been only an hour or two into the start of his shift.

Unannounced cops were never a good sign, even if they were related to you. Perhaps especially so.

"Here's your, uh, supplies." The muffled bass notes of a mortified and distinctively uncomfortable older brother reverberated through Bridget's open window, though Steel's senses were strong enough that he could pick up on the conversation through the walls if need be.

There was a hurried squeak of a door partially opening, presumably the one for the hallway bathroom. "Thanks." The door slammed shut again. A minute or so later, Bridget's calm, if a tad overly cheerful, voice flitted through the second floor.

"If you're going to barge in on me like that, you'll have to learn to reap the consequences or give me my house key back."

Heavy boots shuffled uncomfortably against the worn hardwood. "Noted."

"Now, what's got you all hot and bothered?" The voices had grown louder, as if they had wandered into her bedroom and were closer to the open window. Steel tucked himself behind the small chimney lest any of the neighbors who happened to be home get a rooftop show.

"A fire was called in at Jan's Java Hut this morning."

A chilling tension speared through Steel's body, and he muffled a curse. After a heartbeat, Bridget responded, though her tone was not the animated bludgeoning voice she'd used on Ryan a moment before but one of meek uncertainty in the way of unpracticed liars who were out of their element. "Oh no. Was anyone hurt?"

There was a pause before Ryan responded, and the delay threaded that snaking coil of tension more tightly around Steel's chest.

"You tell me, Bridge."

Another beat of silence and then a soft gasp floated on the wind's whisper through the veiled curtains.

Ryan cleared his throat. "You want to tell me why I'm staring at a picture of my baby sister sidling up with some blond dude in a coffee shop in the middle of a goddamn fire?"

Terror, not tension, crept icy fingers along Steel's spine.

"I don't see any flames. All I can see are clouds of white smoke. Is that from a fire extinguisher?" she asked, though Steel, and presumably her brother, didn't miss her blatant avoidance surrounding the subject in question.

"Look at his legs."

A few more ticks of silence passed before Bridget responded. "Those scant blue wisps could be anything, and there's so much white dust and blurriness in the photo, I honestly don't even know what I'm looking at."

"Don't bullshit me." Ryan's words were tight, and his tone was one of a police sergeant questioning a witness, not one of an older sibling looking after his younger sister. "Is that you?"

Steel swallowed down the bile that threatened to rise in his throat and cursed his carelessness and, above all, his brazen selfishness when it came to her. A single, spur-of-the-moment decision four years ago had led to this woman thoroughly winding herself around nearly every single one of his thoughts and actions. He couldn't escape her, no matter how hard he tried to forget the black-haired beauty with soft features and blue eyes that had seen far more than they should have. He had never been able to forget her, though, and it seems that fate was now catching up with him.

Inside, the bed moaned as a body sank onto it, then another. "Yes," Bridget said.

Steel gritted his teeth, shuttered his eyes, and let that single word slam into him, sealing his destiny.

"This photo was taken this morning. You actually left the house today?"

Another soft "yes."

"You drove?"

"Yes."

"How did . . . how did you feel?" A glimmer of that older sibling's softened tone began to poke through the tough-as-nails police interrogation.

"It was . . . fine. Good. Hard but good."

Each breathy word was a slice through Steel's heart.

"And this man? How do you—"

"He's a friend I met recently."

Met.

That three-letter word held all the implications that big-brother nightmares were made of. Tack on *friend* and Steel was pretty sure Ryan was going over takedown maneuvers in his mind.

"Is he hurt? What's his name? Is he dangerous? Did he start that fire? God, Bridge, who the hell is this guy? When did you meet him? You never told me about him." Hurt, accusation, and worry all blared loud and clear in Ryan's voice as each one of his questions tumbled free. Steel waited on a razor's edge for Bridget's response, biting back his rage at the situation he'd put her in.

You knew this would happen. You fucking knew, and you still couldn't stay away.

"He's a friend, and no, he didn't start any fire."

Steel got the impression that particular wording was deliberate, as it was possibly the only truth she could say about what happened.

How would Ryan take it if he found out that *she* had been the one to ignite the flames?

"We met online and have been playing video games for a while. This morning, I finally worked up the courage to meet in person. It was a huge deal, Ryan, and not something I wanted to talk to you about because it was a big personal step for me, as I'm sure you can understand. His name is Ste . . . Steven. I chose to meet at Jan's because it's a public place, it was broad daylight out, and it's not far from home. I followed all the safety rules you've always taught me. These were *big* steps for me, and I don't want you screaming at me about it. I was going to tell you when I felt comfortable enough to do so. I love you, and I wouldn't ever keep something like that from you. You know that. I just needed it to be on my terms."

Lies, lies, and more lies bled out of her, and each one landed in Steel's chest like a honed dagger. The poor, foolish, beautiful woman who had been a prisoner of her own mind for so long was lying to her family to protect Steel.

A sagging, exhausted sigh filled the silence. "I know, and if you want to keep it to yourself a while, I'll respect that. It sucks, though, and don't expect me to be happy about it, but I get it. I do. I just want to make sure you're okay." A rustling of clothes and a soft kiss of affection mitigated the tension in the room.

Steel loosened his grip on the chimney slightly. Bits of mortar and crumbled brick fell away where his hand had dug into the structure. Ryan needed to leave, like, *now*, so Steel could jump back into that bedroom and confess every single thing he'd kept from Bridget all these years, knowing full well the hate she'd undoubtedly fling at him. It had been too long and too hard for her, too agonizing for him, and she deserved so much better than what his actions had saddled her with.

He angled his body into a crouch and waited with patience he didn't have for the two of them to say their goodbyes, until Ryan's next words nearly knocked him off the roof.

"If you go out with that guy again, just don't let me find out on social media like this, okay? That fucking sucked. You have any idea the kind of shit the guys gave me down at the station for that?"

Social media. The handful of people at the coffee shop who, when Steel's fire erupted, had reached for their phones instead of running for the exits. He thought he'd gotten out in time before any photos were snapped, but he was clearly wrong. That painful grip behind his sternum returned, this time spreading farther down until every part of his body recoiled with roiling apprehension.

If there was a photo floating around that linked Bridget to him, and especially one that showed him using his fire, it wouldn't be long before the charmers got wind of it as well.

Steel's heart was an icy crystal of dread in his chest. His stupid little morning excursion had just resulted in the charmers knowing where Bridget was and, more importantly, what she was to him.

CHAPTER 17

Bridget didn't see Steel for the rest of the day.

After Ryan, who showed more hurt in his stoic features than he was no doubt willing to let her see but couldn't hide anymore, left, she stormed to the window to search for the angel, only to come away with a whole lot of nothing. She'd run herself ragged tearing her house apart until she was damn sure there was no angel hiding in it anywhere. In a scrambled moment of panic, she'd even run for her phone, thinking that Steel was just another casual guy she could call or text whenever the moment struck her, but she didn't have his number. She had seen a phone on him when she first found him and stripped him of his weapons and gear, but she'd never thought to inquire further about reaching him on it. Some part of her assumed he'd just be around. Well, she was certainly kicking herself for that naive thought.

Now, however, with her once again alone and tucked inside the echoing halls of her too-quiet house, that black hole she'd once prayed would swallow her up was threatening to do so.

Steel had left, and she had lied to her brother after everything he'd done for her. Guilt and remorse lay thick and oily along her skin, coating her until her heart struggled to beat a steady rhythm beneath all the grime. Even Elliot had chosen to ignore her, refusing to come off the couch after she'd refilled his automatic feeder. Judgmental mongrel.

Her dragging heels scraping softly across the hardwood filled the oppressive silence as she shuffled downstairs. Outside the large picture window in her living room, only the barest wisps of orange remained before beginning their eventual descent beneath the horizon. Tires bumped over the slightly raised edges of granite curbs, announcing the arrival home of the working-class commuter brigade. Car doors slammed, and front doors opened. Children's laughter soon followed when babysitters released their charges into the welcoming, though exhausted, arms of gone-all-day parents.

It was all so perfect, and while Bridget couldn't honestly say that sort of daily routine wasn't one she ever yearned for, what hit her squarely in the teeth was the overwhelming sense that she was missing out on something.

For the first time since her self-isolation, that loss gnawed at her like a rash that had taken over her body until the itching was so bad, she couldn't ignore it anymore and had to look elsewhere for blessed relief. Relief didn't come from her usual methods, however.

When it became apparent Steel was nowhere to be found and didn't want to be for whatever reason, Bridget escaped to her work studio in the room across from her bedroom. The space wore many hats and, therefore, had many names—*work studio, den, gaming center*—but her favorite was *sanctuary*. When she was in that safe haven, she would draw and sketch and make marks on top of marks until the calluses on her fingers grew calluses. She'd only consider stopping when her drawing tablet burned hot beneath her hands and all but pleaded for a break to recharge. But she would never truly stop when the thrall had her so firmly in its grip. Instead, she would grab her sketchbook and colored pencils, scribbling and shading every fantastical creature in her head until her hand screamed from the cramping and the pads of her palms were plastered with multi-color smudges. It was gloriously messy and rewarding for nothing and no one except her soul.

None of it—the drawings, the sketches, even the occasional paintings—had been enough, however. That pervasive itch had turned into a burning, and the irritant had spread so thoroughly that it threatened to tarnish and strangle her from the inside out.

That was how she found herself in her garage, staring at her vehicle, car keys in hand and purse tucked up on her shoulder.

She wasn't exactly sure where she would go or if she could even bring herself to leave, but somewhere between lying to her brother and Steel disappearing on her, the urge to flee had crept higher, and the incessant pounding in her skull had turned into a war drum beckoning her. A challenge.

Her hand jostled, and the keys' delicate tinkling echoed its soft staccato through the cavernous garage. Each reverberation tapped out more of that urging rhythm. The unassuming door behind her, the one that led back into the house that had become so familiar it was hardly palatable, was a bleak reminder of the other atrocity Bridget had committed that day. The lies she'd told Ryan . . . she'd never done that before. Sure, there had always been personal things she'd chosen not to share, and he had respected that, but she'd never flat-out *lied* to him. And seeing Steel so angry, with that entirely different heat threatening to erupt off his powerful frame like simmering brimstone . . .

It had all led her here, where she stood on top of her very own precipice.

With unsteady hands, she grabbed her phone and tapped out a quick text to her brother. *Thank you. I'm sorry. I'm going out tonight, just for an hour or so. Be back by 8 pm. Love you.*

For a moment, she debated even sending the text. Would he demand more details? Abandon his dinner plans with Michael so he could be with her? God, she hoped not, and she prayed he'd see this as not just a gesture of peace but as an act of a still-healing sister showing her big brother that she saw him and she was wrong.

A heartbeat later, her phone *pinged* softly, though it may as well have been a lifetime. She glanced at the text, let out a whimpering breath, and beamed.

Have fun.

That was all. No barking or third degree. Just a simple message, a simple nod of acceptance and understanding. Of love.

After pocketing her phone, Bridget squared her shoulders and reached behind her. With a sharp tug, she closed the door and walked to the driver's side of the car. The car door handle's soft click and release was her first step off the ledge, but it wasn't until the garage door had fully closed in front of her and the car's front wheels had cleared the lip of the driveway that her second foot followed suit.

A tumbling, terrifying sensation gripped her throat and settled in the pit of her stomach. Sweat dappled along the thin skin of her palms as she moved them smoothly around the leather steering wheel. Houses adorned with ornamental shutters and HOA-approved shrubberies just like hers whipped by her window.

And then she laughed. Again and again. A chilling glee sprang free from her until she was near to cackling at the windshield. The backs of her hands swiped against her eyes and came away wet with happy tears a long time coming. With each passing intersection, that terror turned to thrill, as if she had just scaled the slope of a mountainous roller coaster and was whirling down with bone-chilling delight.

Oh, the fear was still there, simmering just below the surface like a bubbling cauldron, but good lawdy, it had been replaced by something she'd never thought possible. Relief and excitement.

As Bridget relaxed into her seat and drove to the one place that would keep this high going, she did her best not to look up at the faintly orange sky and wonder whether she'd see wings.

———

THE BOOKSTORE'S warm bronze door handle kissed Bridget's slightly chilled palm. The weight of the old oak door tugged comfortably against her shoulder as she opened it and slid inside her other sanctuary, though she hadn't been able to visit this one for some time. It was a slight she was eager to correct. All around her, worn leather, crinkled plastic-wrapped dust covers, and weathered paper greeted her, calling to her like long-lost friends.

The bookstore in Aurora had once been Bridget's refuge. The owner, Amanda, had a particular fondness for high fantasy epics and, oddly enough, papier-mâché. She'd always made the most enchanting book displays, crafting stool-sized cupcakes for Bake Like a Bookworm month, then a life-sized anaconda that snaked around the entire front of the store the following month for Snakes, Eels, and Banana Peels to highlight the newest children's books on colors and shapes. Bridget still remembered leaping over the snake's tail, nearly clipping it in the process on her way to score her next fantasy romance.

Her feet led her to that hallowed section now, and each bracing step tingled with another familiar thrill. God, why —*why?*—had she not done this sooner?

Because you needed someone to show you the value of experiences.

A few patrons mulled about, but as it was near closing time, the stacks were pretty sparse. Bridget managed a few kind half-smiles and was surprised at the ease with which that casual anonymity returned to her. Likewise, the handful of customers she'd greeted returned her mediocre gesture with a mimicked one of their own, as if they didn't want to interact with people any more than she did. She had to smile at that and wondered whether Amanda would do well to sell customized sweatshirts emblazoned with an explanation for her customers' common penchant for pages over people.

Unless you want to talk about books, no comment.

She'd buy it in a heartbeat, one in every color.

Bridget reached the back of the store, where the fantasy section was separated from the main stacks by a three-step riser. She took the three-in-one great leap like she used to, and even during that small taste of flight, she couldn't stop the images that had accosted her all day from flaring brightly in her mind.

Fire. Wings. Phoenixes. Angels. Metal. Great shifting beasts. A warrior's kisses. More fire and wings . . .

Through the window, the sharp oranges of daylight had firmly dissolved into the burgeoning tendrils of the creeping night. The sun had just set, and she used those final rays of light, mixed with the garish fluorescence of the bookstore's overhead lighting, to resume her hunt. Her eyes danced over the book displays and titles, searching for something, anything, on—

The man turned the corner before she even noticed him.

"Oh!" Her hands flew to her chest. She pressed the great leaping thing behind her ribs as if doing so would keep it from falling out.

"My bad. It was totally my fault."

That voice. Smooth, butter-coated, gleeful arrogance. She glanced up at the man before her—and glanced up some more. Manuel's tall elegant form loomed over her. He must have hovered somewhere north of six-foot-five, for he had a natural slouch to his shoulders, as if he was used to spaces not accommodating his stature. Nevertheless, those sleek horn-rimmed glasses wrapped around sensual hazel eyes that flashed so brilliantly in the shop's lighting, they almost appeared gold.

Bridget let out a frustrated desperate breath. "What are you doing here?"

Manuel tucked his hands into his pockets and shuffled his weight from one leg to the other. "I guess I could ask you the same question, huh?"

That simmering cauldron of fear in Bridget's stomach bubbled more furiously, but no, she would *not* allow for a repeat performance of this morning. "Just looking for a book."

"Yeah, I'm looking for something, too." The tone in Manuel's voice changed. The haughtiness was still there, sure, but his words had come out deeper, more rumbling and less immaturely boyish. The cuffs of his long-sleeve button-down shirt were rolled up to just below his elbows, revealing thin forearms. His skin, however, had somehow lost its slightly golden hue she recalled from the coffee shop that morning and seemed to increase in pallor before her. Bridget's breath stilled, and something urged her to take a step back.

"Where you going?" Manuel asked. His voice had completely altered now and held none of the lighthearted characteristics of her colleague's natural tenor tones.

The cauldron within her danced, roiled, and protested. Every erupting bubble of fear in the pit of her gut burst with the same frightful message: *run.*

"I gotta go." The words were an effort to get out, but she hardly cared. Bridget whirled away from him and made for those small three steps that would lead her back to the main part of the store, back toward the exit, when a firm hand clenched around her bicep. She cried out, not in pain but in surprise, and another hand secured her mouth.

Trapped. She was trapped. It wasn't the metal of a car's frame that held her but something just as strong and terrifying. All along her back was a solid wall of unending strength,

strength she had never before associated with the lean frame of her colleague. Something about him was different, bigger, more menacing and heated. No matter how she twisted and writhed, kicked and jolted, Manuel wouldn't budge. Her efforts were little more than the flutter of a moth's wing against him. How? He was tall, yes, but lanky. She should have easily been able to knock him off-balance or *something*. She craned her neck back to look at Manuel, but her colleague was no longer there.

In his place stood a hulking specter of bone-white skin pulled taut over straining muscles that bulged beneath the costume of Manuel's clothes. Teal and gold tattoos, almost tribal, snaked up each forearm, over the backs of his hands, and completely covered his sneering face and bald head. The man whipped off the glasses still resting along the bridge of a now bulbous nose, and instead of Manuel's arrogant hazel eyes she expected to see staring back at her, irises of gleaming molten gold had taken their place.

Gold to match the two gold bands circling his neck like some warrior's battle adornment.

"Hello, Bridget. I have someone who'd like to meet you very much, and he's been waiting a *long* time. Best not delay any longer."

CHAPTER 18

As far as cowards went, Steel was pretty sure he belonged so firmly in that camp that he could chair a committee made up of assholes just like him. He'd even bring the doughnuts and coffee to the board meetings.

The cavernous echoes within the den's armory were welcome accompaniments to the melodies of raging war clamoring through his mind. His skin itched with a discomfort he didn't recognize, and a sharp insistent tug within his chest had his attention focused not on the short sword in his hands but on the fierce woman across town who'd lied to her brother to protect Steel's anonymity.

Tempered anger had his fist gripping the hilt of the sword more tightly as he slowly arced the blade's edge along the Japanese whetstone's abraded surface. Steel had lived long enough to appreciate the mortal advancements in weaponry and had long ago lost any remorse about staying true to his once-preferred sharpening techniques. That meant it had been out with the old grinding stone and in with the new—well, new by his standards—whetstone, and he'd never looked back. He rather liked the simple improvement, but he sure as hell drew a line in the sand at those electric grinding monstrosities that had all the subtlety of a bull in heat and the attentive care of a lumbering tyrannosaurus.

Mages spare him.

The calm, slow rasp of the blade against the stone sang through the armory, though it did nothing to crowd out Steel's racing thoughts as he'd hoped. Still, the action soothed him, as it always did. He could just as easily manipulate the metal with a simple twist of his magic, honing its blade precisely to Steel's preferred sharpness, but that would do nothing to steady his frazzled nerves or that unabating hunger swirling within his gut.

He had so many questions. And one, in particular, he wasn't sure he wanted to know the answer to. But oh, if it *was* true . . . if he was correct, as he suspected . . .

Hard heels clipped on the stone behind him, and by the weight and drag of the footfalls, Steel didn't need to guess who had just joined him. Lovely.

"You look like shit."

Steel cocked a brow at Chrome's muscled mass behind him. The angel just popped another square of peppermint gum into his mouth, then lumbered down the few steps to where Steel was seated. Chrome's square hard-lined jaw worked back and forth religiously. Steel couldn't keep his eyes from tracking the slight divot in his sentinel brother's chin as it rose and fell in slow steady circles.

"Did anyone ever tell you that you look like a cow chewing its cud when you do that?"

A flicker of amused challenge danced in the angel's eyes. "No, but as long as we're on the subject of the animal kingdom, did anyone ever tell you that when you bury your head in the sand and let your ass hang out, as you're doing right now, you look like an ostrich?"

"What?"

"Yeah, except you've got prettier plumage." Chrome nodded that still-circling chin at Steel's mop of shaggy hair, then smiled his trademark shit-eating grin. To Steel's credit, he *had* trimmed the mess, but despite its closer crop, errant waves still stuck out from the sides on occasion as if voicing their protest to his pruning.

Shit, maybe he *did* resemble a bird.

"Fuck off. I'm not in the mood."

"Of course not. Why do you think I came down here? I'm a magnet for pissy dispositions."

"Just say what you came to say." Steel swiped his blade once more and then went to work refining the edges with an emery cloth.

Chrome sighed and grabbed a seat next to him. "You don't even try to make this fun."

"I don't think our definitions of fun exactly jive."

"No, they don't." His brother's teasing faded until the soft rhythmic swipes of the cloth against the high-carbon steel were the only sounds around them. "You remember a few months ago when Tung told us how he'd given a vial of his blood infused with his fire to Cyro in exchange for using the demon's magic so Tung could try to make contact with the Empyrean again? And you remember how stunned we all were when we found out?"

The cloth slowed against the newly honed edge until all that remained between the two angels was the veiled echo of the material's raspy kiss.

Tungsten, the prime sentinel and leader of the fallen brothers, had made a deal with the head of the demons himself. Though the celestial mages had appointed Tung to lead the heavenly guard at the time of the Empyrean's creation, the mages could never have accounted for the crippling weight of sheer desperation that would land on their brother, nor the drastic decisions such circumstances would force him to make. In the end, his bargain with the charmer had been nothing but a farce, and Cyro had exploited his manipulations to his fullest advantage. What the dark charmer didn't witness, however, was the toll it took on their family once Tung revealed how he'd kept the whole thing a secret. The fallout had been brutal, the betrayal its own sort of infliction. Among the angels, Chrome had taken Tung's slight the hardest.

Steel's throat bobbed on a swallow. "Yeah."

Chrome's face was void of its characteristic humor and smartassery. Only solemn determination filled out those angular features, and any remaining resolve Steel may have had sank within him like a lichen-infested stone.

He knows. Shit.

"The others?" Steel asked, though his voice wobbled slightly. There was no point in beating around the proverbial bush, not with Chrome.

A single nod.

Steel looked down at his sword. "You saw the photo."

Another grim nod.

Then the confession Steel had kept locked behind silent lips for far too long finally sprang free. "Yeah, I found her."

He didn't need to clarify who *her* was. Months ago, Steel and his brother Titan had tortured a mystic charmer—a class that harbored and wielded magic—for its part in the abduction and trauma of Tung's soul bond, Tammy. Even though the thing was little more than charred flesh and hacked-off body parts by the time Steel and Titan were through with him, the bastard had enough juice and gall still kicking around its skull to throw Bridget's name in Steel's face before the putrid thing went lights out. At the time, his brothers had only shared expressions of worried confusion, but for Steel, the name had been thrown at him as a mocking taunt. It was the matador's red cape flung in his face. The charmers knew who she was, but didn't know where she was, or what she was to him. So, he'd had to decide whether to attack and silence the threat or play along with his brothers' confusion.

He had attempted some sad cobbled-together version of both and had failed spectacularly. But he couldn't do it on his own anymore, not with whatever charmer business was going on at the resort and not with Bridget's association with him out in the open.

"Everyone's upstairs," Chrome added.

Steel sheathed his sword and rose from his seat. "It's time. It's long past time."

Chrome stood and clapped a comforting hand on his brother's shoulder. Steel jerked, not from the jarring motion, but from the pang of unease and guilt that had suddenly come unlocked inside him. They both turned toward the steps.

Their brother Brass whirled into the doorway, his long leather trench coat flaring, then settling around his tall-booted calves. Tight fists pumped and glowed with twin rings of blue fire. Swirling ochre eyes pinned the two angels. "Charmers."

Chrome tensed. "How many?"

"At least three, possibly more."

Steel lifted his eyes to the ceiling as if detecting the daylight through the great mountain they lived beneath. "The sun has only just gone down, not even to the minute, but perhaps seconds ago."

Flames flashed and pulsed higher up Brass's arms. "They're getting bolder," he hissed. "Iron and Bronze were on patrol and spotted them first. They're there now."

Steel checked the buckles on his weapons and beat feet past his brother up the stairs. Blood and fire surged through too-idle veins. The brief glimmer of the full power he'd experienced when he kissed Bridget was a cruel tease that had ignited every part of him, from his cock to his core.

Release sang in the concerto of his battle cry. He'd fight his fury out, confess everything to his brothers, then return to Bridget on swift and unburdened wings.

MANUEL—NO, not Manuel, but whatever the thing was that had pretended to be him—dragged Bridget through the emergency exit at the back of the library. They were so far from the front of the bookstore that any muffled screams she'd managed to release were lost among the drab worn carpet and tall lumbering book stacks.

Before the weighted fire door could close all the way, she kicked a foot out and managed to snag it on the inside. Her toes curled desperately around the lifeline of the doorframe. Watery eyes squeezed tightly shut against the piercing cramps in her foot.

"None of that now."

A hard heel slammed down on her extended lower calf. Bridget roared behind the hand. Her leg slackened instantly, and the jarring thud of the fire door slammed home, sealing her away from help. Pain ricocheted down her leg, though the bone hadn't snapped thankfully. A small miracle. Her foot and ankle, however, throbbed with fiery spasms.

Bridget thrashed and kicked with every muscle in her body still capable of responding, but nothing she did managed to loosen the thing's iron grip even the slightest. Faded striped lines of empty parking spaces stretched around her, and she vaguely recalled the small parking lot next to the bookstore that also abutted the high school's larger back lot where the school buses were kept.

A school and property that, due to spring break, had no after-school or evening activities going on and was otherwise completely deserted.

Amid the expanse of asphalt, one shorter school bus stood

apart from the rest, and it already had its doors open. The pulsing dread roaring in her ears could already foresee how this would pan out. He meant to take her somewhere.

Bridget dug her heels in as best she could and whipped her body in hard spasms like a hellcat. There was no way she was getting in that thing. No fucking way. She thrashed again, but the muscled bands around her only clenched tighter. The one beneath her breasts fell away for the briefest of moments—only to clamp around her more fiercely, but this time, the hand that gripped her also held the tip of a curved white knife under her left breast.

"Keep thrashing about and I'll start slicing things off you that I'm sure you'd prefer to stay right where they are." To emphasize his point, the blade's tip punctured through her sweatshirt, top, and bra, slicing a slow trail along the underside of her breast. Bridget hissed deeply, but she refused to cry out, even as the stinging along her skin burned and warm wetness trickled down her abdomen.

Fear silenced her, but the thing holding her only smiled, though whether it was because of her terror or his appreciation of himself she wasn't sure.

"Attagirl." Then he tugged her forward until her feet hit the prominent grooves of the school bus's bottom step. Her legs strained against the stairs, but his weight at her back was too strong, too insistent. He pushed her again, lifting her a bit. Her legs were crunched and folded onto the higher step, farther into the vehicle that would rip her away.

A hammering crash erupted behind them. Bridget and her captor whirled around. A dark form had landed in the middle of the parking lot. The shadow's resplendent wings splayed wide toward the horizon and rippled with a blazing blue fury she'd never witnessed before. Blinding white light, the amalgamation of every known color, consumed fiery eyes with terrifying power.

Steel.

Around the angel's body and all along his wings, blue flames sang and hissed as if they were lurking, writhing creatures of the deep just begging to be called into service of their master. Though he wore his scabbard and the hilt of his sword peeked over the curve of his shoulder, he palmed no physical weapon, though those flames and his power spoke of something else entirely. His face was a calm, smooth mask of destruction, so unlike the jovial joker she'd come to know. No, this man was a harbinger of a different sort.

An angel of death.

"Let her go." Steel spoke the words calmly. His eyes were so blinding that Bridget could hardly look at his face directly, but some part of her felt when he settled that blazing stare on her.

The creature holding her just bobbed a meaty shoulder and gripped her more tightly. "Nah. I'm having too much fun."

"It wasn't a question."

"Speaking of questions, I've got one for you. Care to take a ride with us? I mean, there's just so much room. We could even spread out if you had a mind to keep her horizontal. The more, the merrier, especially with the others on their way."

Steel didn't answer, but the flames around him brightened and whirled their menacing response.

"You sure? Bus is leaving." The thing's taunts were a thick heavy sneer in the air. "No? Hmm." The creature paused a moment as if to give Steel's nonresponse some great consideration, then leveled that putrid gaze back on the angel. "Pity."

Bridget felt it before she saw it. The slick slide of a hard, smooth weapon being unsheathed from some hidden place behind her. The movements at her back were so slight, she wasn't even sure her captor was aware she could detect them.

But she could, and if that cold weapon the creature inched out from his pant leg was meant for Steel, she was going to stop it. She had to.

The infinitesimal jostling behind her stilled as if preparing to strike, but not before she would. With biting fury, she raised her good leg and slammed the heel of her sneaker down onto her captor's foot, knowing full well the action would only stun him rather than hurt him, but it was all the distraction she could muster.

She was right.

The creature had heaved the blade, but with Bridget's attack, the weapon arced wide, missing its target. Howling in annoyance, her captor hurled Bridget to the ground. She barely had enough time to throw her hands out before she almost ate the pavement. Her wrists screamed at the impact, and her slashed clothes hung limply over her torso. The cut the thing had made wasn't particularly deep, but it was deep enough for the blood to have welled up and already begun drying in crusted patches over her skin.

The flash in her periphery froze her against the pavement.

Steel lunged, not with weapons but power. The charmer, for Bridget now realized what her captor truly was, had used her diversion to release a white plate the size of a deck of cards from beneath its sleeve. Once in its hand, the plate expanded in a heartbeat until it was the size of a ballistic shield, but not one made of metal. No, one made of *bone.*

The charmer crouched, shield in front of it, while Steel's targeted flames beat at the thing in wave after wave of celestial fury. Bridget stifled a scream of pain and crab-walked backward, away from the wall of heat, until a calm gloved hand settled on her shoulder. She cried out and whipped around.

"Be easy. Allow me to get you away from here."

A red-haired man with a quiet resolve about his features leaned over her. Black leather covered his body, from his gloves to his trench coat to his boots, but beneath the open flaps of his coat shone the glinting handles of many firearms that still radiated heat from what she suspected was recent use. Grimy smudges on his temple and a faint blossoming bruise on his right cheek suggested he'd been in a fight of his own. Tucked tightly behind him, however, so close she hadn't noticed them at first against the backdrop of school buses, were gleaming wings of shimmering brass. His strained amber eyes pinned her with expectant worry, but she sensed he was holding something back, as if his fire wished to quake and burn as well.

"You're an . . . angel, too."

He nodded and gave her a small answering smile that blessedly spared her from the embarrassment of stating the obvious given her proximity to his very real and in no way hidden wings.

"It's best to stand back. This part tends to go pretty quickly." He helped her to her feet and shielded her behind him.

"What part?"

Before he could answer, a hissing crackle ignited in front of them. The charmer cried out as he was pushed back farther against the bus by a second blast of blue fire. Behind Steel, a large brawny man—no, another angel—with wings the dark russet of cooled iron added his fire to the fray, hammering that shield back, back, then back some more. The strength of the inferno sent the demon flying, limbs splayed, through the open door of the bus.

The fires immediately extinguished. Steel, teeth clenched and chest heaving, lifted his arms in front of him once more. The door to the bus slammed closed. Bridget jerked with each violent slash and kick made by the trapped creature against the door, the windows, the windshield, but there was no escape. And then she heard it.

A slow creaking moan filled the parking lot. Metal scraped and sliced against welding points, until great yellow sheets of the bus's steel snapped entirely and crumpled around the charmer imprisoned inside. Tires popped and glass shattered. Screams soon followed. Each new sickening noise caused Bridget's heart to leap into her throat. She ducked her head and covered her ears with her hands, but she couldn't take her eyes away from that school bus as Steel's power manipulated it until it was no more than a wadded-up ball of metal about the size of her car.

When she finally dropped her hands, nothing but silence greeted her.

Bridget stammered back, just as the angel next to her inched forward. Steel had dropped to his knees in exhaustion. That blond head of his sagged to the asphalt until his forehead nearly kissed the pavement as if in some silent weary prayer. Even from where she stood, she could still make out the tremors in his shoulders and the ragged expansions of his ribs. God, he looked drained. No, not just drained but wholly depleted, as if all the power and energy he'd used had robbed his vital organs of optimal functioning.

Then those heated eyes shifted to hers. Steel only stayed down for a moment or so before he rose and lunged for her. Meanwhile, the two other angels let their fire blaze once more, coating and engulfing the bus until the metal began to melt and ooze into a smaller writhing ball.

Steel reached for Bridget, and every wobbly bone in her body was just about ready to throw itself at him, but as soon as his eyes settled on her tattered clothes, he halted.

"You're hurt." He gripped her shoulders, then carefully plucked at the torn sheets of her sweatshirt.

Her weary head had only managed a slight nod. It was hardly sufficient and nowhere near what she wanted to tell him, that yes, she was hurt but it wasn't that bad, that her slight chin raise had nothing to do with her well-being and everything to do with her fear over his. But God, her throat burned, and each sobbing swallow seemed to rake more fiery coals over her hoarse vocal cords. She wanted to scream, to cry out his name, to wail and weep over everything that had happened to her, at all she had witnessed.

But she could do none of those things, and as her brain filled with far too many questions to count, she merely walked up to him and let her heavy head fall against his chest. As if in silent camaraderie of the mutual horrors they'd both witnessed, he simply stroked his fingers, still warm from his power, over her trembling back and held her closer.

"I'm taking you home. My brothers will clean up here. And then, in a few hours, I think it's time you meet my family." His words held all the soothing gentleness of a guardian angel.

It was exactly what she needed.

Home safe.

Bridget tapped out the short text to Ryan right as Steel finished doing his patrol of the property, whatever that entailed. Those two little words that hovered across the screen in such an innocuously common chat window were a blaring mockery of what her life had become. A frickin' *Supernatural* episode, apparently, complete with demon deception and moody angels. Well, one moody angel, at least. She'd reserve judgment on his brothers until she met them. She wasn't totally heartless, after all.

The deceitful text she'd sent may as well have been a neon road sign pointing right at her, lit up for all of Aurora to see: Liar, Liar, Pants on Fire. Though, in her case, the element of fire in that proclamation wasn't that far off.

A door shut below, then even footsteps made their way up the staircase from the garage. Steel's wide shoulders pushed through the doorway. His haggard form slid around her house with a weary grace she hadn't thought possible. Though she still knew very little of his power, the sheer force of what he'd expelled had been extraordinary. She marveled at whatever source of will or stubbornness he tapped into that allowed him to still move with such purpose and intensity through his obvious exhaustion.

"All clear downstairs. Car and garage are locked. No one's outside. The others will be over in another hour or two." He strode toward the kitchen and hung her keys on the little hook by the back door. From behind, Steel's usually prowling, powerful body had slowed. It wasn't in how he walked so much, but how his efforts and movements seemed to require a lot more consideration and direction before everything got on board. Even the simple task of walking up stairs had forced her confident angel to have a more weighted and measured step.

"Is this what happens when you use your fire the way you did?"

That broad back stiffened, and she immediately wished she could call the words home, but as her mind scrambled to figure out how she could pull her foot out of her mouth, he simply turned and leaned his tall frame against the side of her kitchen cabinet.

"Our power is limited. Well, I suppose not all of us anymore, but for most of my brothers, our fire reserves are just that—reserves. Once it's gone, it's gone until we can replenish."

"Underground." Bridget tested the word he'd mentioned to her once before and the knowledge of what she'd learned about this man and his kind.

He nodded in confirmation.

"That thing that took me that looked like Manuel was a charmer. Those are the demons you fight, the ones that hunt and destroy souls of innocent people. People like me." The realization was a sobering pall, and it settled like ash in her mouth.

"Yes."

"So, when you said—"

"I know you have questions, and I'll answer every single one of them, but—" He cut away, but those searching eyes quickly returned to the slashes in her clothes. If anyone else would have stared at her chest like that, with a swirling mix of fire and rage, she'd cross her arms and tell them what's what, but she couldn't bring herself to do that under Steel's assessing gaze. Something about it spoke of more.

Does he feel guilty?

His clipped words broke through her thoughts. "It's fucking killing me seeing you sitting there torn up like that." He stalked toward her with that subdued intensity she suspected was due to his exhaustion and gently took her sleeved arm to guide her upstairs.

"It's not bad, I told you. The cuts have already stopped bleeding."

"Looks bad to me."

"I had a lot of layers."

"Layers that prick cut through like flan."

Bridget halted on the top step and whirled at him, flinging his hand away. "Flan? As in a giggly dessert?"

Steel stilled. "Yes . . ."

"I'm sort of struggling with the analogy here. Of all the things in the world that one could easily cut through, you choose a giggly, mucousy dessert to compare my body to?"

The red flags of warning finally dawned in Steel's eyes. "No! It was just the first thing that came to mind."

"To compare my body to."

His eyes sank to the floor. "Bad choice of words."

"No kidding." Bridget stormed into her room, leaving a cloud of indignation in her wake. It wasn't that she was self-conscious or anything, but with the way he'd looked at her when they were in the kitchen, she could have sworn there had been something more, something beyond just wound care and welfare. For one brief inexplicable moment, the intensity of those glacial eyes fixed on her and had her wondering what it would feel like if—

"Would you have preferred I said butter? Or, more specifically, the sweet creamery butter from the Brittany region in France?" His voice had steadied some and turned oddly wistful, cooling the fiery edges of her confusing tirade. The playful tone she was used to hearing from him returned, but this time, there was a deeper contour to it, like when a mountain cat's mischievous purr turns into a warning rumble right before it leaps on its prey.

Steel prowled closer. "In Brittany, the farmers lovingly tend small herds of dairy cows that feast on grass kissed by the northwestern sea breezes off the Atlantic. The milk is churned, not in minutes by some commercial metal mixer but slowly and lovingly by hand for as long as it takes the milk to give up its secrets and bend for them. It's all about patience and promise . . . the anticipation and reward."

Bridget stood in front of her dresser. Her hands had every intention of grabbing fresh clothes and kicking him the hell out of her room, but that rolling voice was wending its way around her, tugging up goose bumps everywhere it caressed her skin.

The wooden floorboards near her groaned, and the shade of Steel's muscled arm moved into her periphery. Then his deep voice continued, dripping an unfamiliar warning into her senses.

"Once formed, the butter isn't the pale anemic stick of fat common here, but a golden mass of the vibrant wealth of life that the dairy makers can only hope to encourage and mold into a solid arrangement. Only then is it wrapped delicately in a cradle of wax-lined parchment. Only then is it gifted to others who know its worth enough to appreciate its truly priceless essence."

Bridget's hands curled around the dresser knobs, but she didn't manage to pull the drawers free. Her skin prickled hot and tight beneath her clothes. Were they talking about the same thing? How on earth could butter, the same thing some ridiculous coffee snobs and social media food influencers put in their coffee, make her want to strip away everything and be eaten up by this man?

More creaking, more tightening of the space between them, until he was so close his heat nearly singed her shoulder.

"*That* is how I think of you and your body."

Then it hit her. That was worship in his voice. It wasn't disgust or even duty, but *worship.*

She offered up a prayer that her voice was strong enough to carry the words she wanted to say before letting them fly. "That's a big statement."

"I obviously needed to clarify some things." Steel's eyes darkened, but a barely controlled restraint seemed to dance just below the surface of that arresting gaze. He flicked his eyes toward the window behind her, then to the floor, though whether he was searching for or avoiding something, she couldn't tell.

"And what's your final statement on the matter?" she breathed out.

His throat bobbed, and Bridget had a foreign inexplicable urge to drag her lips over the tendon along his neck and kiss that skittering tension away. Then those chilling blue eyes returned to hers, and a weary gentleness stared back. The rawness of it stole her breath.

"That precious things in small packages should be savored thoroughly, so when they're eventually gone, the memory of their enjoyment will be as potent and vital as air and just as life-sustaining."

Steel's jaw ticked with a seemingly painful impatience, as if whatever fragmented bonds that held his true thoughts and secrets were a heartbeat away from breaking, yet his mouth told a different story. Those lips, which had been pressed firmly together a moment ago, were now parted with a panting harshness. She wanted those lips on her skin, wanted to be as precious to that mouth as the butter he'd described, to see for herself whether his skin tasted just as sweet.

Bridget had no idea what compelled her to do it, but a strange boldness sang through her veins whenever she was around Steel. It was a seductive confidence she had long ignored and dismissed, but every fiber within her revolted at the thought of shutting that part of her out any longer. Of shutting *him* out.

Slowly, she lifted her hands toward the ceiling. "Help me get out of this."

Steel hands tightened into fists. "No," he breathed. "I can't touch you again. Not your skin."

"Why not?" Her arms dipped slightly as she tried to ignore the sting of his rejection.

"Because if I touch you again, Sunshine, there's no going back. My fire, it might . . ." His words faltered. "There's a chance that we might be . . ."

Not rejection, then, but something else, something even *he* was afraid to explore. That new boldness inched higher within her until the wisps of his earlier rejection floated into the background on dying butterfly wings.

She surged forward to grab him. "I want to take my chances with you," she whispered.

Then she placed his bare hand underneath her tattered sweatshirt and top. The rough pads of his calluses scraped over her stomach's sensitive skin.

A scream tore from her throat just as he lurched forward, and they were both engulfed in an inferno of blue flames.

THERE WAS no time to speak or warn her, only scream.

Some lurking alien thing speared through Steel, rifling through his core as if hunting for some vital part of him with unrelenting fervor. A worm of power born of no mortal land battered through him the moment Bridget placed his hand on her bare skin. He grimaced against the blinding intrusive tunneling. Some baser part of him knew what it was seeking. Would the power weep when it came away empty-handed, when the kernel of flame it sought to rip out of him no longer simmered in his core because he had exhausted it in service of the woman whose life he'd ruined?

For he was utterly drained, wholly and completely, with nothing left to give.

And then the great writhing thing found its prize, not dead and depleted, but small and slumbering within him. A hibernating beast.

The blue flames of Steel's fire erupted around both of them like before. Again, he had no say in the matter. His power was at the mercy of Bridget's wicked seeking touch. Did the woman know? He had told her some small scraps concerning what happened when their skin touched previously, but nothing substantial. Nothing that would explain the progression of the power she now called forth.

Steel hauled her to his chest tightly. He was devastatingly powerless when his fire swept over her hair, limbs, and features etched so tightly in pain that he knew she felt all of it, as if the fire were real carbon-born flames.

"Bridget! You're doing this! The fire can't hurt you, but I can't control it either. You need to stop the flames, call them back before they burn the house down." He shook her slender shoulders once, twice, thrice, until finally, those blue eyes flared open and searing recognition flickered through her traumatized awareness. He placed his hand on the side of her neck, cradling her tense jaw with his thumb, and gripped her firmly.

"Call it back. It's yours, Sunshine. It's all yours, every ember." His sweat-slicked forehead found hers, and he breathed in her heated cries. "Call it back. I'm not going anywhere. I promise."

The skin of Bridget's stomach tensed and tightened beneath his clenched grip, but instead of celestial heat stiffening the delicate flesh, a chilling softness was left in its wake. Around them, the flames had begun to recede, tangling and coiling in on themselves until they burrowed into that familiar core of power within him once more. Her screams had quieted, and against his chest, her breasts pressed closer, her peaked nipples spearing him with unspoken intent.

He reared back. "Bridget, are you all right? For fuck's sake, say something. Are you hurt?" Panic and fear made him a beast, and he nearly screamed at her for some answering sign that she was well.

Her silent panting was steady, easy, but . . . hungry. He exhaled a cautious breath but never took his eyes or hands from her. Instead, those eyes speared right through him, and every muscle in his body tensed, then swelled in answering kind.

"That was . . . hot," she replied through steadying breaths. "*You're* hot."

And then, never breaking eye contact, the little minx lifted her arms above her head in a silent resumption of her earlier command, as if the celestial spark inside her soul hadn't just ripped his power from him and cradled it in her palms for her to wield.

And still, she wanted him, wanted whatever *this* might be.

He grabbed her wrists and slowly backed her against the wall. Gravel edged his panicked voice. "You have to know that what just happened is the start of something very significant among my kind." His head dropped to her neck, and he pressed hungry lips against her skin.

"How significant?" Her back arched in a delicate curve of enticement.

"Very. Life-altering."

He dropped his hands, and still, her arms remained above her head. He tunneled beneath her tattered clothes and bracketed her ribs. The outlines of her breasts, still shielded from him by the scrap of fabric that was once her bra, rested just above the tips of his fingers. Gone was the shallow slice of the bone knife that marred her skin.

The celestial magic of the soul bond—born from the very power of the Eternal Flame's creation itself—was doing its work, the beginning tendrils of the symbiotic healing connection already snapping into place.

Holy shit. That means . . .

"In my world, Sunshine, when a female steals an angel's fire, she also steals his soul."

"Soul?" That certainly got her attention. Her hands fell and landed on his shoulders. Lucidity was inching back into her eyes, though the cloudy heat of arousal still flared prominently. That curious gaze flitted across his brow, hairline, nose, lips, even a peak over his shoulder at where his wings would be if he unleashed them, until finally settling on his eyes again. "This is a serious thing, isn't it? What happens next wouldn't just be casual, would it?"

The dawning connection of her words had his cock bobbing beneath his jeans. He fought everything he had to lean closer and press his shaft against the valley of her legs until the pounding pressure was enough to undo them both, but he willed his body to stay utterly still and prepared for Bridget to shatter his heart in one fell swoop. Her confession from earlier rang loudly in his ears. She'd never been kissed, never even been touched, except by him. And yet she was here, in his arms, after almost being taken from him by his enemy, and fuck it all if he didn't want to sink into her with every ounce of mated savagery coiled inside him. One word from her, though, and he'd fling himself out the window. If he had to die, who better to destroy him than his soul-bonded mate?

So he bit out the words that would seal his fate. "Serious, yes. Casual, fucking never."

Look at me, Bridget. Look at me, and tell me you don't feel it, too.

A shocked gasp left her, puffing over his jaw and mouth and hitting him with one final caress of her sweet essence. Then she lowered her arms from his shoulders. His fiery soul pummeled and raged against the empty walls inside him—until she didn't move.

Then that small corner of her lips rose on a sly tilt, and she pulled her clothes free until she was bare before him from the waist up.

CHAPTER 20

Bridget had never known what it meant to be craved until the blue of Steel's eyes, now rapt upon her bare breasts, morphed into contained conflagrations of white heat. *Barely* contained if the pulsing vein at his temple and the power thrumming through every muscle on his lean frame was anything to go by. His intensity rivaled a tempest or any of the mystical beasts she dreamed of and drew in her quiet care-free moments.

It was enough to make her second-guess things. Was she truly ready to offer that part of herself to this man, a part she'd given to no one else? And that power, holy hell, that *power*. Even now, her skin and muscles remembered the feel of that fire, how some unknown part of her had yanked it free and taken owner-ship of it as if finders-keepers was the unbreakable law of the universe and not just some silly kid's game. However, once that fire retreated and was called home to the angel before her, something still lingered, and her body could only tremble at its loss.

Could only beg for the connection to the man who still held that fire.

Steel didn't say anything or even move. He did nothing except stare at her bare skin. Her nipples tightened under his gaze as if preening for his approval, for the barest of touches to put her begging body out of its misery. The moment that swirling white fire in his eyes flared brighter, she tensed impossibly tighter, and that scorching heat ran a simmering graze between her legs. Holy crap, he hadn't even touched her yet!

"Steel," she rasped out.

Then he was on her.

Her mouth was a willing victim of his punishing plunder. Insistent hands lifted her legs, urging them to wrap about his waist. She complied and pressed herself into the solid wall of his chest. His arms were iron bars at her back as he marched them into the hallway bathroom and slammed the door behind him.

She tore her mouth from his. "What . . . what are you doing? I thought these things usually happen in beds. I have one of those, you know, in case you missed it."

Laughter smoothed over her mortification as she stumbled for words. With his hands that close to her ass and her bare chest hot and flush against his, speaking was the last thing on her libido's super-charged agenda. All she wanted was this man touching her, kissing her, consuming her, and she was content to combust under his fire, except that damn pearl of curiosity kept poking its stupid insistent finger at the back of her mind.

Steel lowered her until her backside met the firm lip of the tub. He leaned over her shoulder, flicked the taps on, and reached for one of the hand towels she kept folded above the toilet. "There's still some blood."

"Oh." Right. Shit. Because she had been hurt. Targeted and hurt. She glanced down. "You're healed."

"How?"

"Your power." His tongue caressed chilling patches along her neck before his firm lips claimed ownership of every spot he licked and tasted.

"I have power?" She bit her lower lip in time with one of those decadent licks, and parts of her she'd sworn were in years-long hibernation perked right up.

A shuddering groan echoed through the bathroom, and Bridget wondered whether one fierce grip from Steel was all it would take to shatter her porcelain tub into feeble shards that never stood a chance. "Sunshine, you have no idea the power you have, especially over me."

She gasped as he slid a warm wet towel along the underside of her breasts. Slowly, gently, he buffed away any remnants of her nightmare, until all that remained was the heated angel of her daydreams.

He dipped his head. "Do you have any idea how long I've waited to touch you here?" A single fingertip joined his breaths as they both swirled around her nipple in a wicked dance.

"No," she breathed out.

Her breasts heaved and ached under his taunting touch. Every flick, press, or—holy hell—pinch had her arching her back farther, as if she were a python answering his charming dance and call.

"Long fucking time. Too long." The heat of his tongue replaced the heat of his breath, attacking and suckling the scorched skin of her other breast until there was nothing left for her to feel but only what he insisted. Demanded. Her frenzied mind had no time to sort through the sensory confusion. That was a luxury of women who didn't find themselves under Steel's velvet and commanding smoothness.

What a happy pauper she was, and the more insistent his mouth became, the hotter her skin flared.

"Steel, that heat . . . the fire again . . . Do you feel it, too?" Her heart beat a rampant tattoo behind her chest, and she frantically tossed her head to the side. Her hair hung sweaty and limp against her cheeks.

The delicious weight of him eased away from her skin, and

chilly air swooped in. Was he moving away? *Actually* moving away from her?

"No, no!" She lunged for him and gripped the front of his shirt. Parting of any kind was unacceptable. Her grip turned to an insistent pull, then a solid yank. Off. She needed his shirt off. If she was going to combust, there was no way she'd do it alone, not without seeing him bare as well.

A dark teasing chuckle had her thighs clenching more tightly around him. "Damn, you're like a cat with a bird between its claws."

"I want to see you." She cringed at the plea in her voice and hoped he didn't think she sounded as whiny as she feared.

"I'm not in the habit of saying no to you."

"Well, that's good. I'm not in the habit of making demands unless it's something I really, really want."

Steel grabbed a handful of his shirt behind his neck and pulled it free. Admiration for the abundant strength on display had her grinning even wider. The fabric glided over his muscled skin almost wistfully before settling on the floor. Bridget had all of three seconds to appreciate her personal Adonis and then his mouth was on her skin once more. This time, his scorching lips traced a loving trail right down the center of her abdomen. Soon, a light flick of his tongue at the lip of her jeans hinted at his fiery intentions. That small nugget of doubt and insecurity came a-knockin' again, and despite how much she wanted this, wanted *him*, she couldn't stop her body from tensing in his hold, and that questing tongue paused its eager search.

Shit.

She scrambled for words, simultaneously cursing her inexperience. "No, I didn't mean . . . I mean . . . Shit." Bridget waited for it, braced herself for the look of uncertainty in Steel's eyes.

He pulled back a bit, looked at her for a fleeting moment, then shook his head. "This isn't right."

Her heart sank. Frantic words clogged her throat, words she struggled to grasp that would convince him she truly, utterly wanted this. It was just that her stupid body was still new to the idea. Anything to keep him here, to keep that connection.

Steel scooped her up and carried her to the bedroom, where he assured her that yes, he did know where her bed was, and promptly nestled her on top of it. Once she was settled, he rose, keeping her cradled between the bracket of his strong forearms, and brushed a tender melting kiss against her mouth. A quiet soothing promise.

"There is no expanse of time in this realm that I wouldn't happily endure if it meant your comfort and happiness."

Bridget's stomach bottomed out. Her throat tightened, and she strained to swallow against the dryness. Was he saying he would wait for her if that was what she wanted? The hard-set jaw and earnest gaze of the man holding her was a completely different look than any she was used to receiving from men, especially those in positions of power. Steel was nothing if not powerful; yet as she searched his features for any hint of a disingenuous motive, she came away with a whole lot of nothing.

He would truly wait for me.

She traced the smooth fullness of his lower lip. A gentle kiss pressed back against the pad of her thumb. "I'm not asking you to wait for me," she clarified. That hard mouth thinned in uncertainty, and Bridget worried he'd misinterpreted her comment. "No, I mean I don't want you to wait, because *I* don't want to wait, not truly, not with you, but that doesn't change the fact that this is still all new to me." Her core still ached around that emptiness and threatened to inch closer to that pressing weight above. Just then, an idea came to her, tempting and tantalizing in its newness. "But maybe I can show you what I like? Would you be willing to watch?"

As soon as the words left her mouth, light flared in his eyes, and he dropped his warm mouth to her shoulder. She gripped his solid body to hers and smiled.

"Hell, Sunshine. If you're trying to kill me, that would be the way to do it. I can't imagine a better way to go, either."

Her smile turned wicked at the corners. "Sit back," she urged and forced all that panther-like prowess onto its knees with the light push of a single fingertip.

Uncertainty turned to sensuality, and the newfound slink in her spine, the jut of her hips as she unfastened her jeans and slid them away, was a surprising power all its own. Steel sat there, watching her like a good dog who had to remain still before he could pounce on his treat. When the last of her clothing fell to the floor, she lay back against her pillows and let her legs fall open. There was that initial urge to close her eyes, like she always did when she was alone, but no more could she close her eyes on Steel's powerful beauty than she could shut out the sun.

Her fingers trailed through her trimmed curls until they rested gently at the apex of her opening. She'd never done this, not in front of someone, but seeing Steel's chest rise and fall with every circling torment of her middle finger across that bundle of nerves was enough to make her come then and there.

"Beautiful. So fucking beautiful, Sunshine." His fingers dug into the comforter at his sides, pulsing in time with her increasing speed. A long straining bulge pushed against the front of his pants. He looked miserable, eager, pained, hungry, yet he didn't move from his perch, all because she commanded it—*demanded* it. His earlier words crashed over her.

I'm not in the habit of saying no to you.

Breaths rushed out, and that familiar heat began blossoming between her legs, but it was duller somehow, less incendiary.

Her hand moved on its own. One moment, she was urging herself higher, and the next, she was yanking Steel forward and placing his warm hand where hers had been. A silent request turned order. As soon as he touched her and dipped a questing finger through her pooling wetness before returning higher, their bodies shuddered at the connection.

"Perfection. Utter, brilliant perfection. Is this how you like it?" The angel was a quick study, she had to give him that. He picked up right where she left off, while his thumb teased her opening.

"Yes, shit, yes!" Higher and higher she rose, beckoned by his relentless touch, until the bedding beneath her was a rumpled mess and her mind was no better. She let out a scream as she was flung over the edge, not caring a whit if she ever returned. Pulses and tremors racked her body before meeting Steel's answering growl. Heat without the biting sting swam around them, filling the room with a palpable power. Steel's chest heaved, and his head was thrown back. When the gusts had left his lungs, he lowered his head to her.

Eyes of white flames answered.

"What the hell was that?" she panted, but he only shook his head with a wordless expression. "Steel? What happened?"

"Your eyes."

"What about them?"

That charming smile was back and beaming brightly. "Little thief. *Someone* yanked my fire free, and I think I know who's to blame."

Shocked, though not a little proud, if she did say so herself, she answered him with a knowing playful grin. "Oh yeah?"

"Your baby blues turned white for a moment."

"No way!" she shouted with an exhausted laugh. "And that heat in the room again? That was you?"

He laughed in kind. "Oh no, Sunshine." Then he dipped his mouth to claim hers. She melted against the smooth feel of him. "There isn't a fire in all the realms hot enough to match yours. Around you, I'll be lucky if I can muster enough strength to light a birthday candle or two."

"You're ridiculous."

Then he leaned back and stared down at her. Her breath caught at the brutal seriousness painting his face. "When it comes to you, I'll be anything you need me to be."

CHAPTER 21

It had taken every morsel of Steel's not-so-infinite patience to finally convince Bridget to sit the hell down and stop fussing over his brothers. Just because their sizes clearly indicated the number of calories they usually put away at any given time didn't mean Bridget was responsible for feeding them every single one of those calories in five minutes, at eight o'clock at night, with three bowls of Triscuits, two piles of string cheese, and an entire watermelon he *still* didn't know how she cut up so quickly. Knife skills of a ninja, that one.

When she offered to bring up the *good* salami from the basement, whatever the hell that meant, he grabbed her by the wrist, gently informed her that she'd done more than enough, and settled her on the couch. Oh, sure, there had been objections, but once he'd sat down next to her and caged her body between the arm of the couch and the insistent press of his nope-not-going-anywhere thigh, she acquiesced. A win was a win.

Warmth bloomed below his thumb as he gently squeezed her thigh and stroked lazy circles along the outside of her knee.

"You guys really know how to fill out a room," Bridget said nervously. "Are you sure there isn't anything else I can get you?"

"We're more than fine. All of this is quite unnecessary but appreciated nonetheless." Brass, ever the gentleman, gestured toward the abundant snack spread before them. "We're more interested in how you fare." Assessing amber eyes moved back and forth between Bridget and Steel. His brother didn't voice any suspicions. He never did. Instead, he usually preferred to draw the truth out in slow brutal increments.

Chrome, on the other hand, favored more blunt tactics. "You know, for a woman who recently learned her soul's light is the most coveted currency on the celestial market and nearly got herself abducted by demons, finds her butt in a room full of fallen angels, and still manages to pull out a more-than-halfway decent spread of appetizers on short notice, you seem to be holding up just fine."

Bridget's jaw hinged open. Iron rolled his eyes and snuck another cracker while Brass pinched the bridge of his nose.

She shot to her feet. "This conversation definitely needs the Genoa salami—no, the soppressata!"

Steel grabbed her before her leg rounded the coffee table. "Easy, Sunshine. Just ignore him. Everyone else does. He tends to be grumpy when he misses out on a kill."

Chrome crossed his arms and leveled a glare, not at Steel but at Iron, who'd snagged a watermelon cube and resumed his one-shoulder lean against the wall. The copper and auburn highlights of the angel's bound hair warred for attention under the nearby lamplight. That thick bearded jaw of his made short work of the fruit he'd just popped into his mouth.

"Shouldn't have been late," Iron said with a shrug.

"*You* should know better than to not fucking share."

Bridget eased back in her seat and whispered to Steel, "Are they always like this?"

"Only on days that end in Y." He winked at her conspiratorially and was rewarded with a shy lift of her lips. In the background, Brass had said something, or maybe it was Iron. Male grunts and gripes faded into little more than gruff annoyances in his ear. Steel's attention hadn't moved from Bridget's ripe mouth as he remembered how it moved against his own, how it tasted, that heat . . .

"You know, I wasn't sure how I'd handle seeing all of them in my house after so many years without company, but honestly, they're no worse than Ryan and Michael are when those two go at it over whether to pull the meat off the grill or let it go a little longer."

Steel shifted uncomfortably in his seat, then leaned in while Chrome and Iron went at it, but he stopped short at the meat comment. "Your brother doesn't have a meat thermometer?"

"Oh, please. My brother thinks *he's* the meat thermometer. No! Wait. That came out wrong. I mean, he's always going on about knowing doneness based on how squishy the meat is or something. I don't know. It skeeves me out, to be honest. And yes, I know how that sounded." Bridget cringed.

Steel's pointed glare at the others quickly shut down the blossoming chuckle fest. He cleared his throat. "Well, I'm glad they don't make you uncomfortable."

She gave him a small smile. "Me too."

Brass's voice cut in. "The other charmers we cleaned up were all planning to meet in the school bus yard. The one who grabbed you, Bridget, meant to have backup."

"Oh. Lovely. How did he know where I was?"

Brass exchanged a look of discomfort with Steel before replying. "There was a photo of you and Steel that made the rounds online. You guys weren't the only ones in the picture, though. There were people in the background, people who looked like they had just been talking to you. Charmers can change their appearance and walk around in any human form. It would be a simple thing for one of them to disguise themselves as someone you know or had just been seen talking to." A sad smile tilted his lips. "They must have recognized you from the photo. The rest is an easy thread to unravel."

"Do you think they know where I live?" Before Brass could answer her, she added, "My house isn't actually in my name, though. It's in my brother's name."

Brass shared a glance with Steel. "That helps, but it's not foolproof."

"Only fools out there are the ones trying to get in here. It ain't happening," Steel assured her, wrapping a hand around her waist and tucking her in close. The other angels' eyes widened, but they didn't say anything. "Where would they have taken her? The underground facility at that Superfund site where they'd held Tammy before isn't that close. And what's the connection to the resort?"

"Don't know," Chrome added. "You're right, Steel, about something going on at Torrey. Operations vehicles haven't left the mountain again since that caravan you saw a few days ago, but they're loading up on something. Titan and I tracked some unusual shipments going into a few of the unused bays, but based on what we could glean from the events on the resort's website and what we know of the facility's routine yearly operations schedule, we don't know what those shipments are and what they'd be used for. They're out of the ordinary, for sure."

Iron pushed off the wall. "Their base ain't there. If anything, it's at that lab. We left it alone for far longer than we should have. I say we go back and dig around a little."

The lab. A former chemical composition laboratory turned highly polluted and abandoned grotto for Cyro and his charmers to manufacture magical warfare and mages knew what else. Months ago, Tammy had been briefly held prisoner at the underground facility. Even though its location was now known to the angels, the sheer size and scope of the operation was beyond what they could conceivably manage. The frustrating realization chapped their asses to no end.

"No," answered Chrome. "That's Tungsten's decision, and one we certainly aren't about to make without him and the others."

Iron leveled those mismatched eyes at the giant angel, and Steel remembered why it wasn't wise to push too hard at his wounded brother. They never spoke of Iron's history, but the angel had suffered enough for thousands of immortal lifetimes. They had long ago promised him any free rein of destruction he wished to carry out on Cyro and the demons, but only when the Empyrean's gates were opened once more and the Flame restored. As the years dragged on, they had all noticed Iron's willpower thinning just a little bit more. Whether that reckoning would arrive sooner than they were all ready for was a constant worry.

"Then what the hell is the connection?" Steel spoke up, eager to draw the spotlight away from his brother. When none of the others offered up an answer, he cursed. "Chrome, how many vehicles did you see loaded up?"

"Three or four."

"I don't know how slow their shipments are to arrive, but if that caravan that came through here is any indication of what they're used to having ready before they ship out, it sounds like they're close to making another trip."

Chrome nodded. "Based on their current loads, I wouldn't be surprised if they're ready to move out tomorrow."

"Then we track them. Start at the resort and follow them down the mountain, through the development, until we find their endgame and see what they're transporting around."

Brass's auburn eyebrow vaulted northward. "You don't just want to take out the caravan, now that we know where to expect them?"

Steel shook his head. "No. I want to finish what I started before they blasted me out of the sky. We need to confirm where they're heading first. If we were to fly in and steal one of their rigs, especially now that we both know Bridget's on their radar, I wouldn't put it past them to retaliate."

"Tomorrow night," Chrome responded. "We'll track them tomorrow night and see where the breadcrumbs lead." Then he snatched a string cheese before he and the others strolled toward the back door. Chrome held the cheese up and shook it at Bridget. "Thanks for the snacks."

"Oh, yeah. Sure. Anytime."

Brass paused in front of the couch where Steel and Bridget were sitting, then he leaned down toward Bridget and jerked his head in Chrome's direction. "Don't encourage him. Once you leave out food, he's impossible to get rid of. He's like a raccoon that way."

She chuckled softly. "Got it."

Iron lingered a tad longer before he joined the other two on the back deck. That square-jawed chin marked Steel across the room, but he addressed Bridget instead. "Take care of him."

She let in a whispered, startled inhale. "Sure."

A firm nod was Iron's only response before he pushed his bulky frame through the back door and took to the skies, taking all of Steel's questions about his brother's comment with him.

It had only taken three giant angels leaving Bridget's home and flying off her back deck to suck all the air out of the room with them. Go figure.

Bridget rummaged around for the plastic wrap while Steel locked the back door.

"I should have sent them home with leftovers," she muttered, trying to figure out what the hell she was going to do with a few cubes shy of twenty pounds of watermelon. "I'm definitely giving some to Ryan, that's for sure."

Shit. *Ryan.*

A searing pang punched through her, eclipsing any burgeoning happiness she'd gained from hosting a bevy of fallen angels. The lie she'd told her brother still burned, and while she was doing her best to appease that particular slight, she still wasn't texting him as often as she normally would. A small silly part of her thought he might realize that it was because she was finally talking to someone other than him, and wasn't that what he'd been trying to get her to do, after all? With a man, no less?

Well, maybe that last argument was better left unsaid. Still, the wrongness tainted her interactions on so many levels. Sooner or later, Ryan would stop by unannounced again, as was his way, or call her when she couldn't talk, or wonder why this strange distance was growing between them when it was the last possible thing on the planet she'd ever want.

The back door slammed shut, and she peeked around the corner at the other source of her heart palpitations. Steel's muscled flanks bracketing his spine stretched as he bent over to pick up his weapons and stow them in his closet, because yes, she now thought of her hallway closet as *his*. The door opened, and while his torso dipped out of view, his gorgeous denim-clad derriere filled in the lustful gaps of her view quite nicely. For Christ's sake, the man gave her one orgasm and it seems her mind had nothing better to do than wonder whether she could go back for seconds. Or thirds.

There was absolutely nothing to be helped for it. Bridget didn't see any possible way she could stay in Steel's orbit and not want him.

The plastic wrap ran out just as her frustrations reached a new peak. "Gah!"

"Granita's your best bet. Or agua fresca." The angel hovered over to her side in the kitchen.

"Well, I'm glad you know what to do with all this fruit, because my refrigerator shelf space is paltry at best. I wasn't planning on opening that monster up here."

"Oh no? You're not in the habit of buying full-sized watermelons for yourself and diving in with little more than a fork and a smile? Be careful with that type of behavior. You'd put the ice cream manufacturers out of business. I do believe they have the market cornered on single-utensil binge eating. I could be wrong, though."

There he was again. Amid the most harrowing day of her life, that unflappable angel swooped right in and wrapped her in a petal-soft cocoon of his lighthearted charm. It was so *easy* to be around him, to bask in his carefree nature and never get tired of the newfound smile lines she could feel developing around her mouth. But if that was true, why did a part of her recoil at their attraction like he was some foul secret?

Because he is a secret, as are his brothers. They trust you to keep your mouth shut, and in turn, they'll keep you safe. This is all just one big transaction.

"When I had my groceries delivered earlier in the week, I ordered the watermelon with Ryan and Michael in mind. I meant to take it over tomorrow, before everything, you know . . ." Heat crept up her cheeks until the tips of her ears burned. "Michael's Taekwondo studio is closed on Mondays, and the two of them always bring me over on the third Monday of the month for lunch." She swallowed thickly. "Ryan, um . . . He saw that picture of us from the coffee shop. He had questions."

Steel finished putting the cheese back in the fridge. "I know."

"You do?"

His head dropped forward, and a tuft of golden hair fell over his forehead before he raked his fingers over it, smoothing it into submission. "I overheard your conversation when he stopped by. I was still out on the roof."

She nodded, then swallowed thickly. "I think I didn't realize how my actions weren't entirely victimless all these years. How when I decided to stay in the house, I also decided, perhaps without registering it, that Ryan would shoulder this responsibility for me, too. It may have been a higher price than I thought, and lying to him about you, about where I was, well, I know I hurt him."

A few heartbeats passed in the silence, and Bridget busied her hands fighting with the fresh roll of plastic wrap Steel had handed her. When the inside of her thumb was in imminent danger of being sliced open, he gently coaxed the cardboard box out of her hold, stole a bite of watermelon, then finished wrapping it up.

"No more blood on my watch, Sunshine." He gestured down toward where her hand was dangerously close to the box's serrated edge, and she smiled at his attempt at levity. "But I do have to know one thing."

She sniffed away the tingle in her nose, then peered up at him. Eager acceptance brightened his features, and she nearly blanched at it. Then he leaned forward, and the sweet scent of watermelon smoothed her raw nerves.

"What time do you want me to take you over to the studio tomorrow?"

She balked for a moment. "Oh, no, you don't have to drop me off. Ryan always picks—"

"I'm not dropping you off. I'm taking you there, and you're going to introduce me to your family."

"What? But I thought I needed to keep you a secret, keep all of this a secret?"

"While I might persuade you to keep some aspects of my true nature and that of my world private, I would never ask you to lie to someone you love." He moved an inch closer until their chests were nearly flush. "I need you to know me, Bridget, know how important family is to me, so I can know you. How could I possibly protect you otherwise?"

Emotion pulled at the corners of her eyes. "Why would you willingly do that? Why would you risk your family for the sake of knowing mine?"

A dark sentiment flitted over his face. It was a reaction Bridget had noticed a handful of times before but never thought much of. Then Steel's frosted lashes swept down fiercely as if slamming a drawbridge around something her words had crept too close to discovering.

"Because I simply can't stay away from you."

CHAPTER 22

Bridget's nose prickled, almost standing to attention, against the familiar antiseptic aroma of Michael's *dojang*. With practiced efficiency, she toed off her shoes and threw them into the cubbies to the right of the door. Michael was nothing if not immaculate when it came to his facility. She'd even known him to give the poor mail carrier an icy reprimand after the careless postal worker, who made no secret of his daily countdown until retirement, once trekked slushy sidewalk snow inside onto the pristine blue mats. A mistake that had never been repeated.

The strain in her shoulders lessened with each step of her intimately known routine. The studio had been one of a handful of haunts she'd let herself take up space in the past few years. The blue mats, well-worn yet still pliable, were a welcome escort.

Behind her, Steel's soft ministrations echoed her own, and his socked feet joined hers at the edge of the practice floor. "You want me to take that?" He gestured toward the carburetor-sized container she held that housed her watermelon bounty.

"No, it's okay." Because if she didn't have anything anchoring her to the floor, she was pretty sure those skittish urges to turn tail would have their day in the sun, or fluorescent lights, as it were.

"Bridge? That you?" Ryan's booming voice floated over from the office/breakroom tucked in the back corner of the large, blessedly empty *dojang*. The simple wooden door was cocked halfway open due to a rusted hinge that was as stubborn as the man calling her.

The door was the only thing that broke up the expanse of mirrors and heavy decorations adorning the practice space. Korean and American flags embellished the wall to her right. On the left were framed paintings of sweeping calligraphy and boards depicting each technique the students would practice. All along the perimeter, various pads, barrels, and equipment lined up like good little soldiers. The sight of orderly rows had once been a comfort, a testament to the power and uniformity of everything knowing its exact place and purpose. Now, however, with the heat from Steel's nearness buffeting her back like a bracing furnace and strengthening her in a different way, the neat lines of erect padded barrels reminded her of her self-erected prison bars.

"Bridgerton!" Michael sauntered out of the back office with that same loving smile he always had for her. The front of his black hair hung in a sharply angled slash over his right brow before he relegated the locks to their usual place behind his ear. His hair wasn't tied back at the neck like it was when he wore his *dobok* and was instructing students, but rather, it hung free and loose around his shoulders.

Bridget felt, more than saw, the moment Michael took in Steel behind her. That spine of hers, which she'd given a stern reprimand on the way over, did its best to lock up in protest at the questioning concern in Michael's black eyes.

"This is my friend, Steven," she said hurriedly. "I'm sure Ryan already flapped his gums about our conversation from earlier."

"Hello." Steel's quiet greeting was all charm and light. Not a hint of hesitation or nerves. Or knowing more than he should. The bastard. Could he at least *act* like this wasn't going to be a monumentally awkward experience on her part and a potentially violent interaction on his if Ryan no doubt had his way?

Michael calmly padded across the mats, giving no indication of where his thoughts might lie. Unlike Ryan—whose stink-eye assessment served as her brother's automatic greeting for anyone he didn't have a last name, social security number, and blood type on yet—Michael had a different set of skills when it came to reading a person. Bridget had never inquired about the how of it, but whatever silent scrutinization he managed to enact was a true testament to his generally serene life and practice. He'd never had a troublesome student, never spoken to a parent he couldn't reason with, and had never been in a relationship as long as the one he'd been in with Ryan. Oh, he'd had his fair share of bumps in life, but they had been anthills compared to her Rocky Mountains.

Stupid, infuriating, wonderful man.

Michael, his face a calm mask of amiability, extended his hand toward Steel. Before Michael's fingers opened all the way, however, Steel stepped around Bridget and brought his heels together. His long arms dropped flat against his sides, and the space between his fingers closed so his hands were flush against his outer thighs. Those mighty shoulders, ones that had commanded solid sheets of unflappable metal wings, rolled back as if Steel was carrying those condor-length wings now. Then slowly, he dipped his body at the waist. It was a flawless execution of the formal greeting Taekwondo students would grant each other before starting a match. She studied the long slope of his aquiline nose pointing down at Michael's feet, and her mouth fell open.

A perfect bow.

Before Bridget could question the whys and wherefores of

what Steel was doing, one key bit of the gesture's significance stood out to her, and Michael as well, judging by the proud lift of the *dojang* owner's chin. She'd been exposed to the fighting traditions enough times to know.

Steel's golden head remained lowered, as it was customary in the Korean martial art form for a junior to bow to a senior, regardless of location. They could have been in the middle of a Texas rodeo, and the respect Steel had just shown Michael, who Bridget was sure the angel had never met, was tantamount to a show of utmost admiration. Before Steel could raise his head, Michael executed a mimicked timeless bow of his own, acknowledging the respect paid and reciprocated. When both men rose, Michael extended that hand of his again. Steel took it without hesitation, and Bridget almost ruffled Steel's T-shirt with the force of the breath that shunted out of her.

"I'm so glad you'll be joining us for lunch." Michael's sparkling gaze slid from Steel back to her. Not a hint of uncertainty peppered that wide-eyed look, only the glimmer of what she now understood Michael and Ryan had been hoping and fighting for after far too long.

Hoping and fighting for *her*.

She tossed Steel the container of melon and flung herself at Michael in a bear hug to end all bear hugs. "Thank you," she whispered against the column of his neck. The warm encouraging hands at her back pressed in farther than any comforting hug could possibly reach, crowding out the fear and smashing that heinous cauldron inside her into fragments so tiny they'd be impossible to meld back together.

"Always, Bridgerton."

Steel's soft laugh rose behind her. She groaned, then pulled away from Michael, but didn't disentangle herself from the hug entirely. "Really? You couldn't keep that to yourself?"

"Nah. I've waited a long time to embarrass you, and Ryan's going to absolutely lose his mind when you give him the green light to go to town on some of the things he's been holding in reserve. He's got several years of big brother embarrassment to catch up on."

"No. Absolutely not. No way."

A deep voice vibrated off the mats of the *dojang*. "Way."

Across the room, standing just outside of the door to the office, was Ryan. Even without the presence of his usual shit-kickers, everything about his bunched muscles and tight mouth sent a message as he took in Steel's powerful form at her side: Ryan would be giving no fucks today.

Bridget winced, but Michael, ever the respectful referee, simply slapped Steel on the shoulder and ushered them both toward the back room. "It may comfort you to know, Bridge, that I took pity on your brother and made his chicken wrap with the boring rotisserie stuff you two always eat."

Steel glanced at him. "No *buldak*?"

Michael threw his head back. Great peals of laughter bounced off the mirrored walls before he clapped Steel on the shoulder once more, then leveled a censorious glare at Ryan. "Consider yourself warned, my love. Behave or I'm swapping out the wraps. I like this one."

Her brother glared daggers that were all blades without the honed edges, thankfully, and turned on his heel.

Bridget chuckled to herself and followed the most significant men in her life into the breakroom, wondering just how much fire chicken she and Michael would have to slip into Ryan's lunch for her and Steel to get out completely unscathed.

"STEVEN, tell me, you go to Jan's often?"

Steel marked how Bridget's back tensed again as she helped Michael clear the table. It had been doing that every time Ryan would lean into his interrogation routine. Steel didn't mind the game of twenty questions. After all, one didn't exist as long as he had without perfecting deception techniques along the way, but up until now, his deception had only ever been a survival mechanism for him and his brothers. With Bridget in the picture, he'd have to craft a different tale and toe a line he'd not found himself teetering on before. Normally, he'd be thrilled at the challenge, if he wasn't also so terrified at the implications of what this all could mean. And what she couldn't know.

Steel twisted in his chair to face Ryan, whose semi-permanent scowl had only lessened incrementally in the past hour. "Yup. I'm there at least two or three times a week. Woman's got the best chai teas I've ever had, and I've spent a fair amount of time in India over the years to be confident in the comparison. Whatever she does is magic."

"You in the habit of referring to the proprietress of Jan's Java Hut as 'woman'?"

The ceramic coffee cup Bridget was washing out clanged against the lip of the sink. "Ryan! Lose the interrogation act. You're being a piece of shit and you know it."

"What? It's a fair question. Easy and loose language like that is a simple slip into full-blown misogyny. I've seen it too many times to count, and up until a few days ago, *you* would have been the first one to remind me of that fact."

The line had been drawn. Ryan was standing guard over it, Bridget was firmly whisked behind his back, and Steel was well the fuck on the other side.

"Low blow, brother," she seethed through clenched teeth.

"Actually," Steel interrupted, hoping to prevent the mug in Bridget's hand from becoming a fixture in Ryan's face, "I hold Jan in the highest regard and use the moniker as one of extreme affection because her confidence and directness simply wouldn't have it any other way."

Ryan lifted his brow but said nothing.

"When I met Jan, her husband, Jonathan, was about as shy as

they came. He'd hardly say two words to a customer, if he had to deal with them at all, and I could never figure those two out, like, not even a little bit. She had the light and life of a shooting star, all but demanding anyone in her wake to stop what they were doing and gaze upon her in awe. He was simply just another star in the sky that had to move out of her way for her to pass through . . . until he wasn't."

Michael took his seat next to Ryan and smirked. "It's those quiet ones, I tell ya." Then he nudged Ryan's shoulder to force some acknowledgment from him and was rewarded with a mild grunt for his efforts. Michael rolled his eyes.

Steel continued. "How many people have stood in front of Botticelli's *Birth of Venus* painting but have acknowledged its beauty as something so inconceivable and beyond them that they just keep walking? They all know it's a priceless work of art because they've been told so. Therefore, it's untouchable in their eyes. They take it for what it is, an amazing painting by some dead guy, and they move right along—no matter that, for centuries and even to this day, everyone widely regards that depiction of Venus as a representation of a woman with a capital W."

Bridget paused at the sink and turned her chin toward him, but never took her eyes from the mug in her hands.

"Jonathan never kept walking, though, despite his shyness, despite everyone else's obvious enthrallment in everything that Jan was and is. Where others moved right along, perhaps blinded by her boisterous voice and exuberant zeal, he took his shot. He walked right up to her, that woman with a capital W, and married her. No small feat, that, to convince a shooting star you're man enough to soar right along with her in whatever direction that may be."

Bridget's soft gasp was so delicate, only Steel's angelic senses were strong enough to pick up on it. Ryan and Michael made no movements to indicate they'd heard it. By the sink, Bridget's eyes dropped to her tense hands. The mug sat forgotten in the sink. He didn't miss the crinkle between her brows or the insistent pounding of her heart.

"So, you see, I hope you can appreciate where my respect for Jan comes from, along with my respect for her husband." He glanced at Bridget. "And for your sister as well." A tense ache flared brightly within his chest. "There isn't a gallery or starry sky large enough that could possibly tempt me away from taking my shot with her, and anyone who would dismiss her, who would just keep walking by, is a fucking fool . . . and I'm damn lucky for it."

Bridget's sable hair barely concealed the faint blush reddening her round cheeks. Those full trembling lips parted with an audible breath before pressing together, as if holding back some emotion she didn't wish her brother and Michael to see.

Then through that sheet of hair that was just as soft as the delicate skin on the inside of her thighs, she caught his eye. He froze, though his cock twitched insistently against his leg, tapping out a starved rhythm.

In Bridget's muted blue gaze, which swirled with the force and color of the Aegean Sea, pure incendiary heat stared back.

CHAPTER 23

"Did you mean all of that? What you said to my brother?"

The silence within the car had become as oppressive as the crowding, tumultuous thoughts knocking around in Bridget's head ever since Steel's own thoughts had been let out of their cage.

There isn't a starry sky large enough that could tempt me away from taking my shot with her . . . Anyone who would dismiss her is a fucking fool . . . And I'm damn lucky for it . . .

Never, in all of her twenty-eight years as a carbon-based creature swimming and breathing among the billions of other living organisms, had any of said creatures ever spoken about her in such a vital, soul-essential way. Her brother and Michael loved her as one loves a sister. Her colleagues valued her, she supposed, for her reliability. Her employer appreciated her dependability and—she suspected, more importantly—her quiet preference to never make a single wave or even take a single sick day ever again.

But what Steel had declared to her family blew all that out of the water. He had made it sound as if she were essential, as if everyone who'd ever shirked or disregarded her was somehow less off because of it and would never know some great wonder of the world.

The scope of his words was so expansive and humbling, she'd had to grip the edge of the counter and lean into the rim's sharp bite just to ensure that yes, she really was still alive and kicking.

Bridget spared a peek at Steel or, rather, his talon grip on the steering wheel. She hadn't been able to bring herself to meet his eyes since the breakroom in fear that she'd somehow be so wholly consumed by him, she wouldn't know the woman who'd come out the other side.

"I meant every fucking word." His growl eclipsed that ever-oppressive silence she wasn't aware had become a standard feature within her four-door sedan. Everything on her body tightened in response to him. Her very skin had become too confining, never mind her clothes. Threads of fabric once soft and comfortable now rubbed her heated flesh raw with every word that left his lips.

"Why?"

"Why?" He scoffed, as if she'd just asked him why ice cream was delicious or why cool water was refreshing. His golden hair jerked with a stiff head shake, and he pulled the car into the driveway. He still hadn't answered by the time he turned the car off inside the garage. God, the silence was painful and as thick as the real London fog Steel's beloved drink was named for. If Bridget had to endure another second of its choking heat, she was likely to punch out a window.

"Shooting stars aren't that rare, you know," she muttered. "They're far more common than most people think. They're just rocks from space entering our atmosphere—"

"But how many people look up, Sunshine?"

She hitched a breath when the white flames of his fire filled those menacing eyes, which were now trained on her, hungrily flitting over her features like an explorer's gaze caresses a map.

"How many people actually look into the sky, waiting for such a star to slash across their miserable existence? I have been alive far longer than many of those stars, and I can say with absolute certainty that most people never take the time to see what's right in front of them. If a blazing star shoots over their house every fifteen minutes, they won't see it. For them, their literal and figurative skies are simply not clear enough. Their worlds and lives are too muddied with insignificant bullshit that consumes them more than simple wonders."

Dryness pulled at Bridget's lips. Every part of her mouth thirsted for the feel of Steel's lips on hers, for one of the many wonders of the angel before her. Wonders she had never experienced, never *let* herself experience, she realized, which now threatened to consume her the longer she refused to reach for that star in front of her.

Steel's wide shoulders strained against the small confines of the car's steering wheel and seat. Strength born of the ages rippled over a body strung taut with the practiced repression of one denying himself for the good of others.

"My skies are clear," he hitched out. "I see you, Bridget." Storm clouds gathered within his fiery gaze, and her heart pounded in time with their raging flames. "I will always be your champion and fly alongside you, no matter how you choose to soar, regardless of whether I am worthy to do so." His mouth tightened and he clenched his fist around the car keys.

An amalgam of emotions clogged her throat so densely, she could hardly breathe, let alone respond. His words weren't solely blazes of light across the sky but paragons still holding some tinge of darkness that always lurked in the corners of his demeanor. The outward display hinted at some secret locked away, some base part of himself he still refused to share with her.

"I don't want a solemn stranger, Steel," she told him. His features tightened at her confession, but he said nothing. "I don't want to be kept away from whatever it is you think you're protecting me from."

He shook his head. "Bridget, it's not like—"

"Come with me. I have something I want to show you."

Before he could respond, she was out of the car and walking into the house. Only when his footsteps finally sounded behind her did she begin to climb the stairs.

EVERY WHINE the floorboards made beneath Steel's boots was a harrowing gale fanning his fire to near-supernova levels of heat. He was more than happy to give himself over to the flames, willing to combust into the fiercest explosion mortals had ever seen if it meant one more sinful taste of the woman whose hips he now marked in a mesmerized trance.

Bridget strode steadily in front of him, with her hand slightly outstretched behind her, silently urging him along. Each languid sway of her ass was a promise and a song, a pendulum recording every unhurried and agonizing minute she silently dragged him down that hall toward her bedroom.

Bedroom.

The word alone was a prayer he had no right to utter. Memories of the last time he'd been in that room with her still floated around his cock, keeping his lecherous mind company in the rare minutes he could stand to be away from her. The feel of her, the slippery satin of her against the backs of his knuckles, the lush softness of her thighs, the tightened nipples that puckered to attention under his ragged breaths . . . he had no right. No fucking right to any of it, even if that one time with her hadn't been anywhere near enough.

Bridget paused in front of the bathroom door at the end of

the hall, and he halted faster than a grunt trailing behind a drill sergeant. Her back was still to him, and he waited in agonizing silence for her to speak. Did she want him to open her bedroom door first? Did she even want him in there? But instead of turning to the right and into her room, she turned left and stood in front of the shut door he'd never entered before but often wondered about.

"This is me, Steel." She turned back slightly, her chin meeting the top of her shoulder. The tremble in her voice worried him. Before he could question the cause, she pushed the door open.

"By the mages . . ." It was his turn to have words fail him.

Bridget stepped inside, silently beckoning for Steel to follow.

How the hell could he not want to follow? All around him were sketches and drawings of every fantastic mythical creature imaginable, fearsome and friendly. To his right, a large white electric standing desk sported three prominent computer monitors, along with a charging dock for her tablet. Clipped over one of the monitors was a handheld mirror large enough to see one's whole face, and on top of the desk lay a smattering of white papers, each one depicting a human mouth twisted into a different expression.

"I use the mirror to look at myself as I make faces and then try to draw them. These"—she gestured toward the array of mouths—"are actually for an animated germ that's supposed to talk and wreak havoc on someone's mouth before being thwarted by a superhero antiseptic mouthwash." She cringed in what Steel gathered was a public show of disgust, but a subtle tug at the corners of her eyebrows and a pinch of her lips spoke of a deflating disappointment, whether for wasting her talents or for the subject matter she was relegated to create.

The wall adjacent to her desk featured a menagerie of creatures. A corkboard that spanned nearly the entire width of the wall was covered in tiles of nine-by-twelve-inch sketch paper. A long serpent snaked along the base of the board. Its body was a jagged carpet of overlapping verdant-green scales shimmering with undertones of the deepest amethyst. Each piece of paper encapsulated a different portion of its body and was then shingled next to each other. At the far left, the creature's three heads stared back at him. A hydra. The mouths of the three ferocious serpent heads were thrown open wide, fangs snapping around their forked tongues as they danced and roiled beneath the kicking legs of a fighting minotaur dangling above.

Bridget crept closer. "Most people think that a Minotaur has bull's feet, but technically speaking, that's not true, according to classic mythology. They're just supposed to have the head of a bull and the body of a man, with *possibly* a bull's tale. I'm all for creative license, but so many of the video games take it too far. The poor guys usually wind up with abs and pecs and that's about it as far as man parts go." A nervous unease and—dare he say—giggle tinged her words.

Steel arched a brow. "Man parts?"

"Uh, I mean, well, why would you create a character that looks like a bull without it being hung like one as well, you know? Those cosplayers have *preferences*. At least, from what I hear. Actually, you know what? Forget I said that or any of it." Bridget flushed crimson and turned to her desk, suddenly far too interested in tidying up a mess she hadn't previously been concerned with.

By the mages, even flushed with embarrassment, she was exquisite.

Steel shoved his fists into his pockets and bit down the burning desire to make other parts of her flush as well. He choked back a strained chuckle and returned his attention to the creatures on the wall. "Was this for work?"

"No. That's just for me. With the exception of what's on the desk, the rest of this is all for me."

"You don't show it to anyone?"

A quick shake of her head. "The demands of that type of

animation are too cutthroat. Commercial work is easier, and every now and then, I get an interesting job, so it's not so terrible."

"Like superhero bacteria?"

"Technically, the mouthwash is the superhero. The germ is the villain."

"A real battle for good and evil." Steel tried to keep the sarcasm out of his voice, but he would have had more success swallowing his sword. While it was on fire.

"Hey, if you're going to knock it, you can leave. It pays the bills, and I like it just fine."

The denial in her words was as thick as his guilt. "I'm sorry. It's just that all of this is absolutely stunning. I have a hard time believing that you couldn't hold your own against any animator out there. This is a *gift*, Sunshine. Don't you see that? Craft and skill like this don't occur in a twenty-eight-year-old just because she happened to like drawing and got a couple of degrees in the subject. The artists I've known who excel at this level didn't reach it until they only had a handful of a few decent years left in their lives. But this—"

He swung his arm around, across the sketches of exquisite phoenixes and goddesses, of vibrant mermaids and manticores, and halted when he again faced Bridget, this time in front of the wall he'd previously been in front of but hadn't yet observed. She stood with her back braced against the smooth surface that was painted with a pair of end-to-end wings. No, not just end to end but floor to ceiling, colored with a shimmering iridescent gray that would match the coat and character of any wild stallion. Three layers of feathers jutted out in neatly arcing, overlapping rows. They began right at her shoulders, as if she'd stood there many times before and crafted the wings to her height and build.

As if she hoped to be something more than she was one day. A creature with wings.

The realization's depth threatened to crack his soul. He hobbled toward her until whispered breaths were all that separated them. "Why?"

Misted tears clouded her blue eyes, but the steady rise of her chin and soft brows told him she knew exactly what he was asking about. "I modeled the wings after Pegasus. He's considered to be a symbol of the muses, of wisdom and inspiration." Her throat bobbed. "Of freedom."

Steel braced his arms on the wall behind her, but instead of touching her—as his thrumming panicked body yearned to do —he let his head hit the wall next to her ear. "Oh, Sunshine." The words tore free from his ravaged throat. "When did you paint these?"

"A few months after the accident."

He pulled back to look at her and stilled when her hands settled on the sides of his waist.

"I painted them because I wanted some part of me to still imagine that freedom, that ability to drive and draw and paint and soar and be whatever I needed to be if it was just me and the stars. When I painted these, I wouldn't let myself think about how I had survived that car crash when my colleagues hadn't, or how I wasn't tough enough to navigate the corporate requirements of an overbearing board of directors just so I could become an elite animator."

Tears welled up from her overflowing eyes and spilled down her red cheeks. Angst had him gripping her shoulders. Bridget's proud strength held firm under his palms, and it was a dagger through his chest all over again.

Her life these past four years had been a prison of his construction. He'd caged his Bridget like some pampered tropical bird in an aviary, when all she wanted to do was fly. Soul-searing rage ripped through his heart until it threatened to shatter anything still beating.

"I would give you my wings between one breath and the

next, for as long as you'd have them. I'd take you soaring over the peaks of the White Mountains, then dip low as we skim over the lapping waves of the Atlantic to watch the dolphin pods in the summer. I'd fly you to the tips of towering city skyscrapers and twirl you in and out through tangled spruce boughs." His eyes dropped to her lips, especially the bottom one, which was still puffy and trembling. "I would kiss you among the stars at night and fly you so high and fast that not even the sky's darkness could cast a chill over your heated skin when it's flush against mine. By the mages, Sunshine, I can give you this. *Let me* give you this. If it's freedom you want, I would scorch the sky so nothing would ever be hidden from you again."

Those searching blue eyes studied him, ripping his soul from its useless cage. In that one heart-wrenching moment, the monumental truth of their connection—their *true* connection—slammed into him, filling that gaping hole.

He had to tell her, had to confess everything, for how could he offer her freedom without first offering up his own? And then, if she chose him, if she *didn't* want to hack off his wings and melt them down until he was nothing more than a fading dark memory, there would be no bounds to his worship of her.

The words were there, right on the tip of his fucking tongue, but his mouth couldn't push them forward. "Bridget, I—"

"Yes."

The heat of her hurried breath scattered his barely lucid thoughts. "What?"

Then she pulled his hips closer against hers, and the warmth of her beneath her jeans sent shivers over the top of his thigh now cradled between her legs.

"Yes. I want all of that. I want to fly with you, Steel." She paused. "But I want you first."

Her crown of dark hair thunked against his chest, as if her confession had removed decades of weight from her slight frame. He quickly moved to steady her, but then those questing and surprisingly brazen fingers wandered around his waist until they dipped lower and cupped his ass through his jeans. The squeeze had him sucking in a breath through clenched teeth.

"I want you," she breathed, her voice sultry and commanding, "wings and all."

CHAPTER 24

It was the promise of flight and freedom that did it. Well, that and the searing hunger swirling behind star-bright eyes that had never stopped glowing from the second Steel had walked into Bridget's sanctuary.

Eyes that seemed to ache and plead with a need that one million percent matched her own.

Bridget melted into the firm press of Steel's body until that rock-hard thigh of his was centered exactly where she wanted him. Legs quaking with adrenaline and Lord knew what else barely did the job of keeping her upright, but that budding arousal between her legs was a wanton harlot who had little interest in excuses or nonaction steps. Eager to oblige, she canted her hips forward slightly. Steel's hands dug into her waist, steadying her, letting her set the motion of what her body searched for with ruthless insistence.

"Bridget," he ground out. Hot breath fanned the side of her neck and skimmed the slope of her shoulder. "I don't need this. You don't have to—"

"Well, I very much *do* need this. More specifically, I need *you*, so please spare me the objections and virtuous hero crap."

Bridget arched her back, and that delicious scrape of his hard denim-clad thigh against her core had them both hissing. Strong fingers slid under her shirt, then curled briefly over the hem of her pants as if to tear them off her fully before retreating.

"Bridget . . ." he warned. "There's something you should know. I—" His cry was cut short when she yanked his shirt collar down and kissed along the column of his throat, starting with the defined ridge of his clavicle. "Fuck." The hard arcs of his fingernails dug into her more sharply, even as his desperate panting breaths caressed her shoulder. Her mouth was a breath away from finally tasting his when Steel pulled his knee away from her and held her at arm's length. Pleading, clouded eyes pegged her in place. "Will you stop for one moment and look at me?"

Creeping tendrils of rejection weaved their ominous threads under her superheated skin. *Wait . . . Does he not want . . .?*

"You . . . you don't want this? Me?"

It was something she'd never considered. Though once she took in the anguished and drawn features of the angel staring back at her, an emotion she was all too familiar with settled in for the night.

Mortification.

Her hands rose to her cheeks. "Oh God. I didn't read the room right, because you don't want this. What you said . . . I thought it was an invitation or a type of acceptance, but I was way wrong, wasn't I? You don't see me in *that* way. Because I'm a mortal or . . . a . . . a virgin, is that it? Oh, shit shit *shit!*"

She tried to disentangle herself from his hold, but that stupidly infuriating strength of his held her shoulders right where he wanted her. Neither of them moved after a few heartbeats, but her traitorous body insisted on squirming in his touch if only to steal a few final caresses. A single calloused finger lifted her chin and held her in place.

Powerful scorching eyes stared back, illuminating the slashing angles of Steel's hard jaw and bunched brows. To Bridget's astonishment, she wasn't the only one trembling, though while she did it out of embarrassment, Steel's frame seemed to vibrate from a different emotion: unleashed rage.

"Don't see you in. That. Way?" That celestial fire flared brighter with each word he grounded out, and Bridget couldn't be certain, but something within her core preened as if in an answering response to his power. He let out a sharp chuckle of disbelief. "Oh, Sunshine, I didn't want you to stop because you're untouched."

Despite her confusion, her body was still intent on rolling with the previous punches. Bridget's skin puckered every place Steel's heated gaze slid over her. When his eyes returned to her face, the indecision and worry she thought she'd detected before had most definitely gone the way of the dinosaurs. Intense passion had kicked those squatters out of the room and moved in with an open-ended lease.

Steel dipped his head lower and dragged his hands northward until his insistent grip held her mouth prisoner an inch from his own. "I wanted you to stop, Sunshine, because I know that one time with you will never be enough for me. If we keep going down this road, rest will be a mercy I'm not sure I'm capable of granting. I want to . . . Fuck, I want so much for you, but to finally have you—"

It was Bridget, not Steel, who sought the kiss first. The connection was a thunderclap of tempestuous need. It roared in sync with the shackled door of her self-made prison shattering off its hinges. Just as his tongue invaded her mouth, a desperate searching part of her pleaded to invade him as well, to form an eternal tether that wouldn't just pull her free but lift her to otherworldly heights.

Heat was too simple a word for the smooth intensity unfurling within her core. It tightened and writhed with each shift of her hips and drag of her nails along sweat-slicked skin, until she imagined herself as one of her phoenixes, erupting around the only man who had ever been bold enough to get close to her fire.

A fire she hadn't even known she possessed—the fire of a shooting star.

Steel urged Bridget's arms above her head as he torturously peeled her shirt off. The room's ambient air matched the cool chill of the spring's evening freshness. Steel dropped to his knees and lavished playful kisses on every patch of goose bumps that popped up along her abdomen. His roving hands crept higher up her back, and deft fingers made short work of her bra. The simple cotton fare joined the heap of clothing on the floor, followed quickly by Steel's upper layers.

Soft, heated breath tickled her skin as he spoke. "You know, I hadn't realized our height differences would be so advantageous from this angle."

Bridget slowly peeled her eyes open and glanced down, then sucked in a sharp breath when that teasing mouth she loved so much maneuvered an equally teasing nip along the underside of her breast before soothing the hurt away with his tongue.

"Good to know we're . . . a . . . good match."

"We're far more than that, Sunshine." A soft bite on her nipple had her arching her back, bringing the whole of her breast more fully into Steel's mouth. A moan of appreciation licked through her skin, and the vibrations sent shockwaves from her toes to the tips of her ears.

Clearly, the gorgeous bastard had planned that.

Bridget's head hit the wall while Steel continued talking. How the hell was he freaking *talking*?

"Compatibility is for mortal dating profiles," he said with all the arrogance due an immortal being.

His hands traveled to the fly of her jeans, while that mouth rained down relentless torture on her breast. A slow swipe of his tongue had her agonized peak budding impossibly tighter, and then the angel teased it further by blowing a trickle of cool air over her sensitive flesh. Pooling warmth flooded between her legs, and that unshakable heat swirled higher behind her ribs.

"Your body sings for me, like flowers coming alive in sunlight. You're so much more than my match, as you say. You're simply essential." He plumped one aching breast and dove his mouth onto her again.

She threw her head back and moaned a cry toward whatever magic or mages that had brought Steel to her, even as his other hand burrowed into the heated wetness between her legs. With his hand trapped beneath the front of her pants, he had no recourse but to shower her clitoris with relentless attention and she—oh, drat—had no recourse but to lose her goddamn mind.

A virgin she may be, but a stranger to orgasms she was not. Though she had a nightstand drawer full of rechargeables, none had ever come close to giving her even the barest hints of what Steel's touch was cresting her toward.

"Fuck compatibility," she managed to breathe out. "I want you up."

A dark chuckle rumbled over her heart's racing pulse. "I *am* up. There is not a single part of me that *isn't* standing at ready attention. Ow!"

Done playing, Bridget grabbed a fistful of his hair and gave an insistent tug. "Up. Now."

"Whatever the lady wishes." Steel rose to his feet.

Bridget never took her eyes off him as she shimmied out of her remaining clothes. More plops of fabric and shoes hit the pile, until she was naked before him. Her breath sawed in and out of her, and her stomach curled with ravenous energy. Was it nerves or something more? She didn't care to dissect the differences. All she wanted was the angel before her, to be claimed by him in every way possible and to claim him back.

"Your turn." She gestured her chin toward his pants, but he didn't move.

He just stood there, with that celestial fire dancing high in his eyes. A brutal seriousness that didn't belong to his easygoing features darkened his gaze. "No, Sunshine. It's your turn. It'll always be your turn."

Before Bridget could process Steel's words, his hands were at his waistband, shuttling his remaining clothes to the floor.

She hardly had time to admire the goods before the two of them came together in a rush of flushed skin and eager passion. Mouths tangled in messy meetings. Her breasts were crushed against the hard slopes of his muscles. His cock ground into her lower belly with a painful, aching insistence. Her body craved him inside of her, on top of her, wrapping every inch of her in his heat until there was no difference between her fire and his.

Her heels left the ground. A moment later, Steel's solid strength held her steady against the wall. She lifted her legs and wrapped them around him, clinging to him and seeking him out like oxygen to fire. Her core pressed against his hungry cock, and she dipped her hips low to slide against him, learning the feel of his turgid sex and how they would soon fit. God, to have the time to study this man . . .

"If you don't stop that, this'll be over before it starts," he teased against her neck.

"Oh, well, we wouldn't want that."

Steel leaned back a bit and held her gaze. "You have nothing to fear from me. Ever."

He gently grabbed her hand and guided it to his cock, allowing her to take the lead. Heated velvet kissed her palm as she swirled her thumb over the crown before deftly examining the long ridge beneath. Hardness was too simple a word to describe all she held in her hand. And all she brought to the edge of her opening.

Bridget sucked in a breath at the first contact, not the invasion but the heat—not just of his cock, but all around her. Steel's back was an immovable foundation as she encouraged him farther into her channel inch by decadent inch. Their alternated moans of ecstasy kept time with Steel's advance-and-retreat maneuver, until nothing separated them.

"You all right?" Steel cradled her to his chest with all the reverence of an altar enshrining something holy. Her throat tightened against the magnitude of everything swirling around and within her.

"It doesn't hurt. Not really," she whispered, doing her best to keep the wonder and emotion out of her voice. "No, it feels . . ."

"Like fucking heaven."

She laughed. "Yes, exactly like that."

"Then let me show you the stars." He claimed her mouth again and lifted her higher against the wall and his chest. His hands splayed her bottom wide. The fullness that had teased her earlier intensified in breadth. Each slow stroke of him inside her stoked that heavy flame. Her heart pounded in time with his as it beat frantically against her breast. Steel swirled his hips, and a new patch of burning embers within kindled. His stride was torturous, insufferable, and all-consuming.

"Steel, oh God . . ." The words died in her mouth, even as he did his best to swallow them with fervent kisses. That heat coiled more tightly around her, engulfing her in a fiery passion no orgasm ever had a hope of comparing to. This connection had awakened a dormant part of her, giving her wings, calling her to something more.

Steel slid out of her, then hammered in more firmly, yet not with what she suspected was his full force. It didn't matter, because with each thrust, that spark within her wept for a release only he could pry free. And he would. She had no doubt of it. A stilted cry ripped from her lungs, and when her eyes flew open, Steel's body was pure metal against her. Before she could make sense of things, dark shadows entered her periphery, wrapping around her.

No, not shadows. Wings.

Steel's bellowing cry chased her own, and his hips bucked a frantic rhythm into her quivering core. A brilliant light burst from their little cocoon, illuminating every one of Steel's muscles bulging with strain, every metallic feather sheltering her. She slammed her eyes shut and clutched him more tightly, absorbing everything he offered.

Slowly, the fire dissipated and, in its wake, lapped teasing puffs of exhausted breaths. Smooth lips caressed her jaw, her cheekbones, her eyelids. When she finally had the wherewithal to open her eyes, her blond angel's beaming smile warmed her all over again.

"You know, for an angel, you're awfully human."

A soft chuckle, then another melting kiss across her brow. "What makes you think that?"

"Because, despite your good sense, you seem insistent on wanting to care for me. It's a human trait—adopting broken things." Bridget returned his wide smile before giving his nose a kiss of her own. "And I simply cannot see a way of not returning the favor."

CHAPTER 25

Bliss was a hard thing to come by in the mortal realm. Steel imagined that if the fickle occurrence existed at all, a more perfect picture of the wonder couldn't exist than what was currently splayed out on top of him: Bridget, warm and sated, snuggled into the crook of his arm, with her limbs draped over him like an ensnaring ivy claiming an abandoned stone keep. She wasn't asleep, on account of it being four thirty in the afternoon, but her heart had turned over into an idle rhythm that ticked in time with his and a quiet stillness had swept over the bedroom he'd brought her to.

He had become an expert regarding her nonsleeping state because he'd casually checked her wrist no fewer than a dozen times in the past ten minutes under the guise of just needing to feel her, hold her.

Well, it was no guise. His skin thrummed with an aching need to touch her. It was a foreign sort of hyper-awareness that had taken control during their last three—correction, *four*—couplings, and it still churned within his gut. Steel's lower abs clenched at the memory of it. When his muscles finally relaxed, and Bridget collapsed against him in exhaustion, a long-forgotten power had surged through them, filling Steel with a fullness he never thought he'd come to realize again.

"If you keep grabbing my wrist like that, I'm going to take it as a sign that you're checking me for cooties."

Busted, Steel gently folded Bridget's right wrist over his bare chest. "No cooties to be found, I assure you. And I *did* check everywhere." He cupped the swell of her peachy ass against him and gave it a playful squeeze.

"Pervy angelic flatterer." With her cheek squished against his pec, her jibe came out more as *purpy angwewick fwaddeder*.

"I regret nothing." Idle hands went to her wrist again before he could stop himself. He turned the dainty thing over and frowned. Only smooth unmarred flesh stared back at him.

Nothing.

"Okay, why do you keep doing that?" Bridget sat up next to him and tucked herself under the covers. She squinted at her wrist, swiped at it a few times, even sniffed it, but just wrinkled her nose in confusion and shrugged.

Steel's throat tightened, and a cowardly part of him—the *only* cowardly part of him—wished she was still draped across his chest. Confessions were so much easier without eye contact.

He willed his heart to calm. Despite her dark hair that stood up at all ends, and those oceanic eyes still drowsy and slightly glazed from prior exertions, Bridget gave him no quarter. That spark inside her beamed through those windows to her soul in rays of curiosity and concern.

No turning back.

Deflated shoulders sank below his ears. "When we joined, your eyes changed color."

Shock froze her features. "They did?"

"They took on the color of mine, not the blue of them, but the light of my angel fire manifested by my metal. They turned white."

"White . . ." Bridget turned over the word as if it was spoken in another language. "White, like how your eyes glow?"

Steel nodded woodenly. "That particular phenomenon has . . . implications."

"I don't feel any different, though." Bridget held her arms out, turning them over, scanning for any abnormalities.

"You may not feel different. You may not feel anything at all." He stared out the window at the sun dappling the leaves of an ancient oak tree. "But I do."

"Are you all right?"

"All right." He snorted at that. What a ridiculous word. "No, I'm not all right. I'm about as far from all right as they come."

"What's going on?" Wariness crept into her voice, and he hated himself for putting it there in the first place. "If there's something wrong with—"

Steel extended his arm, and blue flames sprang free. Angel fire sprouted from every pore and clung to him like a shadow. Muscles tightened and grew with the force of it, stretching and rolling like a mountain cat long slumbering in the sun and finally ready to pounce.

Bridget gasped and reared back. Soft blue hues glowed brightly against her pale cheeks and across her bare shoulders, bathing her in the sheen of his power.

"I have my full fire back. When I call it forth, there's no longer that impression of time that I may only have use of this power for so long before it leaves me again." Wiggling fingers drew into a tight fist, and still the flames raged under his control. "It all came back to me. Because of you."

"Me?"

"You, Bridget. I've seen this happen twice before in two of my brothers. They—" Steel cleared his throat. "It happened when they found their soul bonds, when the celestial light inside two beings finds each other and claims them as—"

"Mates," she whispered. Bridget's eyes never left his fire, but her awareness of his suspicions was painted plain as day across her face.

Steel extinguished the flames and hastily grabbed her hands. "When the soul bond was discovered, at least for Titan and Tung, it restored their full powers somehow. They no longer need to charge their energy beneath the earth each night. It means the connection that was forged between them and their partners is one of . . . well, I suppose you would understand it as soulmates."

He risked a glance at her to gauge for skittishness or fear, hatred or disgust, though he hadn't a fucking clue how to handle any of them. He was hardly an expert in facial tells, as evidenced by his panic over every twitch and wrinkle that snared his gaze, but by the mages, she was lovely, winces and all. A primal urge nearly had him keeling forward to count every single one of those enticing freckles with his tongue just to see whether there was any part of her that *didn't* taste like cinnamon.

When she didn't respond, he gestured down toward her wrist. "I was checking for a tattoo. It appears once the bond has snapped into place."

That galvanized her into action. Bridget yanked her wrists free of his hold and examined them under her pert nose a second later, rolling this way and that beneath the slashes of sunbeams trickling onto the comforter through the window.

"I don't see any—" Bridget's sharp gasp broke through his worried brain fog.

"You see something?" Steel huddled closer, gripping her right wrist. Nothing glowed back at him . . . until he turned his attention to her other wrist, the one that had been pinned to his ribs when she was lying next to him. The one he hadn't been able to check as often but was currently illuminated under the sunlight.

Bridget squealed. "Oh, this is so—"

Steel braced for the condemnation, for the mouse to realize the traps that had been laid out for her.

"*Cool!*"

Steel blinked. "Cool?"

Exuberance replaced skepticism, and Bridget's blue eyes brightened with misted joy. "Oh, Steel, it's stunning. And it glows! Well, sort of. I didn't even notice it when I was lying down, but when I turn my wrist just so under the light . . ."

There it was. A symbol no bigger than a quarter flaring bright gold against slightly red skin. His thumb swept over it to soothe the blooming warmth, and he dipped his head to drop a staying kiss on the mark. Then the unthinkable happened. Bridget's deft fingers curled around his ear and cheek, holding him to her. The action was not one of abhorrence, as he expected, but rather acceptance. Compassion, even.

Then her voice, soft as a dove's wing, filled the silence. "What does it say?"

"*Pyranis.* It's a name I haven't gone by since before I fell from the Empyrean, and now it's yours, if you'll have it."

Those strong fingers lifted his head to hers, reminding him of how he had tilted her chin to meet his gaze when they were in her design studio. His chest tightened at the tenuous fortune the mages had bestowed on him, and all because this wondrous woman hadn't had the good sense to leave a dangerous man for dead on her back porch.

Wonder and a hint of something he couldn't quite name stared back at him. "You just gifted me my very own mythical existence, complete with a kick-ass tattoo and soulmate." The smile that beamed out of Bridget rivaled any fire he could conjure. "I'm in, Steel. Up, down, all around, I'm in for whatever this is, under one condition."

A tight breath *whooshed* out of him, and he let his head, still cradled in her hands, fall to her collarbone. "Name it, Sunshine, and it's yours. Forever. For always."

That perfect mouth crept closer to his ear. "You fly me to the stars, as you promised."

Her sharp yelp hardly registered as he unleashed his wings and curled them around her. Their bodies rolled until she was settled securely, and still wonderfully naked, against his chest.

"Done."

***

"OH GOD, it smells like sex in here."

And that was the comment, announced by Chrome when he led the rest of the angels into Bridget's house later that night, that made her realize she could *definitely* see herself adopting a few more big brothers.

Emphasis on the *big*.

After Steel's elephant-in-the-room-sized reveal—and, holy hell, what a revelation that was—the two of them dove feet-first into some serious talk. The most worrisome was the little fact that they hadn't used any protection during sex. Steel had only kissed her forehead and explained how all celestial beings who were created from the Eternal Flame—by virtue of being created and not born, per se—couldn't create life themselves. In essence, angels and mages alike were sterile. Who knew?

They talked all through dinner about everything and nothing. The angel had patience in spades and tolerated every nagging question her dazed mind could conjure—about his brothers, the Empyrean, even the other mortal women who'd bonded. To Bridget's *great* surprise, it all felt right. She kept waiting for that terror to latch onto her, for the prospect of leaving her home to explore a world of powerful angels and elemental magic to clamp down on her with chilling fear.

None of that happened. The fear stayed good and gone. There was even the added boon of Steel's constant touch that thrilled her to no end. The freedom for her to reach out and graze her fingers along his toned forearm or indulge in the desire to reach beneath his shirt and splay her palm against his lower back. All simple things, but they were shiny and new and bolstered whatever spark lived inside her.

Steel, she'd also learned, had the same affinity for touch, and boy, was she not complaining. During one of their more animated conversations about his ability to bend steel-based metals, he'd abruptly paused to lift Bridget onto the counter. A sharp yank of her leggings was her only warning about his particular intentions before the angel dropped to his knees. He'd mumbled something about wanting to see whether other parts of her tasted like cinnamon, whatever that meant. She'd hardly cared and hadn't come to truly appreciate the development builder's choice in durable countertop material until then either.

She sure as hell did now, especially as Chrome, Iron, Brass, and another red-haired angel, Bronze, leaned their bulk against the counter. Steel joined Bridget on the loveseat, while his other two brothers, Tungsten and Titan, took up space on a couch normally suited for three. The angels' wide thighs and sporadic fidgeting against the cushions gave the impression they were far more snug than snuggly, despite the furniture's large size.

Tungsten, the golden-haired prime sentinel and leader of the angels, turned toward Chrome, and heat crept over Bridget's face as she recalled the giant angel's earlier proclamation. "Shut it. We're in Bridget's home. Be respectful."

The angel to Chrome's left, Bronze, snorted. "Yeah. Easy for him to say. He wasn't the one who walked into the armory shortly after a certain bonded male's sweat session. And I ain't talking about exertion from target practice. Well, actually, maybe that's not entirely far off— *Ow!*"

Iron smacked Bronze on the back of the head and resumed his stoic stance against the counter as if he'd done nothing more than swatted a pest. Given the dynamic, Bridget supposed that wasn't too far off the mark.

In what she suspected was a practiced maneuver, Tungsten disregarded the exchange. "Ignore him. We're beyond ecstatic for the both of you." Ashen eyes softened, and a trim smile lit his stern features. "Bridget, welcome to our family. In time, I hope to introduce you to my soul bond, Tammy, and her twin sister, Rose, who is bonded to my second in command, Titan."

The bearded angel next to Tung nodded, and a flicker of understanding curled a corner of his mouth as well. A co-conspirator. One who, perhaps like Tungsten, had a certain appreciation for the physical effects of the soul bond.

"Thank you. I look forward to it."

Steel leaned his elbows on his thighs. "Yes, there's a lot to look forward to, but first, we need to shut down the charmer threat that keeps driving through Bridget's development. Find out what they're doing." Darkness dimmed the usual brightness in his voice. "They know about her, and even though the house is in her brother's name, it's only a matter of time before they connect the dots and realize she lives on their freaking paper route."

Tungsten nodded, then glanced at the clock above the stove. "It's eleven now. If we fly fast, we should reach the resort right as they're ready to depart, if they plan on keeping to their prior schedule. We follow the trail, see where it ends up."

Titan turned to Tung. "What if the trail ends at the lab again? The highway exit at the rear of the development could easily take them there."

"As well as any number of other places," Iron added. His russet beard volleyed back the terracotta hues illuminated under the kitchen's lights.

A few of the angels shifted on their feet, though whether from unease or an aversion to being idle Bridget didn't know. She slid more closely into the shelter of Steel's arm.

"Something about their cargo is off," Steel reminded them. "My metal didn't like it. I say we see where the caravan winds up. If it's the lab, Cyro's aware we already know the location and he hasn't acted on it yet. It's been months since we last saw him or any big moves out of the place. That metal, however, isn't anything I want to risk him getting his hands on."

Tung leaned forward. "What are you suggesting?"

"I'm suggesting that, even if the cargo isn't going to the lab, it's just more bad news waiting for us down the road if we don't take it out." Steel gestured between the two angels on the couch and himself. "The three of us are at full strength now, and Cyro has no fucking clue. We may be able to combat whatever the hell his minions are cooking up. We have to at least try. Whatever that shit is, it's an easier target above ground than it is below. Even with Iron's help mapping out the lab's layout from old schematics, there's no telling how big the space is now or what the charmers equipped it with, not without going in. If we take out what we can see, we have a better shot of gaining an advantage either through knowledge or enemy arsenal destruction."

Silence permeated the small living room, and searing tension thickened Bridget's once airy and comforting home. These sentinels were far more than the stern law enforcement officers and stealthy martial artists she was used to. Steel's brothers wore masks of brutal determination that belied the warmth shown her mere moments before. It was a different painting from the one she'd imagined while in Steel's arms, from the one he'd promised to help her explore when she was ready.

A heavy weight settled over the space, until finally Tung spoke, breaking the trance. "If we find the caravan is heading toward the lab, we identify the cargo first. *Then*, once we know what we're dealing with, we eradicate the threat. Understood?"

Solemn nods of chiseled chins bobbed around the room.

Beside her, Steel's blond head did the same. "Your brother's still coming over tonight?" He asked her.

"Yeah, he had to cover a half shift for one of the officers, but he'll be over around midnight."

"You told him the story?"

She nodded. "I told him there were some strange cars parked outside my house recently and that I wanted him to stay the night."

"Good."

Then in a practiced maneuver that no doubt spanned millennia, the angels rose to their feet. She scrambled upright as well, though she needn't have bothered. Steel hauled her to him with all the effort one would exert picking a kitten off the floor and slashed his hungry mouth across hers. Unlike the others they'd shared, this kiss was a searing promise that ended before it began. When their mouths parted, Steel lightly brushed his lips across her forehead before following his brothers out and leaping into the night sky.

But the ghost of his nearly imperceptible whisper, one she wasn't entirely sure he meant for her to hear, lingered on her skin.

Soon.

CHAPTER 26

The arid breeze tickling the back of Steel's neck was the oddest sensation for a New England spring. It would have alerted the crisp hairs on his body to stand at military attention if they weren't already on high alert.

The wind was parched and ominous as it carried him and his brothers over the roving brigade of hodgepodge trucks—vehicles that would take him no time at all to cave in on themselves and roll into neat metallic boulders. Chrome had been correct about the charmers' readiness to move out, and it sure as hell chapped Steel's ass that patience needed to win out over pain.

Their pain, not his.

The cloying air whipping against Steel's wings called to mind dragon's breath, oddly enough. How apropos, then, that a slew of entirely different fiery winged beasts now stalked its moving prey—one that most definitely hoarded some sort of metallic treasure.

Coffee-colored freckles and sable hair wove within his thoughts of hoarded riches and mythical creatures. The invasion had become an increasingly common occurrence, one that both soothed and stirred him.

Hard and lustrous silver wings leveled out beside Steel, joining his own.

"They're getting off the exit for the lab," Chrome observed. "Any clue what's in those crates? I'm a heartbeat away from gnawing off my skin with my eyeteeth. Whatever's in the back of those trucks is foul as fuck and making my metal skittish."

The caravan of vehicles consisted of two operations pickup trucks, a landscape vehicle, and a van, all of which sported the Torrey Mountain Resort logo on the doors and sides. Stuffed into the bed and rear of each vehicle were black rubber storage bins with bright yellow tops, all neatly stacked in arrangements that would make any *Tetris* aficionado nod in appreciation.

"No, but at least we know where they're headed." The vehicles bounded down the same small dirt road—and Steel was being generous with the word *road*—they'd all come to know far too intimately in the past few months. This dusty stretch of pebbles barely wide enough for Steel's shoulders, let alone a proper box truck, had all the feel of a runway leading into abandoned airspace. There was nothing for miles around, except the noticeable cap of a landfill and acres of polluted greenery long abandoned by mortals.

Above them, Bronze, Brass, and Iron soared in tight formation, their sheathed blades and hidden firearms nothing more than misted shadows among the clouds. Tungsten and Titan trailed behind, ensuring no surprises followed their contingent. Not that there ever were, save the occasional curious raptor, which was the only bird bold enough to investigate.

The trucks turned off onto a patch of grass worn with tire treads. Steel scanned the compound. "I don't see anything that could accommodate cargo. Where would they unload it? There are no garages or loading docks anywhere."

"No clue, but now that we know where that crap's going, whatever it is, I don't particularly have any plans to let it get that far."

"Same."

The angels banked low and landed in a tuft of trees not far from where the resort vehicles stopped. The trucks had parked alongside a caged-off masonry building that looked no bigger than a cluster of restrooms one might find at a municipal park.

Brass was the first to step toward the clearing. Ochre eyes of heated fire blazed through squinted lids. "Why are they stopping near that building?"

Steel joined him. "That's not a garage, though."

"No," Iron supplied. The brush of his mace's chain against his leather wrist cuffs was the only sound of his approach. "It's a sewer pump station. The lab's at a lower elevation than the sewer lines, so the pump station pumps up the wastewater to the municipal sewer system."

Chrome crossed his arms. "Well, apparently, that pump station's seeing a heck of a lot of action, and none of it concerning the shit it *should* be dealing with."

Steel braced himself, waiting for Bronze to offer up his own hilarity at the obvious opening Chrome had given him, but one by one, truck doors opened and closed. Charmers in various states of concealment stepped out. Some wore mortal skin and effects, while others' gold and teal tattoos glowed over ashen skin illuminated by the trucks' halogen lights.

Titan's wings flared behind him. "I count eight, and there's about to be a shit ton more, I suspect, if they go through that pump station's door. I'm willing to bet that thing's been retrofitted with an elevator of some kind and the original building's just for show." He scanned the charmers as they milled about. Some were talking. Some were beginning to wheel out hand trucks and loosen ratchet straps over cargo.

Tungsten stepped forward and, to Steel's delighted surprise, was the first to palm his weapons—two tungsten-plated, chrome-reinforced Desert Eagle firearms. "Chrome, any mystics?"

The telltale waft of the brawny angel's peppermint gum mingled with the verdant approach of spring flora. "Nah, they're all elite. They need the muscle to move whatever the hell they've got in the back." Warrior class, then, like the charmer who had attempted to abduct Bridget.

Steel cocked a brow at Chrome, unimpressed by his brother's self-certainty. "There were mystics in the caravan I ran into earlier. That's how I got Bridget into this mess."

"No, you got Bridget into this mess because you couldn't resist kissing her before you got your coffee, then you forgot all about the prevalence of social media and facial recognition."

Steel's muscles swelled with visceral rage. He reared at his brother, hand already cocked for a blow. "Open that fucking mouth one more time—"

"Save it." Iron stormed forward, his mighty ax and mace gripped firmly in each hand, and with two giant flaps, he leaped into the night sky. Wind gusts bit into Steel's face, but before he could either join his brother in the air or pummel Chrome into the ground, Titan's strong hand landed on his shoulder.

The knowing iridescent eyes of a bonded male glowed fiercely and pinned Steel in place. "Let's take care of this so you can take care of her."

A moment later, Steel's Lakonian short sword was in his hand as his bootheels left the ground.

BLACK BLOOD SLICKENED Steel's blade before his feet had landed. The kill was hardly one to savor, regrettably. Oh, he was certainly in a *mood*. For bloodshed, bed sport, vengeance, anything that kept his cock up and his blood heated. Blue fire coursed through his sword as he looked down the slope of his nose at a gasping elite. The demon looked ridiculous, feebly holding its hands against the two-foot-long gash sizzling away across its belly. Honestly, had anyone in the history of battle ever had luck trying to put their insides back in their body once their guts had sprung free? It was like trying to put back one of those prank snakes in a can. What a waste of dying breath.

At Steel's feet, tan skin and eyes of an indiscriminate blue flashed and faded, and the demon's mirage gave way to the truth of its ugliness, along with the single gold band adorned around its neck.

A mystic.

Steel couldn't have kept the amusement off his face if he tried. He had never been so gleeful as he lunged, plunging his blazing sword to the hilt inside the demon magic user. Gurgled gasps creaked through lips stretched wide. Black eyes danced an unfocused rhythm in Steel's general direction, but the writhing bastard was beyond lucidity. Electric fire crept along its torso in an incendiary delta of webs, ashing everything it touched. Before the thing was a total loss, there was one small token Steel couldn't resist claiming. He drew back his sword and, with an effortless hack, relieved the demon of its right arm, which sported the single gold armband signifying its class, and not the double gold bands of the elite. He held the arm aloft and turned to Chrome, who had just emptied a full magazine of bullets into his quarry.

"See? Mystic." Smugness warmed Steel as he tossed the arm in his brother's direction before incinerating the thing.

After firing one more bullet, this one between a demon's eyes, Chrome reached down toward his toppled prey and made to retrieve a token of his own. When he stood upright again, he offered up a certain, very intentional finger. "See? Fuck you."

"Asshole," Steel muttered but didn't linger. He ran toward the back of the nearest vehicle, the one hitched with a landscaping trailer. Already, a dry revulsion filled his veins, and his fire, which had sung brilliantly through his body a moment ago, raged for a wholly different reason, like a feline's hairs raised in warning.

Grunts and shouts echoed around him. A few choice curses came from his brothers, but urgency forced him to focus. He grabbed the nearest container, yanked the lid free, and cringed. Billets of titanium, tainted with some form of otherness, sat in neat orderly rows. He flipped over another lid, then another, and was greeted by more of the same, except these bars were bronze and chrome. They appeared harmless, yet something about them hummed with an inky crudeness. What the hell?

Around him, groans and cries rent the night as his brothers dispatched the remaining demons. Then he heard it, the low hum of a vibration, almost a tempered whine.

A portal. Shit.

Titan's roar was barely audible through the approaching din of magic. "More are coming! We've got to move *now!*"

Steel's eyes flashed to a lone box in the far right corner. Without thinking, he grabbed the thing, then shoved it against Brass, who had hurried to their side, heedless of the blood welling against his auburn hair.

"Take this back. Chrome needs to piece it apart." Then Steel turned to his prime, who'd just finished firing off another shot, and his second in command. "We've got to torch the trucks before more charmers arrive. The others are too gassed, but the three of us might be able to."

Understanding sparked between Steel and the other soul-bonded males. Tung barked the order, and the remaining angels took flight just as the depressed sound, now mimicking a plane's engines approaching full bore, grew louder. Any second, the portal would open, and mages knew how many charmers would come through.

Solid metal rippled over Steel's body, encasing him in fluid armor. Wings spread wide in an extension of his power, and flames erupted from his outstretched arms. Tung and Titan assumed similar forms, until all three backflapped high into the sky to get well out of range of what their fire would do.

The second blue flames hit the gas tanks, the trucks exploded in a symphony of devastation, sending debris and shrapnel straight into the swirling vortex of the portal. Every speck of the vehicles whirled in a viscous funnel cloud swallowed up by hungry vile magic. Once the dregs of tire parts and sheet metal were sucked away, sharp pops and hisses resounded through the barren field like a newly doused campfire. The explosion had forced the portal to close before it could fully open. When the thick, oppressive smoke finally began to dissipate, not a single vehicle or demon remained, only scorched earth.

Titan grabbed Steel by the collar and half flew, half dragged him back into the trees. The pitched sounds of the portal's abrupt closing had been its own treacherous assault. A buzzing whine rattled Steel's ears and made for a choppy-as-hell flight pattern. A glance at the others revealed they were suffering right alongside him. Tung's right wing sagged with his displaced equilibrium, and Titan kept his hands over his ears as he bobbed in the air, struggling to maintain his altitude.

Eventually, Steel's stride returned but not before his worry over the charmers' cargo settled into his mind. Flight feathers rippled inward as if cringing with the memory of whatever coated those metal billets. Something foul and unnatural. Something even Steel's fire and metal cowered from.

As he banked higher, settling into a much-needed thermal he could glide through without expending tons of energy, an ominous hesitation quivered in his gut.

Just what the hell, exactly, were they bringing back with them?

CHAPTER 27

All clear. Lots to analyze. Need to regroup. I'll be over first thing in the morning. - S

The delicate ping of Bridget's phone was the sound she'd been waiting for. Even though the clock crawled past midnight a good twenty minutes ago, her body had decided that sleep wouldn't be on its agenda.

Because she was the sister of a law enforcement officer, her life came with a larger amount of worry than most. Early on in Ryan's career, when he was a patrolman, she had become fast friends with the troublesome emotion, especially the instances when Ryan had to draw his firearm during a shift. Steady helpings of peanut M&Ms and white Bordeaux got her through the worst of her nerves, but she'd never been able to truly settle until he called her, usually with a minimal damage report.

Old habits died hard, it seemed, though her relief at the sight of Steel's text was entirely new. The backs of her eyelids prickled. That strange budding sensation within her, which always soared in Steel's presence, now hobbled around in her chest, searching and whining like a penned animal. There was relief, yes, but it was devastatingly temporary and would likely be until the morning when she saw him again.

"Why the hell don't you have your phone on silent?"

Her brother's stocky frame crowded out the hallway's meager night-light—and yes, she still used a night-light. His white undershirt and boxers bore all the signs of bedtime routine completion, but the ever-present shadow that darkened his square jaw mimicked his inky midnight-blue gaze.

"*You* never have your phone on silent," she retorted.

"*I* need to be accessible to the station, brat, and you damn well know that."

She stuck her tongue out just to firmly cement her hard-won brat status. The whites of his eyes flashed before she'd even been able to rear her tongue back in.

Once his usual ocular positioning had been restored, a truly gargantuan task given her brother's penchant for dramatizing things that didn't need it, his gaze drifted from the phone settled in her lap to the small silver figurine on her nightstand. The furrow between his brows was her only indication of his concerned curiosity before he pushed off the doorframe and strode to her side.

"What's this?"

"A dragon. Obvs."

Ryan clicked the nightstand lamp up a tick, then held the thing closer. "This is . . . this is the dragon you had hanging from your rearview the night—"

"No it's not." Bridget snatched the thing back and tossed it into the drawer.

"I'd know that thing anywhere." A wary haze clouded Ryan's eyes. His brow was pulled low with an emotion Bridget couldn't easily identify. "Fucking Christ, that dragon dangling in your face and obstructing your vision contributed to the accident, Bridge!"

Contributed, as in it was one of many factors. Those other

unspoken factors hung heavily in the charged air between them. Alcohol, Ryan pointedly omitted, being the other main contributor.

Confusion once again pinched his features. "How'd you get it, anyway? As far as I know, it wasn't removed from the crash site. It would have been sent to the crusher, along with everything else in the vehicle."

"St— Steven." The lie sprouted from her tongue like a weed. "He gave it to me."

"Well, that's fucking creepy. I mean, it looks exactly like the original. Like, *exactly*, even down to that pronged tail, with all those barbs sticking out from it. How'd he know about it, anyway?"

Unease and a sense of dire defense surged to the surface. "It's not a great secret that I like mythical creatures, asshat. Giving gifts is what you do for people you care about, with special attention being paid to gifts that are *actually* things the recipient would like. If you have any confusion about the subject, I'll refer you to Michael. I'm sure he'd be more than happy to explain what the hell one man can possibly do with *seven* T-shirts that all say, 'I don't need a weapon, I am one.' The answer, in case you're curious, is nothing."

Her brother threw a hand out toward her dresser, as if the thing was a co-conspirator in housing the T-shirts in question. "T-shirts get dirty, and they wear out! They're a completely useful gift, and he loved the joke. Thought it was funny!"

"One shirt is funny, Ryan. Two is ridiculous. Besides, Steven had the dragon made based on the one from the painting in my living room. You know, because he knew I'd like something I'd already had a fondness toward. It's called taking a hint."

"Yeah, well, you should look at your little hint again. Outside of the common reptilian resemblance, the two dragons don't look a thing alike. Ugh, whatever. I'm going to crash on the couch. I've got to be back at the station by seven tomorrow morning, then I'm off for a blessed four days." He clasped his hands together in prayer and threw his eyes to the ceiling. "The pull-out still work on the couch?"

"What? Oh, yeah . . . Yeah, it still works. Sure."

"Great. G'night."

Bridget murmured the words back to him, but she couldn't look up from the phone in her hands. Her memory snagged on something Ryan had said, and her brain stalled out. She threw her nightstand drawer open and rescued the small clump of dragon-shaped steel.

The figurine was about three inches tall, and yes, it very much resembled your classic dragon. The thing flaunted slitted eyes, barbs protruding all along its spine and tail, and enough fangs that would make even Venom think his dental work was lacking.

The dragon in her painting, however, told a different tale. Its wings were more ethereal than membranous, and its tail didn't culminate with a cluster of sharp spikes like on the figurine but, instead, sported a clearly defined arrowhead. Likewise, horns were cast out from the sides of its heart-shaped face, rather than in a mohawk of blades the dragon in her hands boasted.

They were different. No, not just different. Contradictory. One body type was slim and sleek, while the other had a proud chest. The closer she examined the silver figurine in her hand, the starker the incongruities became and the more closely it resembled the dragon in her car four years ago.

Itchy tension flooded her skin, and she frantically kicked the covers away. The similarities were too close. Too exact. "How did he know? How . . .?"

Memories from one of their earlier conversations invaded the pea soup in her brain. There had been pizza dough, grape tomatoes, and talk of dragons.

"I had one exactly like this—exactly like this."

"You seem to have a thing for dragons."

When Steel had first handed the dragon to her, she remarked on its likeness to her original, sure, but she hadn't thought much beyond it. Dragons were dragons, and once her mind had begun to recount the other harsh realities of that night, she'd not really given the little beast another thought.

The dragon in her painting, which Steel had claimed to model the figurine after, was nothing like what he'd given her, though. The lump of metal in her hands, however, was just so specific, almost intentional.

Pinpricks raked up and down her neck, fanning over her chest. With measured worry, Bridget slowly dropped her head and peered down at the silver dragon.

How the hell did Steel know what the dragon in her vehicle looked like the night of her accident?

***

STEEL TUCKED his phone into his back pocket, then resumed his stance in front of the Creepy Crate, as Bronze dubbed the box they'd swiped. No response from Bridget, but c'mon, like he should expect one? It had been an hour since he last sent his message, and it was now well after one in the morning.

The normal considerate male in him should be grateful and content that she was most likely sleeping.

But the possessive soul-bonded angel in him couldn't give a ripe fucking fig about contentment and only wanted contact —*any* sort of contact—with her now now now.

So, here he stood, coiled tightly, with black demon blood still dappling his pants, and stared at a box of metal that his power knew was anything but. A few of the others had already gone to patch themselves up and recharge for the night. All in all, the battle had been more of the get-your-blood-pumping and less of the losing-limbs variety, which Steel was grateful for, but none of it changed his urge to be as far away from the shit in the crate as possible. And get back to Bridget as fast as his wings would carry him.

A centering breath shuddered through him, and he let the heaviness of his eyelids ground him. *Answers. You need answers first, then rest.*

Around the farmhouse table in the den's great room, Titan, Tungsten, and Steel stood over Chrome's shoulders as he dragged a blue strip of paper across one of the metal bars in the crate.

Titan leaned forward. "Is that—?"

"Blue litmus paper," Chrome answered.

The small vial of blue scraps was only one of several tubes and diagnostic equipment sprawled out across the wood table. Not for the first time, Steel wondered whether the scattered array of science equipment was some oddball testament to Mr. Wizard and Bill Nye or, instead, to the chaotic children that made up the target demographics. At least this unorganized mess would make sense to a slew of chaotic and scatterbrained eight-year-olds, because it meant jack shit to him.

Chrome swiped the strip over the surface of the not-steel steel once more, and the powder blue faded to carnation pink.

"What does that mean?" Steel asked.

"It means there's hydrochloric acid coating these puppies."

"How? Acid breaks down metal, most especially steel."

Chrome sighed and leaned back in his seat. "Magic. That's my best guess, at any rate. They've been weaponizing the shit against metal for ages. Who's to say they haven't figured out a way to put these two very opposing substances into some sinister dark magic spin cycle and finally have them come out holding hands on the other side?"

Tungsten pinched the bridge of his nose. "Spare us the colorful commentary. So, what you're saying is that Cyro—using magic—has forged a metal, which is normally at our command, with one of the most harmful substances to our elemental form?"

"Looks like it."

Steel shook his head. "I still don't get it. What good would having such a billet do for them? Just so they can be able to craft blades and bullets from the stuff? They enchant their weapons against us already. Why go through this procedure? Seems like a lot of extra work for not a lot of return. There must be something we're not seeing."

Titan appeared at Steel's side. The bearded angel's muscular shoulder cast a shadow in Steel's direction. "Can you manipulate it?"

"No. I tried. My power literally shrinks away from it. The acid and whatever magic they coated the stuff with is nullifying things somehow."

Chrome snapped the lid over the Creepy Crate. "Well, until I can learn more about it, no touchy."

"No worry," Steel remarked.

Tungsten rested his large frame against the wall. "Regardless, this could have major implications for things we may not yet be able to see clearly. Stay on your guard, and don't let this become a distraction. Our directive is to find and protect the Flame's sparks that reside in the mortal realm. With your Bridget, Steel, we have another soul under our care." He flicked his chin toward the sealed crate. "I won't allow this to split our focus. See what you can discover, Chrome, but let none of us forget what we're truly here for."

Weary heads bobbed with exhausted nods of understanding. Tung was right, as usual, though Steel had never grasped the full scope of his prime sentinel's devotion to the Empyrean's priority until now.

Until he'd found his soul bond.

A few hours. Steel would grab just a few hours of rest, then fly to Bridget. If his eager wings didn't carry him there sooner.

Ryan's tires bumping over the granite curb of Bridget's driveway and barreling down the road should have been a harbinger of joyful tidings. She should have been whipping open the drapes, getting out her fancy coffee mugs, and even putting on a swipe or two of slightly-passed-its-prime mascara.

Bridget did none of those things.

She sat slumped in her chair at the breakfast bar, where she'd been all morning, fiddling with that stupid steel dragon like the thing held all the answers and capabilities to make sense of the mire in her mind. Her smooth thumbnail found a groove along the creature's back and traced the angle until her finger dipped into the arcs of its scales. The disruption mimicked her aggravated thoughts. The joyous highs of breaking through both her body's and brain's barriers, with nothing but hope and happiness on the horizon, only to career through a road barricade and plunge straight off a cliff.

Unfamiliar fury and heart-clogging hurt had her gripping the figurine more tightly. The dragon's scale pattern was one she was more than an expert on because it was what convinced her to choose this dragon over others in the first place. The big fat scales had been shingled and textured, and when she originally considered purchasing it, she'd imagined how rewarding the sensory experience would be while running her fingers over its rigid hide at red lights. Kind of like petting fuzzy dice.

Now, the figure was a cold lump in her palm.

The back door's suction seam hissed its release, and her shoulders inched closer toward her ears. Was she ready to see him? Could she even look at him without those icy-blue eyes stabbing her in the gut instead of stroking her senseless?

A bitter malt scent, kissed with a roasted earthiness and subtle sweetness, permeated her kitchen. And there, beneath it all and hiding like an exuberant kid at a surprise party, was the soft caress of cinnamon.

Steel placed the white to-go cup under her nose, then brushed a light kiss on her cheek. His swipe of affection landed, but it wasn't returned. "I still owed you a London Fog."

Fog. What a completely apropos word for the tangled heap that had been made of her emotions, thoughts, and memories. Bridget's squishy insides had been turned into a congealed mess, as if a three-year-old had gone wild and taken a hot poker to all the things vital to her makeup.

Steel eased his lithe body into the seat next to her, but he didn't settle fully. His movements were wary, rigid. Good. He should feel half as confused as she did.

"Everything all right?"

Bridget slid the dragon across the counter toward him and asked the only question she cared about. "How?"

He eyed the thing with all the trepidation of a man spying a trap but having no recourse except to move forward. "How, what? How did I make it?"

"No, how did you know what to make it look like?"

The delay was slight, but it was there. A tell. "From the painting in your living room."

Bridget deflated at the obvious lie. God, she had hoped . . .

Steel swept a hand through the unruly hairs at the front of his head. Despite his most insistent finger drag, the locks fell back into the chaotic sprawl they were used to. That fluttering, untrustworthy bloom of power within urged her to lean forward, grasp those tenacious hairs, and soothe them into careful order, but the heavy pall cast by the troubling holes of that dragon willed her to remain still.

He's lying to me. Why is he lying to me?

"Those two dragons look nothing alike."

The angel steadied his hand around his cup. "What's going on here, Sunshine?"

"I don't want you to call me that right now."

He sat back. "All right."

Hurt filled his eyes, but she dismissed it. "This dragon is the same one I had dangling from my rearview mirror the night of my accident four years ago. Maybe it's not the *exact* one, but it's most definitely a perfect replica. I haven't seen this thing since then. It's not like it came in a set. I don't have any others lying around for you to copy. So, how, Steel? *How* did you make a dragon figurine that flawlessly resembles something you've never seen before?"

Stern brows slanted low across those glacial eyes, which had peeled away from her face and remained glued to the figurine in question. Shoulders she'd once thought so impossibly strong sank beneath his form-fitting jacket. "I have seen it before."

It was Bridget's turn to stiffen. "When?"

"Let me . . . Can you just . . ." Words failed the usually eloquent angel, which only added to her unease. "I'll start from the beginning. I need to, please."

"I don't give a crap where you start from, as long as you get to the freaking point. Where have you seen my dragon before?"

Fear and worry had her yelling, but she was far too frazzled to rein it in.

"When you had your accident. When . . . when I saved your life," he relented before soaring to his feet and vaulting away from her, startling a snoozing Elliot in the process. His scolding demeanor morphed into one of a cornered predator as he furiously paced throughout her living room.

"Look, promise me you'll listen," he rushed out. White fire blazed in his eyes, a stark reminder of who and what she'd invited into her home. Her life. *Her heart.*

She ducked her chin once in acknowledgment. It was all she would give him.

"Four years ago, I was up in the mountain pass not far from the resort. My brothers and I were taking care of a pocket of charmers that had been preying on some of the tourists. One mystic got away from the pack. I spotted it before anyone else did and chased it into the ridge just bordering the access road up the mountain. I was already spent after fighting for a good hour. My fire was on fumes, and it was all I could do to stay airborne.

"I had the thing cornered in a rocky outcropping not far from the road, and I thought if I could just get one good hit in, it'd be over. The mystic knew it, too. They're magic users, not hand-to-hand fighters like the elite, and they sure as shit don't do well when separated from their packs." He sank onto the couch, and a bit of her ire sank along with him as tortured memories of those mountains flooded in. "We struck at the same time. My sword sliced right into its upraised hands, severing them from the wrists, but not before it managed to release an orb of magic. It knocked me off the ledge, along with several sizable chunks of the mountain." His solemn eyes, older and burning more brightly than any star, punched through her.

"I landed on the road hard, and my reflexes were shot. I was so damn slow to rise. Everything hurt. I could hardly hold my wings up, and the hit made me too weak to even retract them. Before I could get up, though, a set of headlights blinded me. They were so bright and came on so quickly, I didn't have time to move."

Bridget's mouth went dry at the confession.

"The vehicle slammed into me. I was still in my metallic state, though, so the force of the impact was enough to flip the car off its axis. I saw it roll and skid out before it ground to a halt against the rocks."

Steel's words became an oppressive shroud around her heart. The sad caged-off organ quivered and gasped as her broken memories grasped at monumental straws.

No . . .

"My metal skin was the only thing that kept me alive. Even still, despite my injuries, I couldn't abandon whoever was in that car if there were survivors. I just couldn't . . . So I crawled toward the wreckage. I'll never forget it, the demolished car full of all those lifeless and silent bodies—except yours." The final word was a desperate croak. "I couldn't tell what all the injuries were, who had heartbeats and who didn't. I could only hear *your* breaths. They were these short wheezing puffs, almost like a rattle." Again, he fisted his hair. "I couldn't—*wouldn't*—leave you there."

Bridget's hands flew to her neck in a feeble attempt to quell her wobbling throat.

"There was a hole in the door, so I ripped it wider and got you out, but I had no clue what to do. I just remember how pale you were, how one of your legs was bent at such an atrocious angle, the gored marks all over your skin, the blood . . . I didn't dare touch you anymore. I didn't want to make things worse unintentionally." He cleared his throat. "I called 911, waited with you until I heard the sirens, and then hid."

The heated paper cup against her palm had cooled to just

shy of tepid bathwater. She sat there, shaking her head in tremulous disbelief. "The dragon . . ."

"I saw it in your car. The thing had fallen free and landed in the center console." The angles of Steel's beautiful face were edged in harsh slashes of despair and anguish, guilt and . . . Was that regret?

No. No, she wouldn't feel pity for him, not when he'd known about her for *years* and acted like he'd just met her.

Bridget pressed the pads of her palms against her quivering eyes, but her damn hands did little to hold back the hot tears spilling over. "All this time. All this fucking time you knew me? You knew what happened and you never said anything?"

Steel soared to his feet and pleadingly stretched his hands toward her. Whatever good sense he was otherwise incapable of showing finally managed to trickle its way into his brain when he didn't advance. Damn right.

"I've been watching you," he hurried out.

"You've been *what?*"

"No, that came out wrong. I mean, I've been keeping an eye on you, making sure you survived, making sure you were safe—"

An explosion of milk and tea splattered against her cream-colored wall behind his head. The caramel remnants of her drink trickled and pooled at his feet. Like blood.

Her hurled drink didn't faze him. He didn't even flinch, almost as if he wanted to get hit, welcomed it as penance even.

She couldn't think, couldn't feel. The tears came faster, clouding her vision and drowning out the present until all she could see were the tortured memories of surgery after surgery, three funerals she was too injured to attend, a heartbroken brother, the years-long isolation in her home, and the callous men she'd worked for . . .

Men who thought they knew better than the people who helped them claim their corporate titles.

High-handed men who didn't care who they hurt or crushed along the way.

Men like Steel, who had lied to her and kept her in the dark.

"I checked in on you every agonizing day you were in the hospital. When the nurses were overwhelmed, I'd sneak in and leave you cups of ice chips or warm blankets. And when you were discharged, I swiped the parking ticket off Michael's car because he and Ryan had been double-parked waiting too long for the attending physician to sign your release papers."

"I don't want to hear this. I don't want to hear any of this. You *lied* to me!"

"I lied to *myself*, Bridget! I thought it was guilt that kept me coming back to you each day. I thought it was a messed-up form of obligation that had me looking after you because it was *my fault* you felt the need to lock yourself up in that house to begin with."

Looking after you . . .

A rush of curious occurrences, odd puzzle pieces she'd collected over the years that never quite fit but she also never bothered to question, flared brightly in her mind.

Her weekly grocery delivery order, which was always left under the covered awning near the garage and protected from the elements, despite her specified front door drop-off location.

Her walkway when, during the iciest of ice storms, the concrete was always bone-dry and clear early in the morning while her neighbors' properties were still glassed over.

She backed away from him until her spine kissed the lip of the breakfast bar. "The groceries, the driveway, all those strange things that always seemed to work out in my favor. Was that . . .? Did you do that?"

He didn't nod. He didn't need to. She knew.

Yes, Bridget, that was all him. All that time, he'd always been there, and he lied to you about it.

White fire still raged behind Steel's wild eyes. His chest

heaved on great ragged breaths. "I was bullshitting myself every single day, Bridget. Every single day I kept you in the dark, kept my brothers in the dark."

"Don't call me that! Don't say my fucking name! You've known everything about me all along, and you lied about it, acted like I was just some other silly sheltered suburbanite." More muffled memories floated to the surface. "My basement . . . When I took you into my house that first night, you knew exactly which door led to the basement. You've always seemed to know the layout of my house effortlessly, but effort had nothing to do with it, did it? You told me you once considered moving here, that you'd checked out another unit in the development once before, but that was a lie too, wasn't it? You've just been stalking my house all this time." The lies kept piling up, and her heart threatened to fracture under the weight.

"I know now that I kept coming back to you every day, even when you didn't know I existed, because there wasn't a single possibility that had me staying away from you. I realize now that my soul claimed yours long before I landed on your deck, and I'd rather rip it out of my fucking chest than witness one more day where you're too afraid to sketch your heart out, or the only souls you speak to are Ryan and Michael." He surged a step forward, but her hands shot out in a warning. "These days with you have been the best of my existence, and I'd give up any remaining days the mages see fit to grant me if you can just understand—" His words broke off as he finally scrambled toward her, heedless of her protestations, and clutched at her shoulders.

She twisted sharply, wrenching out of his hold. His chest jolted at the reaction, but she didn't care. "Get. The. Fuck. Out."

"Bridget . . ."

"I said, get out!"

Unable to look at him anymore, she ran up the stairs and locked herself in her bedroom like the sad sorry girl everyone believed her to be. The delicate flake who couldn't handle hard truths or the even harder realities of life and the real world.

They were all right.

Her legs finally gave out when the thud of the back door closing reverberated through the house. Bridget tucked her head against her shaking knees and shattered into pieces.

CHAPTER 29

The sun yawned its bolstering warmth over the empty acres of Chlor-Chem Labs's dilapidated remnants, and yet Steel was still miserably frozen. There was a time when switching into his metallic skin and baking in the high heat of the star's energy wasn't a half-bad way to spend an afternoon.

Now, he wished he could snuff the infernal thing out under his bootheel like one of Chrome's flaming cigar butts.

The mossy log under his ass dampened the backs of his thighs through his jeans, another putrid reminder that there were places even the sun's great light couldn't be bothered to illuminate.

It had been a whole week, and Bridget refused to speak to him. For three days following his confession, Steel had tried to reach her. Phone calls went unanswered. Texts ignored. When his bleeding heart couldn't take it anymore, he'd returned to her house and all but thrown himself at her back door like some rain-drenched mongrel begging for sanctuary. When she first ordered him out of the house that final morning, his useless chivalry had demanded he leave the spare key she'd allowed him to borrow. With one click of the lock, he'd firmly planted himself in an escapeless hell of his own making.

Could he shoulder his way into her house and demand she hear him? Could he melt every fucking lock in that structure until nothing barred his way from looking upon his soul bond again?

No. No, he couldn't, nor would he ever, but it didn't stop the desperate pleas and harrowing cries he sent pealing through the back door's glass night after night.

During those endless hours, his miserable soul confessed everything to her, even as he sat hunched over on her deck, with his sad back cozied up to her aluminum siding. Never once did she open the door or even acknowledge his presence. No lights had ever shone through the first-floor windows. He only knew she was still home because his angelic senses refused to ignore her precious heart ticking away from the bedroom upstairs. Such a morose, reluctant rhythm.

Even his very makeup was an invasion.

Still, he refused to stay away, and he shared what he'd never spoken before to anyone, including his brothers. Explanations of those early days following the accident seemed like the best place to start and how he'd arranged his patrol schedule to keep watch over her.

Once he'd started, there was no way he'd been able to put the pin back in the grenade. It all flowed out of him, every brutal confession and pent-up passion his soul simply couldn't contain any longer. With the wall at his back, he'd described what she'd looked like from outside her picture window over the years, when he'd snag those secret early morning glimpses of her curled up on the couch, dappled in the dawn's kiss as she read a book. How he'd spent countless hours envisioning those legs draped across his thighs instead of the cushion she kept under her knees for added support. How his firm thumbs would massage the delicate arches of her fuzzy sock-clad feet in his lap and wagering how long it would take to turn her attention from her book toward other fantasies.

Then when Steel had wrung free any precious memory of Bridget, whether small or secret, he'd haul his bedraggled body into the sky—only to return the following day and do it all over again. There was gluttony for punishment, and then there was whatever the hell he was doing.

By the fourth day, however, no heartbeats called to him from within the house. He'd peeked into the garage, allowing himself yet another small invasion, and was met with an empty concrete floor and the greasy smudge of an oil spot.

She'd finally left, presumably for her brother's place, and had taken his battered heart with him.

"I don't want to be here," Steel muttered, flicking a twig into the ensnaring foliage of a red cedar. All too late, he realized he'd accidentally said the inside part out loud. Dammit.

"So, go somewhere else," Brass replied matter-of-factly. "Chrome and I can handle running surveillance. Your mind's clearly elsewhere, brother."

Steel murmured an unintelligible noise, the only response he could muster. Hell, it wasn't like he was kidding anyone with his too-eager attitude to get out of the den and away from Aurora proper and, most especially, a certain suburban development.

Shit. He knew he was miserable company, but he just couldn't bring himself to care. Yay, self-loathing.

Chrome's gruff tones added a jagged edge to Brass's otherwise neutral statement. "What the good man is trying to say, but is far too polite to manage, is, of all the available parties interested in running surveillance this morning, why would a sad sack like yourself think he was even remotely up for the task? None of us would have blamed you if you wanted to lay low for a bit."

"Your candor is truly heartwarming," Steel retorted, then

bent down and picked up another twig. "I'm not in the mood, all right?"

"For the job or for Chrome's attitude?" Brass asked.

"Yes." Fuck it. They could sort out which one he meant because he wasn't even sure.

Brass nodded his quiet understanding, then leaned back, directed his attention to the other side of Steel's shoulders, and leveled serious amber eyes on their boisterous brother as if to say *now is not the time.*

Chrome's guttural throat clearing was the angel's only acknowledgment of Brass's warning, as much of a *loud and clear* that any of them could ever hope to expect from him.

Tires rumbling over the low grass near the sewer pump station drew their attention across the field. Steel had never been so happy to see what had to be a ten-year-old paint job on an even older sedan in all his life. Anything to draw his brothers' focus away from him. The vehicle parked right next to the chain-link fence surrounding the pump station's small masonry structure.

Chrome stood first. "A visitor?"

"A human?" Brass inquired.

"Gotta be, unless the charmers figured out how to not get all deep-fried crispy in natural light," Chrome remarked.

Brass snorted. "Not helpful."

"Neither was asking the question in the first place."

Steel stepped forward and squinted. A tall blonde woman in a white coat, one that would fit in just fine at a research facility or a hospital, got out of the car and walked toward the only entrance to the pump station.

The one they'd all suspected served as far more than standard access to tanks and pipes.

"She looks like she's heading to work or something," Brass mused.

As little sense as that made, Steel couldn't help but hum his agreement. The woman wore black slacks that even sported one of those proper ironed creases down the front of the pant legs, animal print ballet flats, a powder-blue button-down blouse, and . . . He squinted . . . Was that a freaking ID badge hanging from a lanyard around her neck?

"No shit. She *works* there?" Steel shook his head in disbelief, then sought confirmation from Brass, who was wearing the same dumbfounded expression he himself no doubt wore. Chrome, however, had yet to comment on a situation that most definitely warranted a comment. Odd.

"Hey, you all right?" Steel nudged his brother's shoulder.

To his astonishment, Chrome wobbled slightly. When had Chrome ever wobbled, let alone *not* dropped his two cents into anything? Like, ever? Steel tracked Chrome's hard gaze where it followed the woman's every step until she disappeared through the station door. The angel's expression was subdued, almost haunted.

"I've seen her before," Chrome whispered. "Or someone like her, maybe, I don't know. But man, she looks so familiar. *Too* familiar."

"Do you think the charmers are employing humans? You think they would do that?" Brass asked.

Chrome shook his head. "I don't know."

As they prepared to fly out of there, Chrome took one final glance back at the woman's car before leaping into the sky. Fiery pools of polished platinum flashed in his eyes before he blinked them clear.

OVER THE PAST FEW DAYS, it had only taken six shameless drive-bys and some embarrassingly sloppy streetside snooping for Bridget to determine that Steel no longer stalked her house. That was good. Because if those dark wings shot out of her backyard one more time, she was liable to steal one of Ryan's rifles and try her hand at skeet shooting.

Or lasso them down with her garden hose and shake their owner free of any remaining secrets—of which there were many, she was certain.

Bridget hefted her handbag onto the breakfast bar and tossed her keys down with them. The tinkling *plunk* of metal on marble resounded in her back teeth, much in the way a low-toned piano chord would when an enthusiastic child got to heedlessly smash their hands across the ebony and ivories.

Dejection hung thick in the air of her once-secluded refuge. She didn't want to be here. Every couch cushion and rigid surface retained some ownership of Steel's presence. Leave it to her to have furniture and cabinets with muscle memory and personal preferences. Another byproduct of her fanciful nature, she supposed.

But God, it hurt. After a week apart, her mood had turned from sour to downright putrid. Ryan and Michael had graciously opened their home to her, and heaven preserve Michael, he'd even managed to keep Ryan from prying too carefully into the cause of her abrupt need for a change of scenery. Basics had to be revealed, of course, but she spun the details with careful artistry into what she hoped were universally understandable relationship woes.

Yes, she and Steven had a fight. Yes, she needed some time to herself, but the house was too big and empty. (No way in hell was she going to tell them about Steel's ever-present vigil outside her back door.) No, Steven didn't hurt her (physically, at least). Yes, she remembered where Ryan stored the taser in her kitchen (in the junk drawer with the tape measure and Mini Maglite).

She'd quickly learned, however, that being around a couple in love was *not* the best way to nurse a broken heart. For that was most definitely what she had. What else could explain the chasm that had been torn open in some previously unoccupied part of her? Somewhere around day five, as she lay on top of the lumpy bed in Ryan and Michael's guest room while struggling to fall asleep, the map of her time spent with Steel had taken shape. While studying the whorls and rises of the past several days, she hadn't at all been prepared for the treasure she'd uncovered at the end.

One by one, each of the angel's laughs and lazy grins had peeled away one of her layers—layers she had carefully constructed to keep out the world's cruelty and preserve what little sanity she could still protect.

What a disastrous folly. She'd have had better luck teaching Elliot to tap dance.

Even gone, that damn angel couldn't give her a moment's peace. Every time she closed her eyes, that charming smile and devilish tongue would feather sparking heat down her neck. Another blink and that same tongue and mouth were sliding through intimate flesh as his solid shoulders pushed her thighs wide. She'd blink again and his arms were cradling her against his chest while sharing a laugh in front of the stove.

Steel's soft words and unyielding affections had also unearthed something she'd inadvertently imprisoned: joy. How had she ever managed to hold happiness captive inside her for so long? She didn't even know she was capable of the stuff, not truly, not real soul-kissed happiness that incinerated shadows and blasted through dark corners until the light couldn't help but shine through.

Until *love* couldn't help but shine through.

Again, she scolded her quivering ridiculous heart, which had all the good sense of a battered dog that kept returning to its abusive owner because it simply didn't know any better. Well, she sure as shit knew better, thanks to Steel. Lies, she reminded herself, had no place where love was concerned. The stuff simply couldn't exist without trust, and if there was no trust, then what the hell were they even doing? The next opportunity she had, she'd paint that damn slogan on her studio wall in gory red streaks.

Bridget pressed at her eyes. "No. Nope. Not going there again." She quickly sniffed the tears away, then shook out her hands. "Underwear. I'm here for a change of underwear, and that's it."

A thud outside halted her stride halfway up the staircase. Steel had come back. *Crap.*

Not at all interested in skulking about her own home anymore and infused by perhaps a bit more rage than reasoning, Bridget stalked down the stairs and marched toward the back door. When she didn't see him immediately, she heaved the thing open. The pent-up vitriol lying in wait on her tongue was all the kindling Bridget needed. If the angel wanted to talk, oh, he was about to get an earful.

Cool spring air sailed through the kitchen, though the breeze did little to temper her fury.

"You want to do this? Fine. Let's have at it." Bridget swept her gaze over the empty patio furniture, then the barren backyard.

A discordant rumbling baritone doused her ire and froze her to the deck. *Not Steel.*

"Don't mind if we do."

The blade at her neck silenced her screams.

Steel could only handle so much talk of mortals embroiled in celestial matters before he was so eloquently reminded of one mortal in particular. Oh, he'd tried to hang in there, tried to settle into his brothers' conversation and suppositions about what a mortal woman was doing in the charmers' grotto—and voluntarily, it seemed. Somewhere around downing Iron's third proffered espresso, however, Steel's fire twitched beneath his skin, so much so that if it didn't spring free soon, he feared a table replacement was in his future.

He politely—okay, not politely—left during one of Bronze's asinine, though oddly animated, theories about possible human housekeeping services. Fucking really? Unsurprisingly, with the sun firmly tucked in and night fully dawning, his weary wings had floated him back here, to Bridget's doorstep. Or back doorstep, as it were.

Funny thing about depression, he'd learned. It wasn't a black hole at all. On the contrary, the dark emotion demanded a steady diet of desperation, which—surprise!—Steel had no shortage of. The vibrant and voracious shard of light inside him was now a miserable smudge of dingy lacquer. His soul's tether had been wrenched so tightly, he feared another tug or two would shatter it entirely, and then where would he be?

Right back here, he supposed. The very seat of his torment.

Penance, indeed, and a testament to how vital that woman had become in just a matter of days. *No, years. No more lies, not even to yourself.*

Steel shifted his shoulders, preparing to take up his vigil on the deck, but he nearly tripped over the back doormat.

A doormat that lay askew, with one corner rolled up, and had been displaced five feet away from its usual perch directly in front of the glass slider. What the hell?

"Bridget," he hollered through the glass door. One second passed, then two . . . Steel barged through the door and pulled his sword free. "Bridget!"

Again, nothing. He spun around. A flash of orange bolted from the living room and ran up the stairs. Elliot.

A single slow creak resounded from the floorboards above, too heavy to have been caused by a cat.

Steel took the stairs three at a time. Her bedroom door was the only one closed. He burst through the thing, unseating the top two hinges.

Bridget lay sprawled on the bed. Her wrists and ankles were spread wide and clasped to the bed frame in some mocking display of sacrifice. The iron manacles biting into her skin were saturated in a writhing swirl of green magic, ensuring Steel's power would be useless against them. A similar ripple of translucent magic writhed around her mouth like a boa constrictor, butting up against her nostrils and leaving little room for her to draw full breaths. Fear drenched her features.

"So happy you could join us. I would have prepared refreshments had I known you'd be coming. Do you want something? She's got quite a good selection of treats, I will say."

At the foot of the bed, a shadowy figure stood. Wrathful eyes burned beneath slashed brows. Eyes of gold, like the three gold bands ringing the charmer's neck.

An apex, a combined demon warrior and magic user, and the most lethal of Cryo's fighting force.

Blue fire erupted over Steel. Flaming tendrils arced down his sword, nearly spilling over the curved tip. He shot out his palm and punched his power free, igniting the room in blue fury.

The apex ducked low, avoiding the blast, and tumbled to the side of the bed. Steel roared forward, slashing, parrying, swiping at anything thrown his way. The fucking thing had touched Bridget. Steel would adorn his wall with the demon's hands in payment, then slowly burn off more precious parts of him. Fire and rage orchestrated Steel around the room in a torrent of blinding aggression. He lifted his blazing sword high, poised to strike, but the demon had deftly gained his footing, flashing a cocksure smile with each empty arc of Steel's blade.

The apex sharply shifted. The bastard was too fast for Steel to follow. In a blink, Steel's sword caught air again, and the demon caught up Bridget's neck, his coiled strength hovering over her straining form. The bone knife's razor tip lay an inch above the hollow of her throat.

"Uh-uh, careful now. Wouldn't want to bust this particular piñata just yet. Don't get me wrong, I will if I need to, but I'd much rather snuff out this specific soul by going through the proper channels. A clean slice just bleeds the damn thing out and back into the mortal populace, and then I'd have to start this rat race all over again when her soul finds a new host." The apex stood, casting his gargantuan shadow over Bridget's shackled body. Her pale complexion had grown ashen. Lips tinged with blue stood out through the iridescent green magic binding her mouth. Helpless shaking fingers clawed at the bedspread. The charmer cast a droll look down at the bed. "Though I imagine you wouldn't appreciate the cleanup." His bulbous nose wrinkled in disgust. "Mortal decay takes forever."

He lifted a querying brow at Steel. "You're fond of this one, right?"

Steel couldn't think over the rage roaring in his ears. He clenched his sword's hilt tighter. Pure celestial power pulsed in every cell, and the house's steel supports groaned in supplication.

When Steel spoke next, venom dripped from his tongue. "Consider yourself lucky. You get to choose how you die tonight. Long and slow while an I-beam constricts every last breath out of your lungs, or fast and ruthless while you choke on your own blade. Don't think I won't rip out every steel joist in this house just to see which one fits your thick neck the best. Perhaps I'll do both and save us all the time."

The charmer smirked, then leaned close to Bridget. "Oh, my dear, I do believe that angel loves you." Then the apex stood tall again. "While your offer is certainly creative, I must rule differently. I'm afraid you won't be offering up any such enticements this evening. Though I would *love* to see that I-beam trick sometime. I've heard one of you birds likes to dally with steel. I'm so happy it's you who I get to play with tonight."

A sharp pop boomed above the ceiling. Bridget cast her frightened gaze to the level overhead, then flashed panicked blue eyes back to Steel.

Around them, the house's metal bent and heated from Steel's elemental fury. Fire writhed and pulsed over his muscles, until the flames nearly kissed the edge of the bedsheets.

"Time's running out. Let her go or I'll choose for you."

The apex merely shrugged, as if he were a bored voter who had grown weary of a politician's empty promises. "Impressive. It seems you can be quite the busy bee. Did you know that we too have been busy?" He dipped the blade lower to Bridget's throat, teasing her so it just kissed the valley of her neck, before withdrawing it to its previous height. "This female here is the perfect test subject for Cyro's latest advancements, ones we had yet to perfect when the brown-haired beauty resided as our guest all those months ago. You see, we couldn't quite figure out how to extract a soul containing the spark. Our tried-and-true tactics at bleeding out souls, it seemed, wouldn't do for one kissed by the Eternal Flame."

A series of hissing pops ricocheted through the basement. More pipes and planks sprang free. Steel didn't give a shit if he collapsed the whole block on their heads. Eons of patience and stealth made him stronger, bolder. He simply needed to wait for the right moment, and the charmer needed to keep fucking talking.

"We'd finally perfected the procedure, and wouldn't you know? It had something to do with that little celestial connection you lot are so fond of. You see, we couldn't just snuff out the spark. No, we had to *lure* it out." The apex inched closer to Bridget's splayed leg and pulled the knife away from her throat. Her chest expanded on the first full breath Steel had seen her take, and that tumultuous light inside his core settled slightly.

Then the demon dragged the knife's blade up along Bridget's inner leg, halting it at the juncture of her thighs.

Steel's fire was a few feet away from torching everything in the room. As his soul bond, Bridget would survive his flames, but the apex and the house wouldn't. Just a few more inches . . . Just a few more steps . . .

"That celestial bit was the key, you see. It was all about that link to the Empyrean, and once we developed magic capable of severing that particular little tie, well, there'd be nothing left tethering the soul to the host or any future host. The only wrinkle was finding the correct soul as a test subject—one who also happened to be soul bound to another celestial being."

The apex's words settled like sheets of ice over Steel, immobilizing his flames. He kept his expression stony, but a glimmer of uncertainty refused to be smoothed away. "Nothing can sever a soul bond," he gritted out.

"Are you sure about that, though? *Really* sure? Should we place bets? Here, let me be the first to offer up a show of good faith." The bone knife at Bridget's thigh disappeared in a flash of green magic and was replaced with a different weapon.

Steel threw himself against the far wall. His flames swirled protectively around him. Ivory bone made way for a lethal arc of honed steel, forged from the same tainted billets the charmers had been smuggling from the resort.

Ruthless glee flashed in the charmer's smile—a smile that winged all the way up to his eyes. "Since you appear to recognize this bit of handiwork, I'll spare you the manufacturing details. All you need to know is that it's immune to your little metallic parlor tricks, and the magic imbued within is especially good at severing celestial connections. In essence, one slice can lure her soul out while bleeding that pretty body dry. Quite efficient, wouldn't you say? Oh, and the magical nasties those mystics sank into this blade?" He waved the thing in Steel's direction. "Well, I'm game to test it out if you are, but first, let's get to the main event."

In a whirl of gold and teal limbs, the apex arced the blade over the bed and slashed right through Bridget's femoral artery.

RIVERS of deep crimson and blinding white light melded in a tangle of fleeting essence—not just Bridget's but Steel's as well. Her muffled cries of pain racked her body as she flailed against her bonds. Blood seeped into the comforter, while ephemeral light, freed from its host, floated up to the ceiling.

Steel's knees buckled, but he speared the tip of his blade into the wood to keep from collapsing altogether. Lethal power, which had surged against his ribs a moment ago, roiling to break free, retreated within his chest. The bond that dwelled in his heart's core thudded frantically as if in the final throes of death. His power encircled that dimming light within, as a pride of lionesses would worry over dying cubs.

His soul bond . . . The connection . . .

Severed. The truth rang louder than any other universal acknowledgment.

"No. *No!* Bridget . . ." Steel scrambled to his feet, his fire gone.

The blow to his jaw sent him reeling to the floor. A sharp kick to his ribs followed. His knees and palms dug into the floorboards as he strained to catch his breath.

"I like you, you know. You've made this interesting for me. And as such, I'll do you a little favor. Boy, would I hate to see all that heat in your eyes go to waste. Got to have an outlet, right?" The apex slapped Steel on the back like they were longtime chums, but the weight of the hit toppled him.

Weak. He was growing so weak.

The bond within had disintegrated to no more than a faint whisper. Was the speed at which it was deteriorating tied to Bridget's lessening life force? Steel tried to look up from the floor, but he couldn't see past the edge of the bed.

Boot treads pressed against Steel's neck, anchoring him against the floorboards. He strained under the apex's grip, then burning pain seared into the back of his neck.

"You gave me a great idea, you know. I do have *some* heat of my own. Now, it's not exactly that celestial angel shit. No, it's born from my own magic, but it gets the job done. Lucky for you, I've coated my blade with it, and I get to see whether that mortal technique for killing lobsters humanely and quickly actually has any merit. Apparently, you're supposed to jab your knife right into the base of the neck where the spinal cord begins, then swipe it down straight through the skull. Let's see if that theory holds any water." The apex leaned closer. "Do tell me whether I managed it correctly, all right? I'm nothing if not a perfectionist."

Steel writhed and kicked with the ferocity of a wounded beast, but the fucking demon's weight was like an eighteen-wheeler parked on his back. Sweat dripped into his eyes, and the bond within flickered with the tiniest glow. Pain that had nothing to do with the physical lanced through him. Panic and, for the first time in his long existence, fear clutched at those final wisps of the soul bond. Of Bridget.

Heat kissed the back of his neck. He winced against the fire.

Fire. Burning. *Heat.*

Heat—and fire—that lived elsewhere, beyond his fallen sword and dwindling power.

Steel roared as the searing blade popped through the thin skin at the back of his neck. Acid laced with dark magic seeped into him like a parasite invading a host. His cries muffled his arm's movement down by his waist. Fumbling fingers met their mark, despite Steel's painful delirium, and shakily gripped the hidden *sgian-dubh*. The dagger's handle was a cold balm within his palm, its blade a blessing from the mages.

A blade already imbued with his angel fire.

Steel reared his hips back, knocking the apex off-balance. With a sharp turn and upward thrust, the dagger found the demon's soft meat right between the ribs. The apex's jaw fell open, and clumsy desperate hands fluttered around the handle.

But the damage was done. Already, blue fire hissed and sizzled over pale tattooed flesh, turning every spare inch of healthy muscle to gray ash. Steel wasn't interested in sticking around for the light show. Every cell in his body screamed to get to Bridget.

He bucked and kicked the flailing body off him, then crawled toward the bed. "Bridget. *Bridget!*"

The green magic shackling her had faded, along with the rest of the apex's power. Steel clamored to see her, lifting her sagging form upright in arms slickened by her blood. Above, more of her soul swirled around them, illuminating the room to nearly full brightness.

"Shit, Bridget. *No!*" Steel tried to move and grab the edge of the bedding to stanch the bleeding, but he jerked short and slouched forward, dropping Bridget back against the pillows. "The bond," he croaked out in desperation.

There wasn't enough of her soul left within her body to secure it. Within his own shell, a final flicker, akin to a dying candle at the end of its wick, glimmered from white to orange, then to a muted blue. His power whirled around the bond's expiring ember, frantic, enraged, panicked, as if that apex's blade was still puncturing his throat.

Blade. A blade touched by fire. *His* fire.

Yes. One final blade.

With the dregs of his strength, Steel reached into his cargo pants pocket and pulled his push dagger free. It was one he hardly used and had almost forgotten. The blade was against her gaping wound a heartbeat later. As if summoned, latent blue fire arced down the three-and-a-half-inch chute of steel, cauterizing the torn flesh. Up above, Bridget's soul continued to whirl and writhe around them, hovering like some aimless spirit set on haunting those left behind.

"C'mon. C'mon," Steel ground out.

The white wisps circled in a slow vortex, searching and swirling and seeping into a cyclone of Bridget's weary lifeforce. And then the rotation ground to a halt. Steel's breath caught in his throat. Leisurely, as if time was an inconsequential thing, her soul's essence reversed course, retreating into the healing wound. Steel shuddered out a gasp and draped his exhausted body over Bridget's still form. Bathed in her soul's light, Bridget's illuminated face was stained with an ethereal glow.

The purest of angels. His eternal sunshine.

The room spun with an insistent fervor, and Steel's throat tensed with each swallow against the acid invading his body.

Still, he wrenched himself up higher to cup Bridget's delicate cheek and kiss the back of the hand clutched tightly in his.

"I love you, Sunshine. For me, please . . . you need to live, because one day very soon, I'm going to fly you to the stars." Steel's knees gave out as the pain shooting through his throat seized his muscles. He crumpled to the floor, but he never dropped her hand.

"I love you. I love you . . . to . . . the stars . . . and back," he rasped out toward the darkening ceiling, just before the acid devoured his vocal cords.

CHAPTER 31

An unknown compunction urged Bridget's eyes open, almost like a child's insistent tug at their parent's pant leg. Well, she certainly didn't have children, nor did her standard wardrobe of leggings make it possible for one to find loose fabric to tug on in the first place, so why the hell did she need to wake up?

Bone-weary was an entirely new concept, but whoever had coined the phrase surely had the right of it. Bones, muscles, even her eyelashes sagged beneath a crushing pressure that would convince deep-sea divers to give up their sea legs.

By some miracle of motivation, wake up she did and instantly regretted the maneuver. While there was no light lying in wait to blind her, thank goodness, there *were* many common complaints about consciousness she was intimately familiar with. When one had been besties with depression and isolation for as long as she had been, lucidity wasn't always the harbinger of rise-and-shine the general populace thought it was.

Darkness eclipsed her bedroom, so her vision didn't need to acclimate, but an astringent smell stung her senses so fiercely, she worried her nose hairs would yank themselves out and revolt.

"Uh, gross." She winced at her hoarse words and did her best to swallow past the arid desert that was her throat. Had there been a fire? If stir-fry dinner nights were anything to go by, the hardwired smoke alarms Ryan insisted on installing would have gone off in approximately half a second if even the suggestion of carbon-based smoke was nearby.

Okay, no fire then.

Bridget leaned back and tried to pull herself up. She hissed at her leg's near-violent protest. "Fuck, that *hurts!*"

After a breath or two of blowing out the pain, she clicked on the nightstand lamp and levered forward. Blood drenched the bedding and coated her legs.

"Oh, God . . ." Her stained fingers fell to the garish slash on her inner thigh, a slash that scored her flesh right above where her leg housed vital infrastructure.

Fear paralyzed her, and even though her flight response itched to get her out of that bed and the puddle of gore she'd awoken in, that ever-present curious kernel within just *needed* to have her questions answered first. How the hell was she alive? This much blood loss would kill a two-ton rhinoceros, never mind a one-hundred-and-forty-five-pound bookworm.

The gash was about four inches long, and when she smoothed her hand over it, her nails caught on puckered skin blistered with red and white welts. She lifted her leg, revolting against the stickiness of what she was lying in but determined to test her mobility regardless. Her range of motion abided by the standard operating procedure, thankfully, yet even as she tried out all her remaining limbs, some heavy thudding ache beneath her ribs kicked at her heart like a joey's hind legs pumping their way out of their mama's pouch.

Bridget followed the crimson trail over the edge of the bed and screamed.

Steel lay unconscious on the floor. Black charred skin peeked out beneath shirt sleeves and painted his face and neck in a blanket of burns. Though he lay huddled in the fetal position, his strong shoulders and wide back didn't rise and fall.

He wasn't breathing. How long had he not been breathing?

In an instant, memories of the attack surged through her, and that dull pulsing roar within her chest strengthened to a Category 5 hurricane, threatening to expel her skin off her body if she didn't save him.

Bridget scampered from the bed and dropped down to Steel's side. "Steel! Wake up! Oh God, no no no . . ."

There was no more smooth flesh, only brittle black char beneath pockmarked clothing that looked like it had been riddled with cigarette burn holes. She lifted his head onto her lap. Her heart cried out and fumed over how heavy and lifeless he lay against her blood-crusted thighs. Not just lifeless, but utterly vacant, as if his body had been abandoned by strength and soul alike. She didn't even mark the pain in her leg where she settled him on her.

Her worried hands hovered along his hairline for a place to touch him that was safe. She *needed* to touch him. That bleeding hole inside her knew that, with a body injured that bad, he was beyond CPR. But he was an *angel*, for God's sake. There had to be another way.

Teardrops the size of hubcaps landed on Steel's grimy hair. It was the only part of him not withered and burned, so her hands carded through the strands to offer what comfort they could. "Please, come back. What do I have to do? Tell me what I have to do, and I'll figure it out. Is there a power or a prayer or something? *Please*, tell me what I have to do."

Desperation infused her parched cries, and she clutched him closer. Screams turned to sobs, then to silent gasps of shuddering breaths. She'd cracked her eyes open a few times, only to succumb to the rippling disorientation of a sloshy landscape. It wasn't worth it, she'd quickly decided, so she slammed her lids shut and kept them that way. It simply wasn't worth accessing that sense if all that stared back at her was a bleary world of blood and pain.

She dipped her head forward. "I love you, you know. At some point, it just clicked. Even when I was furious at you, after some time apart, I realized that I'd rather fight it out with you for a chance at happiness than be miserable and alone in my self-loathing again. If the choice is between being right or being happy, then there really isn't a choice. Happiness wins out every time. You taught me that. After all, who cares about being right when all it does is isolate you on a mountain summit? No one is right all the time, and I'd give *anything* to show you how hard I'd fight for you. I don't need to be right. I just need you."

Bridget resettled his fragile neck beneath her palm. His skin was flayed where hers was smooth, and that burning spark within her again preened and pushed toward the surface. Her breath froze. She pressed her hand more deeply against the gnarled patch of skin at his nape, and once more, her stomach tightened with burgeoning power.

No, not power. The soul bond.

Panicked shock punched through her, and the world stalled out. *The soul bond!*

"Please . . . please . . ." She didn't know who she was praying to. She'd never been religious, but Steel had spoken of the celestial mages often. Perhaps they'd hear, or maybe the bond was enough to—

Blazing white light erupted from Bridget's core. All the pent-up power rushed out of her in an inferno of harmony and healing. Snaking milky wisps danced and swirled around their entwined bodies, tightening and pulsing in an ethereal embrace. There was no pain, no heartache, only the existence of two souls in need.

Beneath her fingers, black flakes of charred skin chipped

away, revealing healthy tan flesh. Gray fingernails and ashen lips gave way to tissue kissed with vigor and life. A flaring patch of heat singed the inside of Bridget's thigh right where her wound was, but she couldn't spare it more than a fleeting thought. All her attention and energy centered around the angel in her arms.

An angel whose chest now rose and fell with renewed vitality.

On her gasp, the glow from within her faded, receding into the spark that dwelled inside her. She slumped forward, panting in time with her whirring heart.

When she lifted her head back up, two brilliant glacial eyes lit by wonder, reverence, and something she'd never seen before shined back at her.

THEY DIDN'T SPEAK, and Bridget's emotionally racked body was more than okay with that. She hadn't realized how warm and comforting a safety blanket could be when woven from silence and unspoken sentiments. When Steel woke, they'd both struggled for words. After all, what did one say to a soulmate who had just been dead in their arms a moment prior? That wasn't exactly a cornered market for greeting cards.

Once they were satisfied with their abilities to stand upright on limbs ready for load bearing, Steel had swept her into his arms and carried her to the bathroom. Together, they'd peeled off the blood-crusted remnants of their clothes and washed each other in slow practiced strokes under the shower's no-way-it-was-hot-enough-but-it'd-have-to-do spray. The silent agreement on not using the bathtub was a given. Bridget had woken up in a pool of blood. She had little interest in climbing into a well of the stuff again, even to try and soak it off her.

So much hung in the air between them, so hands spoke where lips could not.

Steel had cleansed every inch of her in abundantly gentle caresses. There were no sly grazes or hints at anything beyond getting clean, just a silent intimate connection. He'd washed her hair and—Lord, help her—even conditioned it twice before buffing her dry and wrapping her in her favorite seafoam terry cloth bathrobe. She'd tried to catch glimpses of his expression to decipher what lay behind those steely eyes, but his deft hand and gentle touch had always directed her attention elsewhere.

There was nowhere else to run now as they both sat, freshly showered and still very much silent, on the couch in her basement—where their entire whirlwind caper started. Her bedroom was solidly off-limits. She'd have to burn her bedsheets, hire a hazmat team to fumigate her room, and re-drywall the space before she'd even consider sleeping in her room again. So, never.

But even Bridget got twitchy with the silence after a while. Just when she worried they'd never speak again, Steel gathered her hands to his chest. "I've been running through every possible way to say what I want to say, and everything just sounds like some pathetic excuse rooted in manipulation."

A wry smile lifted the corner of her mouth. "Okay, maybe don't start there then."

Desperate contrition painted his brow, and his features twisted into an expression he'd never shown her before: vulnerability. "I saved you that night four years ago because I couldn't *not* save you. In my line of work, hell, in my line of *existence*, there are often more casualties than rescued souls. For every one person we spare from the charmers, countless more perish, and it's only gotten worse as the centuries have worn on. So, when your vehicle collided with me, and by whatever blessing the mages bestowed, you were still breathing, I couldn't walk away from you. One day turned into two, which turned into ten, and before I knew it, I was counting the seconds until I could see you again, even if it was only through a window or shadowed under a copse of trees."

Her chest tightened with her own confession, but she refused to interrupt him.

Steel shoved his fingers through his hair. "I suspected you were my soul bond, but I never wanted to voice it. I believe in choice. It was *my choice* to fight against the charmers when they marched on the Empyrean. It was my choice to enact the Sealing with my brothers, knowing full well I might never return to my home again. Just as it was my choice to allow you to feel for me what you would, even though I loved you long before our soul bond snapped into place."

She pressed her palms against his chest, then traced the arc of his clavicle with her thumbs. Anything to keep her hands steady. "Steel, I—"

"When that apex had you strung up on the bed, when he sliced you open and you were bleeding out in my arms . . ." He whipped his head to the side and inhaled swiftly. "I'd never known true fear until I felt your pulse slow to nothing and our soul bond dwindle to extinction along with it."

A sharp yearning traversed the tip of her tongue. She opened her mouth again, but his warm hands merely settled against hers.

"I love you, Bridget. Always have. I behaved shamelessly and lived the life of a coward for the last four years. I turned to deception when I should have turned to your honesty and joy. I should have drowned in your illumination instead of hidden from it. I've been a sentinel for my entire existence, but none of it means anything if I can't guard the one woman whose soul is mine to protect." His chest rose on excited breaths, and his arduous words came faster. "My soul is yours as well, Bridget Olsen. Whether you want it or not, it has always been yours."

The last of Bridget's walls came crumbling around them. She

threw her arms around his neck and whispered her confession against his still-gasping lips. "I love you, too. And I'll take your soul and raise you mine. Two is better than one, I hear, and I can't wait to explore life with you. Together."

It was Bridget who struck first, hungrily slashing her mouth over the last shred of Steel's remarkable self-restraint. His lips met hers in greedy pulls of passion. Melting embraces turned to frantic fanaticism. Power and demand ruled her body, as if her soul required a pound of flesh and it would have it from no other except her mate.

Fine by her.

Steel's exploring hands became eager scavengers. The belt at her waist slid free, and he slipped the terry cloth over her shoulders. Their mouths never separated as her robe and his towel fell away in unison to the concrete floor.

Skin slicked against overheated skin. Steel settled back on the couch, and Bridget sat astride his hips, cradling his power and strength within the shield of her body. She leaned forward, crushing her breasts against his hard chest. Scorching tongues glided in deep tangles that answered for everything they'd yet to share. Words were lost in the language of their bodies.

Steel's hands traveled down her sides and over the swell of her hips, mapping her shape with soul-deep familiarity. He roared up and captured a beaded nipple against his tongue. One lick, then another. She threw her head back and bucked against his hardness. She slowly and tortuously dragged her wetness over him.

He hissed sharply against her nipple. "If you think I'm going to let you distract me—"

Bridget's molten core ushered Steel into her body with another sensuous dip of her hips. The intrusion was so fast and heated, they groaned their bliss together. Strong hands gripped her thighs, squeezing and parting her legs as wide as the couch allowed. She set the pace, slow and tantalizing, and loved admiring the vein jutting out along Steel's throat, which pulsed with each forward thrust. She slid backward again, but before she could bring her body forward, Steel lifted her ass high and plunged her down on top of him.

She moaned. "Ah, shit."

"Two can play at that game, Sunshine."

Bridget's head wobbled as he held her high and slammed her down again.

Wicked lust teased Steel's words. "And I don't accept surrender."

Punishing, pounding euphoria overtook all reason. Bridget rode harder, only slowing to eat up the cries of her name on his lips.

They came together in a frenzy of heat and passion. Every time Steel lifted her skyward, sometimes unseating him entirely, she'd crash back down in a torrent of euphoria. Each height and dip didn't only rock the choppy waters of her life but her soul as well. Her soaring cry was one step closer to those wondrous stars only the select few ever stopped to notice.

But with him at her side, she would notice them and never stop exploring what they had to offer.

Pleasure crested through her with a tidal force. Steel roared his release and buried his cries into the swell of her breasts, only stopping to press a kiss to her heart when he'd wrung every last pulsating tremor out of her.

An impossible undertaking, to be sure, because their love had no end date. They had so much to make up for, and she'd make damn sure they never wasted another minute ever again.

EPILOGUE

Two months later

"The muscles on these characters don't even make sense. Honestly, if anyone actually had traps and pecs that big, with that narrow waist, they'd topple over. Who designed this guy, anyway?" Bronze's grunts carried through his headset, along with a series of repeated insistent thumb taps against his controller. An explosion sounded, followed by several more annoyed male groans muttering the most colorful curse combinations Bridget had ever heard. She bit her lip to force back a smile and took mental notes on which choice utterances she'd share with Ryan.

"Got ya, fucker. Oh, hey . . . Wait, no! *Dammit!* No fair!" Another blast and Bronze's character doubled over into a heap on the ground. A sad red halo pulsed in the lower right-hand corner, illuminating the empty health meter and zero lives remaining.

"My amazing, beautiful, and apparently vicious soul bond designed that guy," Steel remarked through his headset with ill-concealed amusement. "The woman can be quite deadly as well."

"So it would seem," Bronze mumbled. A loud clunk pinged through everyone's headphones. The angel had no doubt just thrown down his controller. Again.

"Love you too, B," Bridget crooned into her microphone.

"Vile woman."

"You did raise a good point, though." She paused, then tapped out a sequence that engaged her character's hidden power. "There's a fine line between reality and fantasy. If the dude can't realistically stand up, how is he going to throw his ax without getting a face full of dirt? I'll work on that. The game's still in beta for a reason." When Steel's character stepped in front of hers to block an incoming attack, Bridget jotted down a few notes.

Titan's teasing voice joined the others. "I wonder where she got the inspiration for all that muscle definition— *Fuck*! Hey, that was my last power-up, asshole!"

Steel chuckled down the line. "Sorry not sorry."

"Pause," Bridget announced. "Snack break."

"Snack break," Bronze commented, his tone accusing. "That's code for kitchen makeout session and we all freaking know it."

"Eyes on your own paper, brother," Steel warned.

"Yeah, yeah. Just go, will ya?"

"Why do you care?" Titan asked. "Bridget already killed you."

"It slows down the pace of play! I'd like to see who wins sometime this year, even if it isn't me."

Bridget whipped her headset off, cutting out the chatter, and walked out of the mostly-packed-up studio space across from her bedroom, which was little more than a glorified closet at this point since Bridget still couldn't bring herself to sleep there. Turned out, it wasn't much of a hardship, as she and Steel had made quite a cozy setup for themselves in her basement.

Steel's headset and controller sat abandoned on the living room couch as he greeted her in the kitchen. Their gaming arrangement wasn't ideal, but they managed. As much as she'd love to play alongside him, the reverb had been unbearable.

A problem, he assured her, that wouldn't exist in her new house. Well, technically, it would be *their* house, but as she accepted the chilled London Fog Steel offered her, complete with her favorite bendy straw, she didn't much care to split hairs.

Following the break-in, it had become obvious she couldn't stay in her old home. The charmers knew who she was and where she lived. Plus, her house carried memories she wasn't too keen on lugging into her new life. So, when Steel floated the idea of a change of scenery, it hadn't been that hard to sign on the dotted line.

Especially when her new roomie offered all sorts of yummy perks not explicitly outlined in the property listing.

The home was the perfect oasis. It was a charming two-bedroom ranch located conveniently close to a highway and not much else—aside from a certain underground angel den. She had neighbors, technically, but none were close enough to see her when she was outside. The nearest exit spat her out into town twenty minutes later, and since the property was located near the main utility hookups, some of which crossed through her land via title deed agreement, she had access to all the deliciously high bandwidth she could get her hands on.

They were small steps, but boy, did they feel good.

Steel rinsed out his coffee cup and grabbed the bowl of barbecue-spiced roasted chickpeas. "You ready to head to Boston next week?"

Bridget grabbed a small handful, shook the dried beans in her cupped hand like they were die she was about to blow on, and funneled a few into her mouth. "I think so. Briar Envoy Games already has me set up at the same extended-stay hotel I stayed at last time for my interview, the one not far from the studio. All meals are paid for, though they said if I wanted to buy groceries instead, I was welcome to do so. The room is equipped with a kitchenette, but Kaitlyn and Noah offered to get dinner with me a few nights while I'm there, so we'll see. It's good to have options, though, and my teammates are really cool. They've all given me a ton of choices, including my boss, and seem totally fine with whatever I decide."

Really cool and *totally fine* being the understatements of the century. Kaitlyn and Noah weren't just animators she worked with; they were fantasy nerds who spoke her language. They were saga-minded kindred spirits in a world of reality dating show lovers and short-form content creators.

And she'd never have met them if it hadn't been for Steel.

Shortly after the attack, Bridget resigned from her job in commercial graphic design. To absolutely no one's surprise, they didn't try to retain her. They hadn't even been able to arrange for her unpaid vacation time fast enough before she logged out of her credentialed programs and quietly quit when her two weeks were up.

That was when Steel read her an article about Briar Envoy Games, a new start-up video game and entertainment operation out of Boston. The company was run by a board of directors, of course, but they were newly incorporated, and their leaders weren't that much older than she was. After some more digging, she'd learned about the company's ideals, interests, and the market segment they'd be targeting: high fantasy video games. Several of the board members had even elaborated in press releases how, at their heart, they were a dream team of gamers who wanted to level their sights on the niche of crafting the best video games out there—and hiring the best animators and graphic designers to do it.

With Briar's standard remote work packages, save for the

one week a month all employees were required to be on-site for client meetings and follow-up corroboration, it was the perfect opportunity for Bridget to ease back into a world she'd long felt content to let spin on without her.

Starting with the weekly game nights with her new family of angels.

The trips to Boston, likewise, would afford her and Steel wonderful getaway opportunities, both as a way to slowly increase her comfort level with physical interpersonal interactions *and* as a chance for her and Steel to vacation properly, as he put it. Meaning food. Lots and lots of food if her angel's exuberance over checking out Boston's dining scene was anything to go by.

"Bronze had a point about his character's muscles. Too beefy," Bridget said around a mouthful of chickpeas.

"Any beefier and Chrome would think you're modeling the guy after him. Though I rather like the long blond hair, especially with the war braids and wings. It gives the whole Viking angel warrior a nice touch."

The compliment landed as Steel intended, but Bridget couldn't manage to smile more than a modest grin. "Is Chrome still looking into that woman you guys saw at the grotto?"

Steel's shoulders slumped a bit, and he hooked her to his side. "Yeah. He swears he's seen her before but just can't pin it down. It's been eating away at him. Kind of turned him into a miserable grumpy bastard, if I'm being honest."

"Oh? How can you tell?"

"He gave up his cigars and is up to two packs of gum a day."

"Oy. Not good."

"No, but we're trying to help him. It's just a shot in the dark, you know? A *literal* needle in a haystack. Short of showing up to watch her enter the grotto each morning or camping out by her car to demand answers when she leaves to go home—which is a level of creepy Chrome has not yet resorted to, thank the mages —he's kind of stuck."

"I know an angel who stalked a woman once. For four years, in fact. It didn't work out so bad for him, I don't think."

Steel brushed a heartwarming kiss against her forehead. "No, it didn't."

Bridget melted into the kiss and lovingly pressed her lips to the dimple on his chin. They pulled away, and Steel handed her the bowl of chickpeas before snatching a few for himself. "Have you guys come up with a name for the game yet?"

"Oh, we have." Her devious eyebrows waggled. Warily, Steel quirked a brow. "It's called *Fallen Angels Rising*."

———

COULD a human woman really be working for the charmers, and why does just the sight of her make Chrome's body stand at attention . . . and possibly recognition? Find out what happens to the sentinels' biggest and brainiest angel when a long-forgotten night of searing passion flares to life, as does the woman he shared it with. But now that he's finally found her, she doesn't remember him—and she's working for his enemy. Start reading *Angel's Light!*

CAN WE KEEP IN TOUCH? Are you curious to see what happens when, after one too many margaritas during family game night, Bridget regrettably issues Bronze a challenge? *Since you don't like the video game characters I design, go ahead and design your own, Mister Smarty Pants.* Claim your BONUS EPILOGUE when you sign up to my newsletter to find out why Bronze is the last person on the planet who should design a video game character.

. . .

THANK you so much for reading *Angel's Devotion!* If you loved seeing Steel and Bridget's relationship grow, let your friends know. Help other readers fall in love with this couple, and all those hunky angels, by leaving a review.

SCAN THE QR code to start reading *Angel's Light* and the BONUS EPILOGUE today!

ACKNOWLEDGMENTS

It's easy to write what you love when there's no shortage of inspiration hitting you in the face. I found Kerrigan Byrne's books at a time when a hard core reading slump was leading into an even harder core writing slump. I'll forever be grateful for the tears, laughs, and book hangovers that woman has given me, and for the words her own words have inspired.

I need to tip my hat to Erin Wright as well, who told me the hardest thing I didn't want to hear: Write the damn book. She was (w)right.

Lastly, to my husband, Ben, forever and always. For all the abundant universe talk he had to sit through, and for never being afraid to tell me to slow my roll.

ABOUT THE AUTHOR

Aimee Robinson is a lover of romance novels in all forms. Her absolute favorites, though, are the ones that offer a little bit of something *extra*: time travel, guardian angels, good old-fashioned meddlesome grandmothers with a supernatural secret to hide, you name it.

She believes romance novels should transport you from the humdrum to the swoonworthy, preferably while being curled up on the couch with chocolate and tea (or a martini . . . or both!). Aimee's overactive imagination lends itself to fun tales with emotional adventures, sexy snark, and happily ever afters.

When not writing or reading, Aimee enjoys spending time with her husband and keeping up with her two young sons.